RULE OF MAGIC

RULE OF MAGIC

THE LEIRA CHRONICLES™ BOOK 4

MARTHA CARR

MICHAEL ANDERLE

DISRUPTIVE IMAGINATION

Copyright © 2020 (as revised) Martha Carr and Michael T. Anderle
Cover Art by Jake @ J Caleb Design
http://jcalebdesign.com / jcalebdesign@gmail.com
Cover copyright © LMBPN Publishing

LMBPN Publishing
PMB 196, 2540 South Maryland Pkwy
Las Vegas, NV 89109

Version 2.02 October 2020
eBook ISBN: 978-1-64971-027-7
Print ISBN: 978-1-64971-028-4

RULE OF MAGIC TEAM

From Martha

To everyone who still believes in magic and all the possibilities that holds.

To all the readers who make this entire ride so much fun.

To Louie, Jackie, and so many wonderful friends who remind me all the time of what really matters and how wonderful life can be in any given moment.

And finally, a special thank you to John Nelson of the Austin, Texas Police Department who patiently answers all of my questions. I hope I made you proud. Thank you for your service.

From Michael

To Family, Friends and
Those Who Love
To Read.
May We All Enjoy Grace
To Live The Life We Are
Called.

CHAPTER ONE

The green Mustang was parked on Viewpoint Drive on the South side of Austin, a few houses down from the rancher painted the colors of a Dreamsicle. Pale orange and not quite white. The tall palm tree in the front yard rustled in the wind as the large fronds lifted, pointing toward the east.

"This is where the magical rainbow ended? Doesn't seem like much." Felix Hagan narrowed his eyes, looking at the broken shutters on the front of the house. "You'd think someone who knows how to use dark magic would fix up the place."

"The necklace leaves a strong trail for anyone magical to follow. This kid definitely had it for a while but it's not here now. It hasn't been long though." Leira centered herself and drew up enough energy to see the bright, glittering trail mixed in with the teenager's weak, twisting magical path. The darkness was already doing its best to pull the kid in closer.

"They're keeping the necklace moving to stay ahead of us and the Silver Griffins. It's not going to be easy to catch someone with it in their possession," said Correk.

"Like they're playing a giant game of Whack-a-Mole with us." Hagan grimaced as his stomach gurgled.

"The mastermind behind all of this chose this kid for a reason. I want to know why. That's the very thing that may help us finally get ahead of the necklace. Lois has it from a reliable source that there's some kind of meeting happening today with the local followers. We wait and we follow." Leira stretched, arching her back. They had already been there for hours. The tip from the older witch didn't include an exact time or place.

"Good old-fashioned stakeout. I like it," said Hagan blowing on his coffee.

It was early in the morning and nothing else was stirring except for a young woman walking a small white chihuahua. Leira watched as the dog took a few steps and sat down till the woman gave a couple of tugs on the leash. The woman gave up half a block later and picked up the dog.

"We should take Yumfuck on walks. It'd be good for him." Leira watched the woman tuck the dog into her jacket till only its head was showing.

"Yumfuck takes himself on walks when we're not around." Correk stretched out in the backseat, drinking a cherry Dr. Pepper. He was wearing his cowboy boots, his feet propped up on the far door handle.

"What would that even look like? Would you put a tiny harness on him like he's a toddler?" Hagan shifted in the passenger seat in the front. His dark blue PDA jacket rustled as he turned. "Tell people he's some kind of South American cat? I'll bet people would buy that."

"Did you remember to keep him in his nest this time?" Correk searched through the bag next to him. He pulled out a plastic sleeve of frozen Thin Mint cookies and slid one into his mouth, letting it slowly melt on his tongue. "Yaaauuummm."

"You're starting to sound like Yumfuck." Leira reached over the back of the seat and took one of the cookies. Correk arched an eyebrow.

"Okay, so you got me on these," she said. "It's a Thin Mint.

Love for them is universal. At least I occasionally eat a vegetable. You should try a carrot or a beet. Think of it as research into something actually grown on Earth."

"I ate a potato last night."

"Chip. You ate a chip. Doesn't count. At some point, if you fry anything it doesn't count as food anymore." Leira was still distracted by the trails of energy. Something wasn't right. She could feel the darkness pulling at the young man's energy. It had a familiar taste to it. *That thing from the world in between.*

"That a rule?"

"Common sense."

"It's true." Hagan grumbled, looking out the window. "Heard the same thing myself recently."

Leira took a long look at him.

Correk slid another cookie into his mouth, staring at Leira as he bit down on the cookie. "I was supporting the small trio of girls in their quest."

She looked back at him and let out a snort. "Those little girls saw you coming. Miniature little geniuses leaning into a badge for marketing. They set up by the Wag-a-Bag and are catching all the early morning party people trying to get coffee. And you."

"This is my first magical stakeout. I gotta say, not as exciting as I pictured." Hagan lifted up off the seat and hitched up his pants as he peered out the window looking for anything unusual. "Just how much magic does this kid have?"

"That's the third time you've done that. What's different about you? Why aren't you eating?" Leira narrowed her eyes, licking the chocolate off her fingers. She glanced at his coffee as her eyes widened. "No cream, either. You've finally gone and done it! You're eating healthy!"

"Errrr…. Healthy-*er.*"

Leira gave him her best dead fish look.

"Thanks, that's sweet." Hagan smiled. "I appreciate that. You know just how to say you care without the rest of it."

"Very touching. Like watching two icicles slowly melting," said Correk.

"Ignore him. Okay, spill it, Hagan. You've raised hiding food to the level of a cat burglar and now you voluntarily quit cold turkey. What happened?"

"I passed that treadmill test, but just barely. Doc said if I kept eating the same way, in a few years I was gonna have some real trouble."

"That was a few years ago, wasn't it?" Leira reached into the backseat for another cookie.

Correk arched an eyebrow again and slowly moved them out of her reach. "No. I offered to get you your own and you turned me down. I warned you about that the last time we got pizza."

Leira pinched his leg. "I don't want a whole box. I just want a few of yours. They'd be happy to sell you more."

Correk sent out a pea-sized fireball as Leira ducked.

"You two are killing me." Hagan frowned as he glanced back at the cookies. He turned toward the window till he couldn't see them anymore. "If you must know, it was only last week. I made the mistake of taking Rose with me. We get home and next thing I know she's pulling out our wedding photos. She was propping up pictures of a younger, thinner me all over the house. My life was flashing before my eyes everywhere I went. She saved the fat me for the door of the fridge."

"Rose should interrogate prisoners. She manages to seem loving while playing with your mind. Eventually you want to help her put you away." Leira glared at Correk. He was putting spray cheese on a Thin Mint. "Dude, that is nasty." She rolled her eyes and turned away.

Hagan looked out the window, sipping his black coffee.

"If it helps, you do look better,' said Leira. "What'd you do with your doughnut stash? I feel like a food pusher, now."

"Hmm, not bad." Correk pulled out another cookie.

4

Leira listened to the sound of the cheese spray and squeezed her eyes shut. "Take a look in the back seat. It'll help your diet."

"No thanks. I want to remember junk food in a good way." His stomach gurgled again as he let out a sigh. "I brought the whole pile to the precinct when I went to say goodbye. Looked like a hero, so thank you for that." Hagan grimaced, throwing up his hands. "Time to turn a page." He stole a glance at Correk but quickly turned back. "Oooh, fuck me that is bad. Don't ruin the memory of food for me. Hey, isn't that the little pisser?"

Leira opened her eyes, leaning over the steering wheel. "Finally. What is he doing?"

The young man took a furtive glance around as he pulled out a wand and mumbled something, pointing his wand at the four corners of his house.

Correk sat up, swinging his legs around as he dropped the cookies back into the bag. "He's doing a kind of glamour spell but in reverse. The house will glow brightly from a block away for anyone with an invitation. Apparently, the meeting is here and is imminent. That spell doesn't last very long."

A blue Lexus pulled up in front of the house and an older man with neatly slicked-back silver hair got out, buttoning his long cashmere coat.

"One lone wizard. Things are getting interesting." The palms of Leira's hands grew warm. She could feel the wizard's energy pulsing in the air. "He's got chops."

"He doesn't look like anybody's flunkie." Hagan set his cup down in the holder between the seats. "Is the necklace with him?"

Leira pulled in energy through her feet as her eyes began to glow. She sent out a stream to investigate his energy. It was strong and full of a shimmering darkness. *That's a first.*

"Never felt such a strong... It's like he's built a wall around his intentions... Really hard to detect much of anything." Leira let her magic coil around, looking for the telltale signs, opening herself up to feeling just a trace of the man's inner thoughts.

"Don't..." Correk leaned forward and put a hand on Leira's shoulder but it was too late.

The man stopped suddenly and sharply turned his head, scowling in the direction of the Mustang. He swiftly lifted his arms, sending out a pulse of energy just wide enough to hit the Mustang and nothing else, making it rock hard on its wheels. Leira clamped her hands on her head as the force of the magic slammed down on her, throwing her back against the seat.

Hagan hit the passenger side door hard, his head banging against the window, knocking the wind out of him. He wheezed once or twice trying to draw back in some small amount of air, while keeping his attention on the man but it was too hard. His chest felt like it was going to explode. "What...the...fuck." His eyes watered as he pressed his palms hard against his stomach.

Correk closed his eyes, shutting out every distraction. He drew on the reserves of his own energy, fighting off the crushing pulse. Every muscle was straining as he raised his arm, the bicep rippling from the effort. He put out a hand, straining toward Leira till he found her shoulder, connecting himself to her energy, guiding the blue and silver stream around the Mustang, shutting out the dark pulse.

At last, the car stopped rocking. Hagan felt a gush of air fill his lungs making him lightheaded. Small bursts of light flashed in front of his eyes as he blinked rapidly, trying to get it to stop.

Leira felt her shoulders lift and she was finally able to take her hands off her head and focus. Correk's magic was calming and she was able to feel him gently steering her.

"What the fuck just happened?" Hagan was finally able to get out a complete sentence.

"Leira alerted a Wizard with very powerful dark magic that we were intruding on his plans. He retaliated with a simple but effective energy pulse." Correk finally sat back against the seat. His entire body ached.

"Was that the fucking bogeyman?" Hagan wiped the drool off his chin, still trying to get his bearings.

Leira let the magic gradually lessen and the glow fade from her eyes. "Sorry about that. I had no idea." She looked out the window. The man and his car were gone. "I'm gonna go ahead and say the kid is gone, along with the wizard. Did you know him, Correk?"

"No, but I recognized the energy or at least his kind. He's very powerful and has been practicing dark magic for a long time. They tend to have short tempers and can retaliate in ways we may not even see coming. Believe it or not that was just a warning shot."

"A warning!" Hagan swallowed hard. "Feels like someone tried to hollow out my guts with a spoon!"

"He's not the one who's behind all of this. I could feel it in his energy. The little I got out of him." Her thoughts were coming to her in pieces as she worked to recover from the blast. "He's following someone else." Leira knitted her brows together, worried. "If that's a new follower of Rhazdon's old teachings…"

"Then how powerful is their new master?" Correk finished her thought without saying what he already knew. *It has to be the traitor among the prophets.*

Leira's phone buzzed and she looked down to see who was texting her. "It's General Anderson. There's a case. Correk, we'll drop you off, first. Figure out our next step with the necklace later."

Charlie Monaghan stood on the wide granite steps of his house on River Road in Richmond, Virginia. Only in Richmond in the polite circles of old families and old money would a mansion with ten bedrooms and just as many bathrooms be referred to as a house. It was a sign of new wealth to talk about money. Charlie was new money, but he got that rule.

He was waiting for the young man, Langston Rogers to park his old Ford Escort in front of Charlie's neatly trimmed English boxwoods along the circular driveway. Charlie kept the smile plastered on his face despite his irritation that he was even having to go through the motions. He only agreed to meet the young college professor because he was from his alma mater, Virginia Commonwealth University and was an old friend's grandson. That and the grandfather reached out personally and struck a deal. *I am all about the deal.*

Fifteen minutes of Charlie's time to get Langston to hopefully let this all go, take on something more suitable, in exchange for the man's proxy on a few keyboards.

Charlie was certain the young man was too coddled and slightly off. His emails all talked about an important discovery made in Peru and a powerful artifact. Charlie emailed him back out of curiosity and asked, powerful to do what, but Langston insisted it had to be seen to be believed and would revolutionize manufacturing.

At first, Charlie deleted the emails, all fifty-three of them but then his grandfather called and asked for that favor.

He raised his hand and gave a short wave as Langston got out of the car. Charlie was neatly dressed in expensive slacks and a cashmere sweater over a soft-collared shirt and soft leather loafers. Perfect for the mild winter. "Langston, good to see you. Your grandfather speaks so highly of you." He stood aside and let the young man go ahead of him, even though he had no idea where to turn once he stepped into the large foyer.

It was a familiar tactic of Charlie's to put someone immediately off their game. The young man blushed and stuttered, "After you," still turning in a circle as he looked up at the high ceiling. Charlie smiled graciously and showed him to the wide doors that led to the library.

"I'm sorry about the limited time. Just about fifteen minutes. This was all last minute and I have a golf game to get to. Can't leave my friends waiting at the first tee." He waved his hands around as he talked.

"Of course, I appreciate the time. I'll get this started." Langston fumbled with an ornate wooden box he was carrying, setting it down with a thud on Charlie's antique oak desk. A momentary wince passed across Charlie's face, but he let it go. *Thirteen minutes.*

Langston put both hands inside of the box, gingerly lifting out a metal wheel decorated all the way around the rim in hieroglyphics. He laid it carefully on the desk and took a short, hollow brass metal pipe out of his pocket, giving the wheel a solid hit in a specific pattern across the symbols. Each time he made contact the wheel let out a loud ding in a perfect pitch of C. On the twelfth ding, the wheel started to rattle on the desk as Charlie took a step back.

The symbols along the rim lit up and the wheel lifted, spinning in a circle, rotating a few degrees to the east with each turn. The smile froze on Charlie's face as he watched. "It's an impressive magic trick." *What the hell?*

"Just keep watching."

The wheel spun even faster until sparks flew out, some of the cinders landing on the heirloom rug, quickly sputtering out. An opening emerged the size of a window just above Charlie's desk and he found himself staring at the backside of a tree.

"How the…" He took a step forward, blinking his eyes to see if he could detect the edges of the illusion. *It's real… It's real!* "It's fucking real!"

Langston looked at him and smiled, a sheen of sweat across his face. "It's a tree in a world called Oriceran."

Charlie stepped closer and felt the warm air on his face while the smell of blossoms filled his nose. "Not Earth?" He cautiously put out his hand and felt the bark of the tree. "That's an elm…" he said in a hushed tone.

"Who goes there!" A loud, angry voice shouted from somewhere in the depths of the forest. Charlie quickly pulled back his hand as the Gardener of the Dark Forest appeared in front of them, his four pupils all focused on Charlie. The Gardener saw the spinning wheel and leaned out of the portal toward the desk.

Charlie froze where he was, unsure for once in his life what to do. Langston quickly hit the sides of the wheel again, sending a shower of gold sparks as the portal shrunk in size, sucking the Wood Elf back to Oriceran, and closing with a loud pop.

The wheel slowed its spinning, finally coming to rest as Charlie came closer, scrutinizing it over and over again, saying nothing.

"You had it half right," said Langston. "It's magic but it's not a trick."

"Can't be magic. Has to be science! Why didn't your grandfather mention this?" Charlie was stunned, his mind spinning.

"Because I never told him. He would have told the world before they were ready. Something like this has to be handled correctly or it could cause panic. I knew you were the right person. All of your connections. I mean, your company stretches across the globe. You know every important politician, every foreign leader. You could help tell the world."

"Langston, what you just did... I'm not even sure what I just saw..."

Langston smiled and shook his head. "Sorry, I do that. I get so excited I forget to fill in the details. But I knew I had to show you before I told you, or you would have kicked me out of here. That hole that you saw just hanging there in space? It's called a portal and that tree you touched is in another world, in another dimension. They call it Oriceran. Over there, magic is commonplace. It's more like a form of energy that runs through everything that lives on the planet."

"In one of your emails you mentioned something about that place. How do you pronounce it?" Charlie walked across the rug where the portal had opened up. *There's nothing here.* His mind worked to hold onto the idea. *It's like bad mushrooms. Never liked being high either. No control. Fuck.*

"Or-i-sar-en. I found all of these ancient writings that talked about gates and portals inside of a large vault, along with that wheel. Think of it this way. The same way electricity revolutionized this country... another kind of magical energy at the time... take that and multiply it by a thousand. That wheel..." He pointed at the wheel, his face flush with excitement. "It's like a battery."

"It holds this energy..." Charlie was taking in shallow breaths fighting to maintain his composure.

"Exactly! The last time the gates were closing the ancients poured their energy into it to store for later use. The missing capstone from the top of the Great Pyramid in Egypt? A crystal artifact that someone else got to first. You see what I'm saying? These artifacts are everywhere." Langston's voice cracked from the excitement.

"Who's taking them?" Charlie sat down in his leather chair, trying not to let it show how fast his heart was beating.

"There's lots of theories. Foreign governments. Large corporations. Treasure seekers. There are thousands of these artifacts so probably all of those theories are correct."

"How did I not know?" Charlie muttered to himself. He was always prepared, always watching the bigger picture, but this got right by him.

"It's not too late. Only a small fraction of what's believed to be out there has been found." Langston's face lit up and he smiled, his eyes shining. "It's not even the best part."

"There's more." Charlie gripped the sides of his chair, doing his best to give his trademark smile, showing every pearly-white tooth.

"Here's the only thing that really matters. Every 25,800 years there are these gates that are much larger than that small portal you saw. Huge gates! These gates open and stay open for thousands of years. Beings from Oriceran crossed over to Earth and vice versa." Langston waved his arms over his head. "The last one was over thirteen millennia ago, and magic was just as commonplace here on Earth."

Langston pressed his hands down toward the floor. "That Golden Year takes thousands of years to get here. But the gates will start to open in just a few more years. Slowly at first, but with each slight opening more of that energy we call magic will pour into Earth."

"That's a lot of information."

"The ability to transform and create using a pure form of energy that comes from within is coming back to Earth. Magic. But we need to be ready."

"I'm going to need more proof, Langston." *I'm all in. I can use this. Transform the economy.*

"I thought you'd say that and I brought along a little more to show you." Langston reached into his backpack and pulled out a wooden goblet, placing it on the desk. "Doesn't look like much. Take it in your hands and hold it. Go on."

Charlie looked up at Langston, hesitating. Not his usual nature. He slowly picked up the goblet and held it in his hands, the smile fading from his face, replaced with a sense of awe. A warm feeling of peace rose up through his body, settling in his chest. It was a new feeling for Charlie and unsettled him. He put the goblet back down and looked at the red glow in the palms of his hands.

Langston smiled at Charlie and shook his head. "It's like it can teach you to be happy or something. I'm pretty sure that's not what it was intended for, but I can't figure out anything more. According to what I've read, there are some artifacts that require you to be magical to access their powers. Like it's part of your DNA or something. Can you imagine? But even still, it gives off this cool vibe."

"Is it your plan to gather artifacts and relics and just wait for the gates to open? Is this some kind of negotiation tool when the beings from Oriceran walk through the gates?"

Langston laughed and shook his head again. "I did it again. Left out an important detail." He slapped his leg in excitement. "That's not necessary. It says it throughout all the documents I've found. They're already here. Thousands of them, living right alongside all of us. A lot of them stayed the last time the gates closed. We can negotiate with them now. Think of the problems we might be able to solve, but we have to get to the artifacts first."

"I see your point," said Charlie, rising out of his chair. "Let me cancel my golf game. We need to talk."

Charlie Monaghan liked to be prepared and he was already a little behind. *First order of business, look for a way to harness the new energy,* he thought as he texted the Country Club of Virginia. *'Start playing without me. Something came up.'*

They'll just have to understand. There's a deal on the table. And it's going to be mine. "Do we need to keep calling it magic? Seems like we just found some new kind of oil but this one is in a lot more places."

"You can call it whatever you want but most do call it magic. Bending the laws of physics from within the biology of the practitioner in new ways to alter the environment." Langston shrugged. "Magic."

CHAPTER THREE

Harkin wove through the Dark Market, dodging under a wizard's arm who was sampling a piece of technology floating in the air. It pitched left to right and, with each turn, changed the air currents flowing around it. Harkin felt the air blow across the back of his neck, then turn and blow again in the other direction.

"That's a children's toy," said the Wizard, eyeing the spinning cylinder. "I'm not paying that kind of money to blow wind."

Harkin shook his head and kept moving. *Neither one of them knows what they have.*

The Wizard was starting to bargain, but he was cut short by a hard nudge to his ribs, knocking him out of the way. The compact engine bobbled in the air, cut off by its source of magic. The vendor put his hand out in time to catch the modified turbine before it plummeted to the packed dirt floor.

The vendor was an old gnome who looked up in time to see the Light Elf, Wolfstan Humphrey, growl at the Wizard.

"How much?" asked Wolfstan as he glared from beneath his woolen hood at the vendor.

The wrinkles around the Gnome's eyes deepened. "Ten pintas." He rubbed his chin, ready to bargain.

"You'll take nine." There was an icy edge to Wolfstan's voice.

Harkin felt a sharp pain of recognition run through him at the sound of Wolfstan's voice behind him. He jerked his head around to get a better look. The crowd blocked his view.

Wolfstan noticed Harkin peering over the crowd, and a smile spread across his face. "Still alive. Good to know," he whispered. "I wonder if Correk knows."

He drew the shadows around him, snatching the piece of machinery and let the money fall to the ground before disappearing in a blur.

"Hey, I said ten!" shouted the gnome, throwing up his hands. "Thieves and liars," he muttered, counting his money as he shuffled inside his booth.

Harkin stood in the center of the path, peering into the still-swirling shadows in the middle of the big tent. "Not possible," he hissed. "You are dead. I killed you myself."

"Harkin! Back for more abuse?" Malik had ventured outside of his tent, surrounded by his large bodyguards. "You seem lost. The exit is behind you."

Harkin glanced one more time at the gnome's booth, the light spilling back in front of it and at Malik. "What are you doing out here? Did the Dark Market finally raise its standards?"

Malik snorted, a smile not getting past his sneer. His wings ruffled and folded in closer to his body. "You get rid of all the thugs and the place would be nearly empty."

Harkin folded his arms across his broad chest and widened his stance. It was as good a place as any to startle Malik into saying something. "You're selling my parts to someone else."

Malik's smile spread as he stepped toward Harkin. "Free trade, Light Elf. You didn't think you were terminally unique, did you? Times are changing."

Harkin steadied his breathing and kept his voice low and

even. "Wolfstan Humphrey will get the best of you, and then he'll leave you for dead."

He saw a flicker of recognition in Malik's eyes and felt a cold dread spread over him. "I didn't ruffle your feathers, did I?" Lincoln turned his head away, his remaining eye scanning the crowd.

"I would have thought you'd known better, Lincoln."

Malik screwed up his face, stepped back, and spat into the dirt. "I've been doing this a long time and traded with a lot worse than you."

"I'm not worried for you, Malik. If you want your feathers plucked, that's your call. You've never come up against someone like Humphrey. I tell you what. Tell me where I can find him, and I'll trade you a little information about him."

"Right, because so many buyers are looking for parts that work in biotechnology." He let out an annoyed breath, his arms still crossed. Lincoln's fingers grazed across the hilt of his blade. "Have it your way." Harkin stepped back and hustled toward the exit, brushing past the booths on the outer ring. He made his way to the treeline and waited, hoping he was right.

It didn't take long before Lincoln slipped through the trees without a sound.

"I see you remember most of what I taught you." Harkin glanced at the ground behind Lincoln. Nothing was disturbed. "You forgot the parts about watching who you keep in your orbit."

"Malik pays better than anyone else. Besides, who else do you think would hire someone who spent time in Trevilsom Prison? I can handle myself with Malik, but Wolfstan Humphrey..." The large Light Elf shuddered, the scar along his face glowing blue for a moment.

"How is he alive?" Harkin's chest tightened as he remembered the day he thought he had bested his rival.

"You took him as close to death as possible. Unfortunately,

someone brought him back from the brink." Lincoln whipped around, an arrow notched on his bow, aimed at the pale brown panther above them in the trees. The panther let out a loud growl and jumped. The long, muscular body stretched out to reach the next branch.

Harkin put his hand on Lincoln's arm. "These are protected woods."

Lincoln lowered his bow. "I've heard all the stories about the Gardener of the Dark Forest. Children's tales meant to scare us." He returned the arrow to his quiver. "Pay attention to the real nightmares. Malik and Wolfstan made an agreement for artifacts and technology like you bought from him, but in larger quantities."

Harkin grimaced. "How large?"

"As many as Malik can get his hands on. Don't be surprised if he cuts you off." Lincoln glanced at Harkin, the scar glowing again. "I know you're trying to save your friend."

Harkin flinched as a long green snake with red diamonds along its back slid over his boot. He held still, letting it slither on its way. "That was my fault."

"And you paid for it, and then some. But what does a cold heart like Wolfstan Humphrey want with all that technology? He was never an inventor like you, and he never wanted to make anything better for anyone but himself."

"Wolfstan may be trying to go big. There are rumors someone is trying to create their own army in the other world."

"If he succeeds, both worlds could be in trouble."

Leira walked Correk to the guest house while Hagan took a walk to calm his nerves. He was still rattled and looked a little pale. "I'll be fine. Just need to shake it off."

Leira slipped through the gate as Correk followed her. The patio was still quiet, and Estelle was nowhere in sight. Leira knew better though than to assume Estelle wasn't watching from a corner by a window somewhere. The bar owner had a knack for seeing everything.

"Leira! Glad I caught you!" Craig popped up from behind the far end of the bar, holding up a credit card. "Forgot this last night! Was having a better time than I realized. Don't worry Estelle told me to go get it. I wouldn't put a toe in that woman's territory without permission. I'm very good at following orders. Are you coming to softball practice? You too, Correk! The Ice Cold Pitchers could use a decent third base player."

"Craig!" Estelle snapped a towel in his direction from the door of the restaurant. The cigarette clenched between her teeth was already mostly ash. "Git! Too early to be running on like that. They'll be there. They're family!"

Craig cracked a smile and winked at Leira as he raced by Estelle at the door. She cracked the towel at him again as the ash fell to the floor and she brushed it away with her foot, leaving a gray streak. She turned back to give a wave to Leira and Correk.

"Love the comb. That's new." Leira pointed at Estelle's head. There was a silver and gold metallic butterfly comb tucked in her tall, red bouffant.

"Felt the need for a little something extra this morning." Estelle shut the door and threw the bar towel over her shoulder, retreating into the kitchen.

Leira turned to Correk, the words tumbling out of her. "Did I just put all of us in danger back there? I feel like I sent up a flare and told some big bad dude we're following him."

"Like it or not, he probably already knew all about us."

"Then why the enormous blow back? Was it because I magically felt him up?"

"Partially, and like I said in the car that was a tap on the shoulder for that wizard. He was giving us just a taste of what he could do."

"Dear God…" Leira's voice came out in a whisper. She turned and walked toward the guest house stopping abruptly at the door. "Is it possible I missed the necklace's trail and it was in the house?"

"Not likely. It's far too powerful to mask. But I suspect they were headed to wherever the necklace is being kept. He was making sure they'd have a chance to get away and we'd think twice about following them right away."

"I would have followed him if the general didn't need us. I'm still going to go back and read the trail he left behind to see where they were headed."

"Be very careful. I'm not going to bother to tell you not to do it. But he will certainly have left traps in his wake specifically designed for someone with your power. They're not taking any chances with this necklace."

"Royal Elven power poured into something for millennia…"

"It should have been fine inside the walls of the Light Elves' castle."

"Till it wasn't."

Light flashed across Correk's eyes. Leira knew she hit a nerve.

"I know the prince was your friend. I didn't forget that," she said softly. Leira pressed against the scar on her belly. It was still tender. "But there's already been a lot of destruction from the loss of that artifact. How is it any different from what the Gnomes have locked in their vault? Even the Silver Griffins see it my way. They locked it up in their vault."

"The difference is obvious. The Light Elves stored the power to be used for good. The intention was always different. The energy held in the necklace is different." He spit out the words, clenching his jaw.

"An important distinction with a similar ending. Set aside in case it was ever needed. I do understand. Humans do the same thing all the time. Weigh the risks. It's the damned unintended consequences that bite you in the ass. It's what bothers you so much about Harkin. You question his motives. But it seems like his intentions were good and went south in whole new ways."

Leira saw Correk flinch and regretted saying anything at all. She quickly changed the subject. "I've never asked you, but are there other artifacts like this still inside the castle?"

"No, none this powerful. It was one of a kind. One...of...a... kind." He drew out each word.

"I get it. Positive energy. We'll keep searching and we'll get the damn thing back. Someday it may turn the tide for something else and we'll all be grateful it exists. Time is funny that way. Look, I've got to go. Case is calling. I want to go in and check on Mom and Nana, and then I have to get back to the car. I want to make sure Hagan is taking long, deep breaths. Are we good?" Leira squeezed his arm, sending out a low, soothing jolt of energy.

Correk arched an eyebrow at her. "Trying to make nice?"

"More like returning the favor. You've helped me stay steady more than once. Estelle's right. We're all family. I'm still going to say what I believe is true, but it doesn't mean I was trying to wound."

Grief passed across Correk's face. "That's the thing about living a very long time. A lot happens but I learned like every other Elf to stop thinking it was happening to me. Still... the pain can linger. The hard truth is my father is not around to explain anything anymore and trying to make up his reasons never ends in anything that feels like closure. All I end up doing is letting go of him again and again."

"What was his name?"

"Harkin." Correk glanced at her and held his hand up in an L-shape, an image appearing of a broad-shouldered Elf who resembled Correk.

Leira glanced at Correk and hesitated but decided to give in to the idea and grabbed him in a short hug, squeezing tight. The picture fizzled in his hand and disappeared.

"A little aggressive, Berens, but appreciated." He wrapped his arms around her, not wanting to say how much he needed it.

Leira lingered a few seconds and then punched him in the arm. "Now I know we're good."

She walked the rest of the way to the guest house and opened the door, dropping her purse on the red velvet chair as she went toward the kitchen.

Correk stayed a moment and brought up the picture again for before closing his hand into a fist and following Leira into the house, shutting the door behind him.

"Mom? Nana?" Leira called out, but the place was quiet. The troll sat on a large frond of a potted fern Eireka brought home. He was happily eating Captain Crunch from a box nestled among the leaves, watching an old episode of *Star Trek*. Captain Kirk was up to his waist in tribbles. Yumfuck let out a trill and made a loud crunching sound as he bit down on a mouthful of cereal.

Correk sat near the troll and held his hand out as the troll poured cereal into his palm.

Leira glanced down. "Classic kind? I didn't even know they still made that stuff. How did you get it? I know I said the spell this time. What else have you been into?" She went into the kitchen and glanced around, but nothing was pushed to the side. A sure sign of troll foraging. She saw the note on the counter by the coffee pot and scooped it up.

'Gone apartment hunting with Nana. Your grandmother didn't like the house I found. Gave the troll the cereal. Don't worry. He can handle the sugar. Be back by dinner. We'll be fine. Took an Uber. Love, Mom.'

So fucking normal. "Thank goodness I have a homicide to go to," she muttered. She folded the note and stuffed it into her pocket, the sapphire ring on her hand catching on the lining.

She went to the living room and grabbed her purse from the chair.

Correk was tossing cereal into his mouth as the troll guzzled a can of Fresca.

Leira put her hand on the door. "What's with the throwbacks? Wait, don't tell me. Nana and Mom did the shopping. Weirdly touching. Careful with that cereal. It has its own little payback. It'll scrape the hell out of the roof of your mouth. I will be back by dinner." She shook her head. "Can't believe I need to let people know that."

Correk gave a crooked smile and waved at her to go. He had his own things to attend to. Leira headed out the door and he waited, listening to Craig shout goodbye before he conjured a ball of light between his hands and opened a portal to Oriceran. A light breeze moved through the living room rustling a pile of papers.

"You keep this between us. I'll be back in a few hours," he said to the troll who gave him a side glance as Correk stepped through to the forest and closed the portal behind him, sending a spray of sparks across the living room. The troll let out a raspberry and filled his mouth with cereal.

———

Leira found Hagan in the food court brushing small bits of taco shell off his shirt. "You caved."

Three young privates in uniform walked by and started when they saw Hagan's jacket.

"PDA, cool dude," said one of the young men, shaking his shaved head. "Didn't even know that was a job."

Another tall, muscular young man held up his hands. "No public displays here. You guys really take that seriously."

Hagan snorted and held out his hand. "Thank you for your service," he said, not bothering to explain. He pulled his hand back and brushed a small bit of salsa off, using his pants as a napkin before putting his hand back out. "Thank you for your service," he said to the young woman, as he shook each of their hands.

Leira smiled and nodded at the group as they walked up to place an order at the taco truck. The woman glanced back over her shoulder before placing her order. On a hunch, Leira pulled in just enough energy and saw the glow surrounding the woman. *She's a witch. Good to know.* Leira took a look at Hagan. "How many?"

"Just three, which for me is good news. Stress eating," he said. "It's progress not perfection or I'd be screwed."

Leira took a long look at him. "You can say no if you want. If this whole magic thing is turning out to be more than you bargained for you can take a pass. Totally understandable."

"Fuck no, Berens. I haven't felt this juiced since I was a young detective. I got sucker punched. It happens! Glad we saw those kids in uniform. They're just kids, you know. They're taking much bigger risks. I'm an old fart with a few tricks still up my sleeve and can still do some good. Hell, I'm doing my small part for Mother Earth."

Leira tried to give him a dead fish look but a half smile crept across her face. "Come on, we have a case to get to and it's not good to be late."

Hagan followed closely behind her. "Have to admit those tacos really hit the spot. Puts me in a better mood. These jackets are a little ridiculous, but I doubt your average college kid would even get the joke. Rose got a kick out of it though and then so did I, if you know what I mean." He let out a snort as he got to the car.

"Never change, Hagan."

"Pretty sure that's not possible. All the grooves are already in the record."

Leira and Hagan found themselves standing in a basement in the upscale neighborhood of Travis Heights behind South Congress Avenue.

"I didn't even know there were basements in Austin. The bedrock stops most people." Hagan was talking in a low voice even though there was no one to bother. The young man on the ground had been dead for days and was puffed up to almost twice his size from all the moisture in the basement. "Damn flies. You'd think winter would kill them off." Hagan swatted at them as they flew around his head.

"First good frost they'll leave for a few weeks." Leira crouched down to look at the body.

Captain Napora came down the wooden stairs, treading heavily on the risers. "Nice to see you Berens, Hagan. Knew we'd see each other again. Didn't think it would be so soon. Nasty business." He stood beside Leira, his hands on his hips. "Third one we've found like this. Some kind of symbol cut into his neck. Other than that, the killer leaves no clues. Very careful. I don't believe we were meant to find the three bodies, either. Makes me wonder how many we haven't noticed. The brass insisted we bring in the Feds and I thought of you two."

Leira glanced up at Hagan standing behind the Captain. He shrugged with his hands out. Leira couldn't do much beyond take a look at all the details. *Not wasted time. Can still learn a few things. Good detective work got the job done all those years when I didn't know what I could really do.*

The Captain leaned forward, peering over her shoulder.

"Sir? You're blocking the light." She looked up at him and waited till he took a few steps back.

A detective appeared at the top of the stairs. "Captain, you have a phone call. They said it was urgent. Sounds like someone who outranks me by more than one star."

The Captain hesitated but took the stairs two at a time calling over his shoulder, "Keep me in the loop!"

"Will do." Hagan took a deep breath and walked closer to Leira.

"You're not going to breathe down my neck in his place, are you?" Leira finally managed a perfect dead fish look at him.

Hagan arched an eyebrow and drew his mouth into a thin line. "Nope, just going to be a part of the case, which will require me to be more than the pretty boy in the background." He stared at Leira, waiting for her to answer.

"Good point," she finally conceded. "Sorry about that."

"Getting a little big for your magical britches is all. Would happen to anyone." He pulled a white handkerchief out of a back pocket and wiped his forehead, sliding it back into his pocket. "That carving was done after the guy died. Just a signature. I'm betting this is human shenanigans. Not magical."

"You'd win that bet. No magical trail. But here's a weird twist."

Hagan interrupted her. "More than one human. It's obvious. Look at the way the stairs are bowing but aren't broken. Doubt they could have taken the weight of someone big enough to carry that body without splintering."

Hagan looked at the dead body. "He has to be two hundred pounds easy. We'd be talking about someone treading on a step with at least four hundred pounds. The wood would have cracked easily. Then there's how neatly that kid is laid out. No bruising on him. Nothing's broken. That would take a linebacker. He had help. They carried him down lengthwise distributing the weight. And he's not from here. Doesn't live here all the time, anyway. Look at those Timberland shoes. That's expensive cold weather gear and they're worn on the bottom. No one in Austin would invest in boots like that or get the chance to use them."

"You've still got it."

"Old human beings can still pull off a few things." He grimaced and stood up straight, stretching his back.

"Watch the stairs for me." Leira pulled up energy from the wet ground, through her body as the fiery symbols appeared on her arms and her eyes glowed. She watched the movement of the energy left behind, snaking back and forth and felt the thin thread of darkness woven through the stream. She shut her eyes and sent her energy out ahead of her, letting it follow the trail, feeling it in the center of her being as the two streams traveled across town to an old church that was turned into a restaurant. More streams appeared. "This dead guy definitely isn't from Austin."

"What restaurant? They haven't officially identified him yet."

"He's not. This was done as a ritual. Humans trying to play at being magical. That made up symbol is a sign of their cult. They think they're creating zombies."

"That's not really possible, is it?"

"I doubt it's possible for ordinary humans but these days I don't rule out things quite so fast. There's no magical trail so they didn't have an artifact. I'm going to go with *no* and conclude they're homicidal idiots. I think I have their meeting place. It'll be the best chance to catch most of them."

"Most... Let that sink in. What is wrong with people? How do we break it to the Captain up there?" He shook his head.

"I'm thinking we don't. We tell the general and let him pass along the news however he sees fit. There's not enough in this basement to give anyone anything substantial but I recognize the restaurant."

"You sure you don't want to try and talk to any dead bodies?" Hagan waggled his fingers. "Try and raise the spirits?"

"I'm not even sure how I did that the first time but I'm guessing it's not a good idea to try and do on the fly. We have enough information. Let's get out of here."

"Make your call."

"You would have figured all of this out on your own."

"No shit. But you got the address a lot faster and maybe with a few less bodies. Don't you worry, Berens. There'll come a time when ol' Hagan will be the deciding factor. I'm in this for a reason. I can feel it in my gut. Make your call. The Captain will be back down here at some point and then you'll have to wait. We need someone on that building pronto."

CHAPTER FOUR

Leira called the general and told him everything she knew. A special ops team surrounded the restaurant in under an hour and took five people into custody with enough evidence on their laptops to charge them with several counts of murder.

Leira drove Hagan home and stopped in front of his house, the motor idling.

"You know I'm still figuring out how to handle all of this." Leira draped an arm over her steering wheel. "I was kind of an ass back there."

"Only a small one and I know it's a lot. You get a pass once in a while. It happens. We'll get our rhythm back in no time. Until then, I'll remind you not to hog the playing field. I guess I take the rest of the day to do what I want until they call again, huh. You'll take care of the paperwork?" He waved his hands in the air.

"Don't keep doing the magic hands. You've never seen me do that even once."

"It's our shorthand. It works. You have to admit you know just what I mean."

"Till the next case. Yes, I'll do the paperwork. Good news is, I don't have to hide how we're doing it."

"We should stop by the warehouse some time, check in." He opened the car door and grunted as he stood up, hitching his pants back into the right spot.

"Furniture won't be there till next week. Not much point just yet unless you like sitting at a card table and staring at me."

"Point taken." He leaned down so he could still see Leira. "Good start to this whole thing. Makes up for the magical brawl earlier. Lost one, won one."

"I prefer to think of that first one as a draw."

"Fair enough. Call me when we're up again."

"Keep your phone with you. I have a feeling it won't be long."

"Roger that," said Hagan, as he shut the door, giving a short wave and turning to the stairs.

Leira watched him go inside before she pulled away from the curb. *That damn necklace will turn up again. When it does, I want to be there.*

Charlie Monaghan finally calmed down enough to look like his old self. Every hair in place, a smile at the ready and his hand out to shake. He waited patiently in a back room of the Capital Grille at 42nd and Third in New York City. It was the perfect place for the select chief executive officers of the most influential conglomerates in the Western part of the world to meet. It was centrally located near several foreign consulates, making it easier for the gentlemen to make their way to the restaurant.

The spot was already a favorite among the different embassies, and no one would have wondered at seeing so many gather there on a frosty winter morning.

The black Lincoln Continentals, the upscale taxis of New York, glided to a stop in a neat line in front of the dark brown building with a flat facade and darkened windows that gave it an unassuming air.

The street out front was regularly swept on the hour and the windows washed daily to maintain a certain sense of order the rich and powerful expected.

Charlie pulled the meeting together in record time in just a matter of days. He made the phone calls himself, using every favor and leveraging every bit of inside knowledge he had of the different companies to get the hand-picked group assembled.

Langston Rogers was already settled in a chair near the top of the table, waiting patiently, just as Charlie instructed him.

Charlie rehearsed Langston's part with him, locked in the library with all of Langston's findings, going over everything. Langston showed him every artifact and relic he had in his possession, along with the video he took when traveling through Peru.

Each new bit of information about Oriceran left Charlie more energized. He was determined to gather a team together from around the world. *No one can win this race ahead of us. If there's one thing I've learned. The meek never inherit much of anything.*

A doorman was there at the ready at the entrance to the Grille, opening car doors and quickly ushering each carload of a CEO, his chief financial officer, several assistants and at least one beefy bodyguard into the Grille.

They were escorted down the slim hallway that ran the length of the restaurant back to the meeting room already set up with coffee and breakfast. An open bar was at the ready for later when the negotiations might become more difficult.

Charlie took on his usual role, clearly in charge of the day's events. He stood near the coffee, smiling graciously and shaking hands, his diamond cufflinks twinkling. He was wearing a bespoke dark blue suit that fit his frame neatly without looking tight across the shoulders as he talked with his hands. A new black and gold silk tie with his school crest was neatly tucked into his jacket. "John, good to see you! How's your wife, Alice? Get yourself some coffee."

An interpreter stood by his side, waiting patiently as he greeted the handful of CEOs from foreign countries. But Charlie was fluent in several languages and rarely needed help. He always liked to be prepared, just in case. No opportunities left on the table. That's what the entire meeting was about today.

A revolution to change our way of life for the better. A new source of energy that's already in a race with others. We will liberate as many artifacts as possible, as quickly as possible, get them into our possession and figure out a plan of action as we go forward. It was his opener to grab their attention.

A new challenge was presenting itself and Charlie was going to make sure they were all prepared to take advantage of it. It was his goal in life and had served him well. *The power of magic on Earth is real and is only going to grow stronger.*

The first report about artifacts came across his desk at the beginning of the year, but Charlie wrote it off as a hoax or a scheme to get rich people to part with their money. Someone at his country club had cornered him after golf one day, going on about an opportunity in a new technology that combined the ancient and the new. Now he wondered if he had passed up another business deal. *What was his name?* He shook his head, letting it go, smiling as someone gave him a nod, reaching for a coffee cup.

Then, Langston Rogers emailed him. Still, he balked. *What sane man believes in magic?* It took seeing magic to make him a believer.

The explosion of ideas rolling around in his head was keeping him up at night, gleeful at the opportunities.

But he would need a way to harness it all. That would take contracted cooperation from others, especially if he was going to convince magical beings to help change the world and build up the economy, all at the same time.

Humans, on the other hand are easier to get on board. Give them a middle-class life, get their loyalty in return forever.

It was only recently with all the layoffs that there were a few sour articles in the press and comments in social media. Charlie smiled harder, determined not to think about it. *Magic. There's fucking magic in the world.*

"Phillip, glad you could make it. Sorry you had to miss your son's soccer game. This is important. I'm sure we all see that."

Priorities. He smiled, all his even, white teeth showing and creases forming around his eyes. Everyone made a point to go up and say hello, making polite conversation for a moment before moving on to a safer part of the room. Everyone understood a basic business rule. Get in Charlie Monaghan's way and pay the price.

He was already leading the most influential and lucrative conglomerate in the world under the name Axiom.

Under his reign, Axiom was run as lean and efficiently as possible, investing everything in research and development, and replacing as much human power with robotics wherever it was feasible.

His favorite saying was that everything that came out of the ground was eventually modified by Axiom, helping people on their path to a better life. *Service and compensation. No reason I can't do both.*

The companies across the Axiom enterprise controlled sixty percent of the crop production in the world for both people and livestock.

Other companies that had to rely on his genetically modified soybeans, corn or wheat took the deal they could get with Charlie and went home. Nobody liked to negotiate with Charlie longer than absolutely necessary. Every minute longer was usually at the expense of something from their side of the table.

Charlie nodded to his private secretary who announced in his booming voice, "Gentlemen, if we can get started. Take your seats." The chatter in the room eased as everyone quietly took their seats. Only the most confident took seats closest to Charlie and Langston. A tall, well-built man in a tailored suit and long dark hair neatly tied back took a seat further away, relaxing in his chair with his leg crossed. He was too comfortable for Charlie's liking.

Who is that? He nodded to his secretary, and the young man glanced nervously at the guest list on his tablet. "He gave his name as Wolfstan Humphrey. British I think, very old money."

"Get me an introduction before he leaves," Charlie hissed, sensing old money meant new prey.

Charlie waited a beat, clasping his hands in front of his chest, looking around the room slowly for dramatic effect.

He launched into his opening lines, watching the reactions. *Good. Shock and awe. Except for Mr. Humphrey.* His brow momentarily furrowed, even as he plowed ahead.

"Before we get into the weeds with the details, a short demonstration." His heart beat faster again. Excitement was overtaking him. He nodded to Langston, who slowly rose and removed the metal circle from its engraved box. This time he placed the ring on a table set up two feet from the top of the large oval table away from the others.

"Okay, first..." Langston looked nervously at Charlie, who shook his head. *Not what we practiced, right...no talking. Just do it.* Langston took a deep breath and wiped his hands on his pants.

He took out the brass pipe and struck the ring in the exact pattern, stepping back as it spun fast enough to create the portal. Gasps were heard in the room.

"Is that a virtual screen?"

"Did you create an internet with just that metal thing?"

"Wait, is that a window?"

"Mother of..."

Langston confidently put his hand through the portal, moving a nearby frond. His hand shook slightly as he listened for any sounds of the Gardener. *One of these days my luck is going to run dry.*

A loud rustle startled Langston. He withdrew his arm, his eyes growing wide, making many in the room lean back into their chairs.

A large bird with iridescent blue and white feathers dove through the portal, spreading its wings in the boardroom, flapping in the air over the heads of the CEOs and letting out a large squawk before easily gliding back through the portal.

"That's enough, Langston. Close it up. I think we've made our point." Charlie sounded giddy. *It couldn't have gone better.* "That is what some are referring to as magic. Bending the laws of physics to alter the environment. We used it to give a glimpse into another planet. A world called Oriceran where this so-called magic is in the air. It's commonplace. But it gets better..."

Langston smiled at his side. Charlie was using parts of his scattered speech, tailoring it to fit the room. *I was right to trust him.*

"There are those among us here on this planet, on Earth who can do this because of their DNA. The energy flows through them and out into the environment, harnessing a kind of power." Wolfstan sat forward, uncrossing his legs, leaning his arms on the table.

"Magic." Langston opened his hands, smiling.

Charlie drew his smile tighter. "Even better, these creatures who look like us..." He patted his chest, letting the idea sink in for everyone else. "They stored a lot of their power in different inanimate objects creating relics and artifacts that act as conductors or batteries. There are thousands of them scattered throughout the world. This wheel is one example."

"Wow." A silver-haired man gasped as he touched the wheel sending a jolt through his body. He sat back in his chair, his eyes wide.

"But there's a catch. We're not the only ones who know about the existence of this stored magic. The race is already on, gentlemen. We need to not only catch up but run right past them. It's in everyone's best interests if we control the story rather than let someone else write it. To do that we will need to hire the best history professors and archaeologists out there and go on the biggest scavenger hunt seen in modern times."

"With very real consequences." A rotund middle-aged man spoke in a clipped British accent. "I'm going to assume you're already contracting with your top choices."

"Yes, Pearson. The first teams are already out in the field."

"We're here to finance this venture." Pearson pursed his lips, leveling his gaze at Charlie.

"Co-finance and mutually reap the rewards." Charlie nodded at his private secretary. A thumb drive with their individual name on it was placed in front of each CEO, except for the extra guest. He waved off Charlie's secretary, earning a scowl from Charlie. "Legal papers to look over and sign, as well as much more extensive background on Oriceran and the artifacts. You'll find it's to your benefit to be on the inside of this venture. This is going to change everything we know about our lives but unlike past inventions or discoveries, at a much faster pace."

"Do you have specific plans for the artifacts yet?" Finally, Wolfstan Humphrey had spoken. "Do you even know how to use them?"

All heads in the room swiveled from Wolfstan to Charlie, no one saying a word. Charlie startled, though it only showed as a slight flicker of his eyebrow. He spoke, making sure his voice projected across the room. "Our R&D department is coming up with numerous applications." Wolfstan nodded and sat back in his chair, out of Pearson's line of sight.

"I'm in, of course." Pearson raised his large hand, waving away any more questions from others sitting next to him. "Don't be foolish. Charlie Monaghan wouldn't bring a half-baked idea to the table. The details will be worked out. I appreciate the opportunity." He scooped up the thumb drive and rose to leave. "I'll be in touch as soon as possible."

Pearson hurried out, his entourage in tow and quickly found his way to his car and driver. He waited until he was settled in the backseat before he called Lacey Trader, the head of the Silver Griffins.

"You were right. The race is on. Protect the vault by any means necessary. Convert the vault entrance and do what you suggested all along. I was wrong. Send out the Silver Griffins worldwide to find whatever artifacts they can and bring them back. I'll finance whatever you need." He hung up and sat back, taking in a deep breath. The stranger in the board room had not gone unnoticed by him either. Pearson had wanted to send out a stream of magic to see if he was a fellow traveler, but he didn't dare risk exposure, and Wolfstan was never in full view to get a good reading. "Something was off about him. That much I'm sure of," he muttered. "But what side is he playing for?"

He reached into the side pocket of the door and pulled out the long, elegant wooden case, opening it up and pulling out the rosewood wand. He touched the tip to the thumb drive, extracting the information and tapped the closed laptop in front of him. "Send it to Lacey." He touched the wand to the thumb drive again, turning it to dust.

Thirty years of being undercover as a Wizard among the more influential humans was paying off.

"Everything alright, Boss?" The young Wizard looked in the rearview mirror at Pearson.

"Yes, Manfreid, it's unfortunately going just as we predicted with a few open questions." *And we'll do our best to control this crash as much as we can.*

CHAPTER FIVE

The other prophets were already in the hidden meeting room at the far end of the post office, one exact mile from where all the mailboxes lined the walls.

The Kilomea prophet chose to walk from the entrance. The rail cars were too small for his size and he never liked the circuitous route the metal car took to avoid the gargoyles flying overhead putting the mail in their proper slots.

A gargoyle swooped low enough over his tall head to rustle the fur on the back of his neck. He grunted and looked up, scowling but the gargoyle ignored him and flew higher, the leather satchel flapping against its gold scales.

A family of Light Elves moved out of his way, the mother putting her arms in front of her children as if she was shielding them.

"Really? You act like you've never seen a Kilomea before. Boo!" He raised his arms and bugged out his eyes. The mother shuddered but the little female Elf in front of her giggled. The Kilomea smiled at her. "You get it. Good for you." He gave a *tsk* at the mother and lumbered on his way, making good time across the long lobby.

At the entrance to the room he stopped and pulled out his folded robe from inside his vest, shaking it out and draping it across his shoulders. He was too far away from anyone else to be noticed at that point. He opened the sliding entrance and went in, the stars appearing across his robe, lining up with the virtual display on the ceiling.

The other prophets were already there, gathered in a circle around the Book of Prophesies sitting in its glass case in the well of the room. He pushed his way into the circle between the Crystal prophet and the Light Elf, Kyomi, grunting a brief hello. Kyomi looked up at him, a strain on his face.

"You already started the meeting."

"We haven't officially started. Only the arguing started early." Kyomi scowled looking over at the Crystal prophet.

"It's time. We can't keep putting this off." A cold mist blew out from the Crystal's mouth and small snowflakes drifted down to the floor. "The gates will start to open soon, and the human beings are already racing each other to find the artifacts and relics we left behind. Our world will be ending, and we will need to make Earth our new home. We need to prepare our people."

"The humans will never fully accept us." The Pixie fluttered at eye level with the rest of the prophets so she could be heard more easily. "We've been over this."

"We must find a way to get them on our side." The Gnome prophet spoke in an even tone. "You know I'm right. Humans respond to heroics. To victories."

"How do you propose we pull off something like that?" asked the Kilomea.

"Wait! The last time we decided we'd manipulate the situation we got Prince Rolim killed." Kyomi was shaking with anger.

"We never intended for that to happen," said the Wood Elf, his pupils moving around, watching everyone. "And just because we failed—"

"Failed miserably!"

"Just because we failed, doesn't mean we give up. What do you propose, Gnome?" The Wood Elf prophet eyed him.

"A ruse where no one can get hurt, at least not permanently. We open a portal to one of their bigger cities and create a situation."

"The exact words used the last time we stood here and plotted." The Light Elf's eyes glowed causing the glass case to give off rolling waves of electric static, protecting itself from anyone practicing magic too close to the precious book.

"Calm yourself. We'll have more control over this situation because we won't bring in an outsider, much less a human. We'll handle this one ourselves. We'll open a portal to Earth and stage an accident to someone they all notice. Someone important."

"A politician?"

"No, we need large numbers to care about the person who gets hurt. A famous person for just being famous. What they call a celebrity."

"We all know what a celebrity is over there," said the Pixie, annoyed. "No one likes to admit it, but we all watch the humans. They're constantly finding new ways to best each other. Singing, climbing obstacle courses, even eating contests. Like watching two Lutea players about to collide. You want to look away but..."

"You laugh when they knock heads." The Gnome graciously smiled, folding his hands over his stomach.

"The Kardashians are all Arpaths. One of them might volunteer." The Arpath prophet fluttered his wings.

"Not one of us. One of them. A human celebrity. Someone who wouldn't know what hit them, and they'd never suspect us. We'd get their undying gratitude across all their ways of communicating with each other. Post, tweets, snap chats, tik toks. There's an endless list. Someone like Penny Ryan. Famous for talking about others and setting trends. Millions of people follow her every move. An accident that leaves her briefly at death's door until one of us magically brings her back to complete health. All in public in the middle of Rodeo Drive and dozens of smart phones recording everything."

"We would be exposing magic." The Wood Elf's eyes widened. "We can't take it back once we do this."

"We can't take back the end of our planet either. We have no choice. The only question is, do we start with a witch that looks just like them or a Crystal and jump in the deep end. No offense." The Kilomea nodded at the Crystal prophet standing next to him. They stood shoulder to shoulder, the two largest beings in the room. The fur on the Kilomea's shoulder was frozen together in clots but he didn't feel it through the two layers of thick skin.

"Put it to a vote," said the Gnome. "Let the majority decide our next step. Our fate is sealed but we can still control how we handle things. We owe this to all of Oriceran. All in favor?"

Everyone raised their hand, even the Light Elf prophet. The Gnome smiled. "Then it's settled. I suggest we send a Witch and the Wood Elf. A little of both. Are you up to the task?"

The Wood Elf grimaced but nodded his head. "It's time we started building bridges even if we have to take matters into our own hands."

"I'm not sure how I feel about harming anyone." The Pixie fluttered her wings, coming to land on the Kilomea's shoulder.

"It's a celebrity. Imagine the publicity this will get them. They'll be set for life." The Gnome let out a chortle. *Always nice when a plan comes together. Not much longer and I can shed this skin.*

―――――

Harkin pulled up to The White Horse Saloon on Comal Street on the east side of Austin. It was a well-known hangout for magicals who wanted a drink but needed to stay hidden. The bar was one story, long with a low roof and two red doors right in the middle. It was affectionately known as a honkytonk that sold beer and tacos. A good description of most bars on that side of Austin.

Harkin walked inside and waited at the door while his eyes adjusted to the darkness and the dim red lights that were always on, giving the place its own kind of ambience. The original owner, a necromancer named Phil, said it could even make the dead look better.

Harkin blinked hard and ambled toward the bar on his left. It made him itchy to stand still for too long in public. He took a quick glance around at the few drinkers leaning over beers at their tables. *Not here yet.*

The bartender stopped mopping the top of the bar and leaned on it with both meaty hands, the usual resting bitch face firmly in place. "Long time, Harkin. You're supposed to be dead. You owe Phil money and he decide to bring you back?"

"Something like that, Jenkins. Still keeping this place a toasty sixty-eight degrees?" The bartender was a large half Crystal, half human with a glamor spell that hid his exterior but not his core body temperature.

Jenkins patted his chest. "Not much I can do about that. What's it been? Twenty, thirty years?"

"Maybe. And this place still resembles a mid-level funeral parlor with a dance floor and a bar."

"When a theme is working, you don't change it." He was already pulling out a glass and pouring two fingers of whiskey, neat, pushing it across the bar.

Harkin picked up the glass and took a nice sized swallow. "I see what you mean."

"Rules haven't changed either, Harkin." Jenkins swatted toward the whiteboard and Phil's scrawled rules. So far there were only four of them, but the magicals knew about the unwritten number one rule. No magic on the premises, ever.

Jenkins leaned across the bar so he couldn't be heard by the nearby man wearing a stained green baseball hat and sporting a beard wider than his chin.

"New clientele I see," said Harkins.

"What him? There's lots of them stopping by lately. Humans have their own way of getting the word out. They all have beards like that. I figure it's the East side's version of a man bun."

"Not planning to break any rules. Just here for a brief conversation."

"Well, there's a first for everything. Break it and I'll throw your ass out of here personally. My back's been bothering me this week, and I don't fancy pulling off another, *never was, never will be* spell and picking grown men off the floor." He gave Harkin a nod. "Mind your business."

Harkin swallowed the last of the bourbon and slid the glass across the bar for another pour. "And do me a solid. Forget you saw me."

"You hurt my feelings, Harkin. That was a given when you walked in the door. It's in the bartender's guide to the weird and magical handbook. Phil wrote the thing. It's a masterpiece."

A door opened and a short, stocky man stood silhouetted against the bright daylight outside.

"Newbie," muttered Jenkins and went back to wiping off the counter. "Gnomes are always too slow to react. That's why they have to hide in holes in the ground."

Harkin smiled and turned the glass between his fingers, waiting for the Gnome to sit down next to him.

"Rankin, you're late. Started to wonder if you were coming." Harkin glanced at him and took a quick look around. No one was paying them any attention.

"I had a helluva time finding this place." He pulled out a white handkerchief and mopped the top of his bald head. "Geez, I'm sweating and freezing at the same time. What kind of mother-fucker runs this place?" He looked at Jenkins. "No offense, of course."

Jenkins curled his lip and let out a low growl.

Rankin put the damp handkerchief back in his pocket and

shook his head. "Cold hearted motherfuckers and still so sensitive. You just never know. You bring the money?"

Harkin slid the envelope across the table. "It's all in there."

Rankin opened it and fingered the cash, getting a quick estimate. "Normally, I'd say I know where to find you, but nobody knows where the fuck to find you!" He smiled, a broken tooth in the front making him sound like he was whistling when he laughed. "Yeah, okay, good enough. You want info."

"Get on with it, Rankin, or I break rule number one anyway."

The Gnome shook his head, letting out a breath and a whistle. "Geez, okay, okay. Everyone is touchy today. Maybe you need another one of those. Hey, tall, dark and freezing. You think I can get one of those too? I got money." Rankin tapped the envelope. "I even tip."

Jenkins pulled out the bat and held it in one hand while he poured a drink with the other.

"Veiled threats, I love it," said Rankin. "I get 'em all the time." He drank back the bourbon in one gulp and wiped his mouth with the back of his hand. "Much better. Now, where were we? Oh yeah, you want info on who's invading your illegal part of the turf. Some dangerous motherfuckers, I can tell you that."

"What makes them so dangerous?"

"They're you without all the niceties, and they have bigger plans." Rankin swiveled on his barstool, getting even more excited and waved his stubby hands around. "I have it from some excellent sources that the company is brand new. Called Fleeker for some reason, I don't know. Marketing. It's a bitch, am I right, Jenkins?" Rankin hitched a thumb over his shoulder, shaking his head. "His kind are never friendly. How can you be if you can never get fucking warm?"

Harkin shifted in his seat. The trip was already worth it. He had a name. "How new and how big is Fleeker?"

Rankin arched an eyebrow and tilted his head. "Interesting question since you didn't start with who's running the place. You came here with a little info already under your belt. You're good, Harkin." He pointed at Harkin, giving him a wink. "You haven't lost your step. Okay, okay, no need to start glowing on me. Fleeker is real new, like yesterday new, but they're already growing at a pace that usually takes years. They're making deals with other companies and word is, if you can't reach an amicable deal, they buy you out."

Harkin tapped the top of the bar with two fingers and Jenkins wandered over to refill the glasses. A nearby human at a table raised his empty beer glass.

"No is not an option," muttered Harkin.

"In the world of dark magic, is it ever? I mean, it's always a contest of whose got the mental strength and the most magic. A new kind of golden rule."

"You have any names inside of Fleeker?"

"No, but I do know of a company they have their sights set on. Should be an easy mark. It's a conglomerate called Axiom owned by a human who has his fingers in Oriceran pots. That would be your weak point. Start there." Rankin emptied his glass. "You're paying today, right? That's just manners. You called me here," he said, his chin tucked on his chest as he held his hands out to the side.

"Never change, Rankin." Harkin slapped cash on the bar and stood, checking his pockets.

"You wound me," said Rankin.

"Just checking. You started out as a clever thief. Why would you stop?"

"Excellent point."

"Give back my pocket watch."

Rankin let out an exasperated sigh and smiled, pulling the watch out of his pocket. "I like to keep in practice. I was thinking it could be like a tip. No?"

Harkin put the old watch in his pocket and walked toward the door, not bothering to say goodbye.

45

"Hey barkeep, how about a couple tacos? This time it really is me paying," said Rankin.

Harkin smiled, despite the growing tremors in his belly, and pushed the door open, stepping out into the daylight. "Wolfstan Humphrey, you dangerous motherfucker. I'm coming for you again and this time I'll take your head to make sure you're dead. Even Phil won't be able to bring you back."

'I have a request while you're in Austin. I'm an old friend of your father's. I knew Harkin well. Can we meet by the edge of the Dark Forest? You can use a tracking spell to find me. Wolfstan Humphrey'

Correk read the invitation and waited for the words to dissolve into worms, holding up the card for the bird waiting on the windowsill. The passenger pigeon swallowed the offering and blinked at Correk with a soft cooing sound.

"That's all I have, Palmer. You'd better get back to the post office." Correk held his hand up to the open window in the cupola of his old room and waited for Palmer to push off, spreading his blue and grey wings.

Correk thought about not going, but curiosity had the better of him. Most Oricerans would never mention his father, much less use his name to gain an introduction.

He gathered his longbow and a quiver of arrows and went to a tall open window. He let the energy flow through him. *"Altrea extendia."* A bronze staircase unwound beneath him, and he set out for the ground far below, steps appearing ahead of him even as they disappeared behind him.

Correk got to the edge of the forest and moved just inside the treeline where he couldn't be seen from a castle window. His eyes glowed as he formed a ball of light in his hands. Singing into it, he let it float ahead of him, tracking the trail of magic Wolfstan had left behind.

The ball abandoned the worn path and bounced over and under branches, heading deeper into the forest. Correk glanced at the clouds behind him where he knew the castle floated. He stopped, wondering if he was walking into a trap and pulled his bow out. He listened for any sound that didn't belong, his ears twitching and heard the footfall of something walking on two legs.

"No need for that." Wolfstan emerged from behind a stand of saplings, the ball of light bouncing just over his head. He waved his hand, and the ball dissolved, sparks briefly illuminating Wolfstan's face.

"I needed someplace private where no one could speculate about anything. The wrong rumors lead to problems."

Correk's eyes still glowed as he observed the swirl of green and black magic surrounding Wolfstan. "When did you know my father?"

Wolfstan grimaced, trying to turn it into a smile. "I thought it was rude to read another man's trail. I suppose under the circumstances, another sage precaution. I knew your father in Trevilsom Prison."

Correk's muscles tensed. He turned to go, magic flowing through him. *It is a trap.*

"Not a trap," said Wolfstan. "That is what you're thinking, right? I come with an offer, that's all."

Correk stopped, but his hand still gripped his bow. "What kind of offer? Your message said you had a request."

"It is a request… not a demand. I've started a company in the other world, and it's doing quite well. Growing faster than I could have hoped." He held his hands out to show he wasn't holding any weapons and wasn't trying to create any fireballs. "I need a Light Elf like yourself to help me bridge negotiations between the two worlds. I'm working on using your father's old research to mix bioengineering and magic."

Correk ground his teeth. A flash of anger passed through him.

Control it, let it go. He heard Turner's voice echoing in his head. *Anger can diminish magic and get someone killed.* "Even less interested."

"Your father's work was groundbreaking. Frankly, it still is. Imagine the possibilities it could do for everyone. It would be sought after on both sides."

"I have no need of money, and I suspect any magical that does."

"So would I, but who doesn't want to push the boundaries?" The magic pulsed through Wolfstan so quickly Correk didn't have a chance to react. Instantly, the day faded to night, and stars appeared overhead. Correk drew an arrow, pulling back on the string, yet the daylight was restored just as fast.

Wolfstan didn't move, a smile appearing that still seemed menacing. "Surely you've given Harkin another chance." The smile grew, the lines deepening around his eyes when he saw a look of confusion pass across Correk's face.

"You don't know, do you? That would be just like him. Noble to a fault, even if it costs him everything. Dear boy, Harkin is alive and well, hiding somewhere on this planet or maybe the other." Wolfstan gazed at the canopy overhead where a colorful macaw screeched. "He still has a few tricks that I can admire. Hiding has always been one of his best."

Correk stepped toward Wolfstan, breathing hard, the nearby ferns leaning away from him. "I don't know what game you're conjuring, Wolfstan, but the answer remains no." Correk turned to go, not bothering to look back.

"Wouldn't you rather keep an eye on things from the inside?" Wolfstan called after him.

Correk didn't respond, his head swirling. *Harkin is alive. No, it can't be.*

"We will meet again," muttered Wolfstan, retreating behind the foliage. He opened a portal back to Earth. "I will get your father's plans."

Hagan and' Leira sat at their new desks in the old warehouse. From the outside, the building still looked like it was falling into disrepair. Inside, everything was rewired and the latest equipment brought in, enabling the Paranormal Defense Agents to monitor magical activity around the world. Couches were set against one wall and a small area with a microwave and a wooden table and chairs in another corner made up what there was of a kitchen area.

A cackle went up from across the warehouse. Lois and Patsy were sitting on the new couches watching *The Price is Right*, laughing at the small yodeling plastic figure making its way up the Alps. "It's going over the top!"

"Lois, we need a couch like this back at the PDF!"

"We don't have room in that closet of an office. This is a couch island. Get it for your rec room."

"Hello, I spend more time with you at work than anywhere else. I want this for the office."

"Then figure out a spell to grow our office or shrink the couch and us along with it." Patsy let out a laugh. "I'm hungry again!"

"News at eleven!"

Hagan put another piece of sugarless gum in his mouth, adding to the bulge in his cheek. "They were brought in to show us how to use everything."

Leira decided not to say anything. "They felt it was time for a break."

A Twinkie went flying across the open space landing in Lois' lap. She scrunched up her nose, stopping her glasses from sliding. "Seven-ninety-nine! Seven-ninety-nine!"

"I have to admit flying food is a neat trick. Efficient too." Hagan chewed his gum, watching the ladies yell numbers at the screen. "I can't tell. Is this relationship working, or not?"

"They came highly recommended and Lois gives off a stronger pulse of magic energy than she's letting on to. I think those two are hiding in plain sight."

"The question is from what?"

Another Twinkie flew across the room. "Told you! Four dollars is too high for a damn roll of paper towels! Even Bounty!"

"Isn't that from Correk's stash?" Hagan licked his lips and chomped down hard on the gum.

"Do you want one? I don't see the appeal. Correk has plenty, and we can get more any time. Hell, I could probably get the Feds to supply us." Leira held one up and peered at the wrapper. "These beauties are some kind of weird invention by humans that will never go stale, never rot. You'd think it'd do a better job of preserving your insides if you eat enough of them." She opened the plastic wrapper and took a whiff. "I don't get it. Does nothing for me." She held out her hand, ready to toss it into the trash.

"You're just gonna throw that away?" Hagan leaned forward in his chair.

"Here, but I don't feel good about this." She tossed it to Hagan, who took a long smell, shaking his head. He looked pained as he held it up. "Ladies, help me out." The Twinkie zipped out of his fingers and across the room.

"Hagan that's one of the more courageous things I've ever seen you do."

"Fuck you, Berens. And agreed."

"Maybe we can get a mini fridge in here and fill it with hummus and carrots."

"Fuck me. Don't do that. I get enough of that at home."

"Alright, if you don't want..."

"A nice sugar free pudding cup wouldn't hurt. The chocolate and vanilla swirls."

Leira looked at Hagan. "Consider it done. I'll even spring for them myself. Donation to the cause. Future you will be grateful you pulled this off."

Hagan grunted. "I'm doing this so there is a future me. Let's talk about something else."

A loud ringing pealed through the room, vibrating against the walls. Lois and Patsy sat up straight on the couches as Lois waved her wand at the screen. Hagan startled, swallowing his gum, jumping to his feet with his gun drawn. Leira pulled in energy from the ground, lighting up the symbols on her arm. "There's no threat."

The ringing was too loud for her to be heard.

Lois and Patsy were frantically waving their wands at the screen closest to them. Both of them looked worried. Leira tapped Hagan on the shoulder and pointed at the two witches. She ran over to get a look at and recognized the symbols flying across the screen. They were the same as the ones appearing on her arms.

"What does it all mean?" She shouted but the witches didn't hear her over the alarm that was still ringing. They were too busy reading as fast as they could. "Hey! Hey!" Leira waved her arms.

Lois turned around and noticed Leira standing next to her for the first time. "Oh!" She waved her wand, silencing the alarm. "Sorry about that. We put that in first thing. It makes sure no one misses anything big and this is big. Big I tell you!"

"All those symbols mean something?"

"Well, sure as shit they do!" Lois was excited. She turned back to the symbols pointing her new upgraded wand, slowing down the ticker. See those swirls? Big trouble. See enough of those and it means someone is dead, kaput! Last time we saw something like that was Chicago and your name kept popping up."

"Is someone dead?" Hagan came and stood beside Leira looking up at the virtual screen.

"Let's see, three witches down from the Order. Oh dear. Fourteen rogues from another country."

"All hell has broken loose!" Patsy was following another

screen, looking back over her shoulder at them. "The Order is fighting with the rogue witches and wizards."

"Let me guess. It's the necklace." Leira clenched her fists. "It's the only thing I know of that would cause this kind of magical battle. Where are they?"

"Latvia. Gets worse. A third party has entered this fray. The local government has sent in their forces to grab it. Human forces! I'm afraid the humans have caught on at last to what's up for grabs. All bets are off!" Lois wrinkled her nose, pushing her glasses back into place.

"This shit has gone global!" Patsy's voice came out in a squeak.

Leira went to call the general but Lois stopped her. "No point, honey. This was nasty and short. Nobody was messing around. The necklace has already moved on. See that string of symbols up there? It's the Order reporting that they missed their chance but so did the humans. Not sure if that's good or bad. Easier to take it from them most times."

"Well, that's odd," said Patsy. "What does that even mean?"

Lois pushed her glasses up her nose and squinted for good measure, stepping closer for a better look. She pointed at each symbol zipping across, pursing her lips. "Hmph, some magical is opening a business. That's not really news. Wolfstan Humphrey. A magical from Oriceran gave himself a last name."

"That part I get. Humans are big on knowing who's not related to who. Wolfstan. That's an old Light Elf name. Never heard of him, though."

"Wonder why Wolfstan made the ticker?"

"Two extremes today!" Patsy patted her blonde bouffant. "Probably nothing."

Lois turned from the screen, not entirely convinced. But no further information was showing, and she had to let it go.

She glanced at Patsy and lowered her voice, stepping closer to Leira. "Look, honey I'm a little surprised, I don't mind telling you that you can't read those symbols. Kind of basic stuff for anyone who's magical. Especially someone like you."

"What does that mean?" Leira's eyes started to glow. She was on the edge of anger and ready to fight. She was tired of doing all the chasing. The symbols lit up on her arms, climbing up her neck.

"See what I mean? It's written across your body! Didn't you notice? The symbols are never the same. These aren't here to let the world know you're fixing to whomp somebody but good. They're the energy talking to you, looking to guide you." Lois waved her wand over Leira's arm, momentarily changing the symbols into words she could read.

'May Sage was wounded but is reported to be in good condition.'

"I know that Witch! General badassery! Would hate to lose her." Patsy swallowed a Twinkie in three bites. "Stress eating! It's how I cope sometimes."

Hagan grimaced and waved at her. "Been there, trying not to do that."

"You're your own virtual screen." Lois smiled at Leira.

"But you can't change the channels, so there's that." Patsy shrugged and turned to the screen.

"These will only appear when you summon them, giving you information about the magic you're tuning into. Like a heads up."

"No mention of the general public squawking about it. That's a plus." Patsy gave Hagan a long look and smiled.

"He's married, Patsy. Cool your jets." She whipped her wand around and zinged Patsy with a small spark, hitting her right in her plum-colored velour pants.

"You bitch!"

"For your own good. You know how you get. Behavior modi-fication." Lois looked at Hagan. "You're welcome, trust me on this one."

Hagan's eyebrows shot up, and he held his left hand up,

wiggling his fingers to show off his plain gold wedding band. "Almost twenty-five blissful years!"

Lois took Leira by the arm as the symbols faded. "You need a mentor who can teach you the basics. Not tall, blonde and Elven hottie. He's too young in Elven years. Has a lot still to learn himself. But you definitely need someone."

Leira's phone buzzed. "It's the general."

"Seems he found out through the more standard channels. Think about what I said. All that wonderful power you have isn't much use if you have to trip over how to use it, bit by bit. Especially if the world is waking up to magic."

Leira answered before the last ring as Lois whispered, "Find a mentor."

"Hello, General Anderson. Yes, I know what happened. We're monitoring the situation." *That damn necklace.*

CHAPTER SIX

The short buses decorated in cheerful colors of blue and yellow turned onto Fleeker Way, the entrance to the twenty-six-acre campus in Round Rock, Texas outside of Austin. The drive toward the main cluster of buildings passed a sculpture garden with a labyrinth for meditative walks connected by walking trails to manicured English gardens. Closer to the main buildings, life-sized statues of popular superheroes posed in mid-flight or performing miraculous feats such as holding a small car over their head.

New employees pressed their faces closer to the glass inside the shuttle, their mouths hanging open.

Lily Sharpton sat on the bus rolling her eyes at the two girls on the opposite bench. "Sensory overload, I remember you well. Visual orgasm. Helps the Kool-Aid go down easy."

Billy nudged her in the ribs with a skinny elbow. "So cynical at such a young age," he snickered. "How's your project coming?"

The smile dropped from Lily's face, and she looked around. "You don't ask questions like that Billy," she said in a hushed voice, glancing at the two girls. They were still pointing and smiling at the sights as the shuttle stopped in front of the largest glass-covered building. "Two lab techs disappeared without a goodbye for sharing dumb stuff with each other. One of them had seniority."

"What's seniority in a place that's been open less than a year?"

"Come on, we're here. Stick to asking about my love life. It's exciting enough for both of us, and we'll get to keep our jobs."

They filed off the bus and saw a large half circle of rose bushes with daffodils and tulips ringing the inside. Everything was trimmed and weeded, not a petal or blade of grass out of place.

Everyone passed through the scanner in an orderly line, holding out their left arm to let it read the chip under their skin. Lily had her daily moment of doubt about letting anyone put a chip under her skin and forced the thought down. "Eight thousand a month plus perks," she whispered. Another part of her daily routine. She held up her backpack and let them scan it, quickly reminding herself where she had left her wand. *At home on top of the dryer. Check.*

Her circle of magical friends had all been recruited to work at Fleeker, and rumors flew that the tenth floor of executives were all magicals, but no one was sure, and Lily needed to keep her job. She waited by the elevator. "Two years and my loans are paid off. Just two years."

Billy looked at her. "What are you always mumbling?"

"Daily affirmations," said Lily, squeezing onto the large elevator, looking up at a big man wearing too much cologne standing next to her. Sensors on either side of the door scanned her chip again.

The elevator stopped at the fourth floor, and a pleasant female voice said, "One" over the intercom. Security knew at all times where someone was in the building and how many should be getting off at any given floor.

Lily pressed forward, squeezing by two techs in blue biohazard outfits. "Scuse me, scuse me."

A large sign on the wall in front of the elevator read, in very large black uppercase letters, SECURITY LEVEL AA. The highest clearance. Others on the elevator examined her and several eyebrows went up. Lily turned around at the last second before the doors closed. "That's right, bitches. Smarter than all of you!"

The doors closed to astounded faces. Morning ritual was almost complete. A few people had complained to Human Resources about her behavior, but nothing ever came of it. Lily's skills were too in demand.

Besides, I'm not exactly human, she thought, passing through the double set of doors that opened to the sides with a *whoosh* as she approached. She stopped at the outer room and put her things into a locker, typing in a short code and turning the dial to lock it. She pulled on a fresh biohazard suit and booties and walked toward the last set of doors. They opened with another soft *whoosh* and an ultralight spray of light emitted from above to disinfect and disable any technology one might be smuggling onto the premises.

No one would be that stupid. She got to her workstation and pulled out the slides that contained particles from an artifact. Some of the slides were mixed with human skin cells, some with different magicals and others with bovine cells.

Lily tapped her pocket. It held a picture of her aunt. "Okay, Aunt Lois, I'll make you proud. Two more years and the loans are paid, and maybe I can join the PDF." Her dream job.

She leaned in and scrutinized the first slide under a laser microscope. She popped her head up and looked around, her face flush. She sucked in her bottom lip and bent slowly over the scope, closing one eye for a better look. "It's working," she whispered, heart beating fast. *The cells are bonding.*

Correk found Perrom near the Dark Market not bothering to blend in, walking toward the vendors who ringed the tent. "I didn't believe the pixies when they told me I could find you here." Correk jogged to catch up to his old friend.

Perrom turned, surprised, his four pupils moving in different directions to see who noticed Correk calling to him. He raised a finger to his lips. "I'm here as a customer. It's good to see you." He grabbed Correk in a hug, slapping him on the back. "It's easier to get to know the different players as a buyer. Merchants tend to say too much all the time, letting things slip," he said in a hushed tone.

A tall broad-shouldered merchant with a small booth near the front of the market was loudly yelling *hello* to everyone who passed by him. Correk looked over at the young Wizard as he playfully slapped a customer's wallet out of their hands.

Perrom watched as the Wizard shook his head, smiling.

"They put the newer merchants out front. They put Louie out front because he's annoying and that way no one inside has to listen to him," said Perrom

"If he's that annoying, how did he get a place in the market at all?"

"He's uniquely gifted at finding small artifacts that pack a punch."

"Ah, a clever thief."

"He gets in and out of strange and dangerous places on Oriceran without a scratch. He's either clever at hiding how powerful he is, or he was born under a lucky star."

Correk stepped close to the table and picked up a metal armband with a ruby set in the middle. "This is quite old."

"No, you're old," said Louie, his blonde curls bouncing as he nodded and pointed at Correk.

Correk arched an eyebrow and stared at Louie.

"I told you his people skills were a bit odd." Perrom smiled. "But he's right. You are getting older."

Louie laughed and pointed at Perrom. "You feel me, right!"

"How much for the armband?"

"Ten gold coins. Worth every one of them. Almost lost one of my arms retrieving it." Louie stood back, his hands on his hips. Correk put the piece down and walked away.

"You'll be back. They always come back to Louie!"

"He's not going to bargain with you. Somewhere under all that bluster is a shrewd businessman as well as a nimble thief. Besides, I hear he has a crew he splits the money with. He has a thin margin of profit."

Correk could still feel the buzz in his fingers from the armband. An ancient and powerful artifact. "I can come back."

"Louie is one of the merchants I've been getting to know. He's good at blending into the background and listening. Bigger players forget he's there. I'm hoping he'll share some of that with me. Doesn't hurt I was able to get my hands on more electronic parts."

He pulled out a solderless breadboard from his leather pouch. It was in a package with Radio Shack printed on the front in red. Perrom smiled. "I can make a circuit. It's fascinating. Imagine if this could be combined with magic?"

Correk bristled and clenched his teeth. "The two were never meant to be combined. There are so many unforeseen consequences."

Perrom patted him on the shoulder. "I suppose some old memories never become calloused." Perrom shook his head. "It's coming, you know. The more the gates open, the more the two sides are going to try to figure out how to combine their talents."

"You have a point." Correk rubbed his forehead. "I need to find a way to let go of Harkin and move on."

"Try not to lose all of him. I remember some pretty good times, too. Your father was a great inventor, always coming up with some new gadget to entertain us. And he always had candy in his pockets. I suppose that's where you got your love for junk food."

Correk arched an eyebrow and picked up a flute, turning it over in his hand, ignoring Perrom.

"Okay, I get it, enough said," said Perrom. *Some day.* "What brings you here? You home to stay?"

"I'm here to find out if you've heard anything else and to make sure I have as much energy as I can keep with me on Earth." *Forget about Wolfstan Humphrey. Rhazdon is a much bigger problem.*

Perrom frowned. "It's gotten worse, then." He took in a deep breath, blowing it out quickly.

"I'm looking for the mastermind behind the new followers of Rhazdon's old cult. They have the necklace."

"There are more rumors about something being off with the old Gnome, and I've seen him a few times passing through the Dark Market on his way to the large tent in the back. That place is invitation only. I don't rate one yet. No one will give me any details. Most are too afraid of him. You think he's the traitor? Makes sense except he's a Gnome. Not exactly a super power, and they're known more for their integrity than treachery. Maybe he has an ally in that large tent. I mean, who goes to the Dark Market with good intentions?" He glanced at the electronic part in his hands. "Okay, good point, I'm here. It's a hobby. But none of this comes as a surprise to you."

"It's the artifact I found that bothers me the most."

"The infinity symbol."

"It's the mark of Rhazdon and now, his followers are playing hot potato with Prince Rolim's necklace. They're even managing to stay one step ahead of the Silver Griffins and an Atlantean agent they've hired. That shouldn't be possible."

"Dark magic can be like that. It has a strong power all its own. Unpredictable though. At some point it always burns up the user."

"We had an encounter with an old dark Wizard who kicked

our ass without breaking stride, but we don't think he's in charge."

"And if someone like him is willing to follow whoever dreamed up all of this. Wow…" Perrom's eyes widened.

"Whoever this is, they're almost as powerful as Rhazdon was in his day. All the stories I've heard… Even if someone had Rhazdon's old artifacts, any of them, they'd still have to be able to use them without blowing themselves up."

"That's not the Gnome. Gnomes aren't that powerful even with an artifact. They're usually smart enough not to play with them. Hell, they guard them so others can't get them. Although, this guy seems to be going against type. There's always an outlier."

"I have to get back. I didn't tell anyone I was coming here." He hugged his old friend, hesitating to say the one thing that had pushed him to look for Perrom. He was the only person he could think of on Oriceran who would hear him out without calling him crazy. Even then, he was close to leaving without saying a word. *I have to say it out loud.*

Perrom was already walking toward the opening to the market. "Perrom." The look on Correk's face drew Perrom back taking large strides. Correk hesitated again. "You know a little about dark magic. It's alright. I've kept your secret."

"My father would kill me if he knew. I figure it helps to stay one step ahead to have an idea of everyone's skill level."

"Do you… do you…" He finally blurted it out. "Do you think Rhazdon lives?" At last, the thought that kept tumbling around in Correk's head came out. Perrom's face dropped all expression and the squares on his skin kept flipping around, matching nearby settings and drawing attention. "Take a deep breath," whispered Correk, nodding at a nearby Nicht who had raised his bat wings into position.

"That can't be possible," hissed Perrom. "You know how much we lost the last time. Don't even suggest it was all futile!"

"Not saying it won't change the truth and ignoring the possibility could be worse. Do you think it's possible?"

Perrom looked Correk in the eye, his jaw set. "For anyone but Rhazdon I'd say no, but dark magic technically has no boundaries. It's the user that can only go so far. If Rhazdon survived that fire then yes, he could still be alive. Don't let that be so."

"Tell no one what I said but stay vigilant."

"Who would I tell that would listen? Are you going to warn King Oriceran? Remember his father. Your grandfather…"

"Not without more proof. I have to go." He put out his fist, and Perrom put his fist on top. The old symbol of agreeing to fight side by side in a battle. It was the second time in his life that Correk had used it.

"Always, brother. Someday soon we may fight with honor and to the end."

"Even if it's the last good thing we do." Correk grimaced, remembering the sight of the old king sacrificing himself.

Perrom pulled back before anyone could see the battle sign. "If I hear anything, I will find you, even if I have to open a portal. You have my word. Now go. We've stood here long enough." Perrom turned without another word and hurried toward the open flap of the market.

Correk strode away as fast as he dared without drawing attention. Saying it out loud made it seem like it could be real. *Rhazdon may live yet. We need to get that damnable necklace.*

General Anderson sat at a long table in front of the Senators that made up the Senate Armed Services Committee. The closed-door session was classified as *no one needed to ever know.*

"Yes, sir, that's our understanding," he said, his hat on the table neatly tucked at two o'clock, the usual spot. He liked order. These days he was not happy with how events were unfolding. "The

Latvian government is believed to have been acting on behalf of the Russians with their backing in an attempt to grab the most powerful artifact on Earth."

"But they failed." A sour-faced senator from Virginia scowled, smacking his lips.

"Yes, sir. We did as well. The necklace remains in the hands of a group of rogue Witches and Wizards. Their intentions are unknown but considered negative to our interests."

"Am I to understand that's not the only artifact? There are thousands of these things littering the world?" The senator from Arizona sat up in her chair, drawing her mouth into an angry thin red line.

"Correct, as well, and a poorly kept secret. Different sites in older parts of the world are being ransacked as foreign governments search for artifacts. Some friendly to us, some not at all."

"An arms race with magic," said the senator from Virginia, narrowing his eyes.

"That is about the size of it. There are rumors that large corporations are getting into the business, but they can't be confirmed. They're doing their level best to stay under the radar."

"So we can't shut them down."

The senator from Maine let out a snort. "Well, hell, I suppose we're about to engage in some kind of new age battle in plain sight." He shook his head. "I thought I'd seen everything. I was clearly mistaken. Your request for funding is approved but remember these are hardworking taxpayer dollars. Make them count. I don't want to have to explain this one to the public. The backlash would never end."

"Yes, sir," said the general. He took in a deep breath feeling some amount of relief.

"What about this necklace?" asked the Senator from Arizona. "Is that worth chasing?"

"As yet to be determined." The general chose to not mention Leira or the warehouse that was a black ops site. Or for that matter, the rumors of someone using the artifacts to experiment on animals. No one else in this room knew anything about any of it. Better to leave it that way.

"Then you have your directive. See that we win this race and soon."

Charlie Monaghan walked into his office, his face buried in his phone, a manicured finger scrolling through messages. He looked up, startled at the sound of Wolfstan Humphrey clearing his throat.

Wolfstan was in a tailored suit with an open collar, relaxing against Charlie's expensive leather couch, his arm resting on the back.

Charlie did his best to recover and regain a position of power without much luck. "Fuck..." He glanced over his shoulder. His private secretary had already disappeared back down the hallway.

"I let myself in," said Wolfstan, rising.

"My security team is supposed to be the best—"

"Times are changing. It is time we met officially," he said, extending his hand. "Wolfstan Humphrey. I was at your summit meeting. Let me cut to the chase. Have you made a decision?" Wolfstan put his hands in his pants pockets, taking a casual stance, but Charlie could feel the pressure.

What an asshole. First the meeting and now this. Charlie had been hoping to avoid giving an answer for at least another week. He flashed a smile, showing all his even, white teeth. "The board is still going over the details. In a worldwide organization like this, decisions can take a while."

"Yes, I have heard." Wolfstan scratched his chin, his eyes glowing as he looked around the room at the trinkets Charlie had on display. "Senator Thatcher spoke of your nice office. Almost as nice as his in the Capitol. Wonderful man, Senator Thatcher. He has really been a friend to Fleeker."

Charlie swallowed, his smile even tighter. A magical was leaning on him. One of his strongest allies was turning his back on Axiom in favor of the new company. He was going to have to rethink his strategy. Maybe there was still a way to save things.

"I'm sure we can come to an acceptable arrangement. You want to facilitate trades between Oriceran and Earth. So do I. Clearly, you have more knowledge of the other world than I do. We can both benefit." He put his hand out to shake and felt his stomach turn over from the vibrations that passed through his arm and spread throughout his body.

"Excellent. I'll look for the paperwork today." Wolfstan held his hand in place a moment longer.

A jolt of energy passed through Charlie's knuckles, making them ache. The strain showed around his eyes.

"I'll let Senator Thatcher know things are progressing. He'll be glad to hear all the pieces are falling into place so amicably. I'll see myself out."

Charlie watched Wolfstan walk down the hallway, then he slowly shut his door. "Not my first thug, and not my last. Something will take out magic and, once I find it, things can go back to normal."

CHAPTER SEVEN

Leira walked into the guest house after a long run, sweat running down the center of her back, and took a deep breath to see what was cooking. She was hoping for Nana's spaghetti sauce or Leira's old favorite from childhood, spicy red lentil soup. *No smell!*

She heard drawers opening and closing in the other room and looked at Yumfuck sitting in the potted fern. He shrugged and held up his little paws.

"Hello?"

"Oh, honey, you're home!" Her mother bustled out of the bedroom, her face flushed and shiny.

"What are you two up to in there? Are you rearranging the furniture? That room is pretty small. Not too many ways you can fit a bed and a dresser."

"Ha! That's a good one. No dear, we're packing! We found a place!" Eireka smiled broadly, brushing a loose strand of hair out of place.

"But... that fast? Is it in a safe neighborhood? Did you check to make sure it's not in a flood plain? Not Onion Creek, right? Are you renting a townhouse?"

Her grandmother cut her off, waving her hands. "You'd think the child thought she raised us! Your mother survived a psych ward. I survived the world in between. We've got this. We know how to pick out a two-bedroom apartment."

"It's for the best." Eireka grabbed Leira at the elbows, kissing her on her forehead. "We're renting for now, maybe forever. Less to do and will leave us more time to do other things."

"She means date." Mara let out a snort. "Maybe I'll figure out how to swipe right myself. You can come visit anytime." Mara packed the few clothes she had in a new suitcase from Costco and zipped it shut. "Good thing all of our stuff was in storage. Have I said thank you to you for not ditching everything? Not sure I would have held on to so much for four years. You didn't even know if I was alive!" Mara wandered back into the bedroom to see if she forgot anything.

Eireka looked at Leira and wrapped her arms around her, kissing her ear. "You're more sentimental than you let on. It's okay. It's a good thing. Kept you from getting too angry all these years and boy, will it help your magic." She whispered it in her daughter's ear and stood back. "You never lost hope. That's why you kept it all. You are more courageous than your grandmother and me put together. No, it's true, don't make a face. It takes so much courage to believe in something for that long, and I know you. You didn't hope, you believed. Hope is just the hole where belief needs to go. You kept all of Nana's dishes and my jewelry stored away, except for this ring." She picked up Leira's hand and looked at the sapphire. "You didn't use any of it because you were determined that we'd be back to use it someday. You have courage in pounds."

"I'm happy for you, Mom. This is the right thing to do. Too many people crammed into one small space, and you've waited long enough to have your own place." Leira shrugged. "I guess I didn't think it would happen so fast. I was kind of used to hearing you sing to yourself in the morning." Her eyes shined as she lifted the bottom of her shirt to wipe across her face. She forgot all about the new scar on her belly, peeking out from the bottom of her shirt.

Eireka winced when she saw it and quickly recovered, smiling at Leira. *So full of heart. If I could take that away from you...*

"You're not supposed to miss me before I'm even gone. What a wonderful thing. You don't miss what you don't treasure." She stood back from Leira and nodded hard. "Well, good. Now I can go and still be sure you'll visit."

"I wish Correk could have even a little of this."

"Good thing you know how to share. He'll be okay." Eireka clapped her hands, her face lighting up. "We can do Sunday dinners! As long as you're not called into some supernatural case! Even then, we'll save you a plate. We'll save one for Hagan on those nights too! And Correk, he's part of the family now."

"One big happy Elven family."

"What a good idea!" Mara came back out of the bedroom holding a glass dolphin. "Remember this thing? Bought it for you in Galveston at that aquarium. Forgot all about it. You had it in a box. Mind if I take it?"

"Ooooooh," trilled the troll. "Beautiful." The troll shook his head. "Leira loves it."

Leira's mouth dropped open and she stared at the troll.

Mara put her hands on her hips, still holding the dolphin. "Well, I wondered when you'd let everyone in on the secret. Trolls can talk when they want to. Little shit is full of wisdom. Just doesn't usually have much to say."

"Yeah, I'm finding that out."

Yumfuck looked up at Leira and shrugged as Mara put the dolphin down. "Take what you love out of boxes and spread it around. Life is too weird and too short for that kind of behavior."

Eireka laughed and picked up her mother's suitcase. "I'll bet if we give you just a few more bits of advice that will help you get over missing us at least for now."

Leira still stared at the troll, waiting for him to say something else. He stared back at Leira and blew her a raspberry. "Is that your wisdom showing itself?" The troll let out a trill and sat back, pulling out an old piece of macaroni from underneath the washcloth next to him. "Oooooh." He licked it and bit down with his sharp teeth, crunching away.

The door to the guest house opened. Correk came in, carrying a brown paper bag folded over at the top with a grease stain along the edge of the bottom. He stopped at the opening and looked at everyone standing around in the living room, the suitcases ready to go.

"Moving." Yumfuck winked at him.

"He's still talking." Correk raised his eyebrows.

"Didn't you know before the kemana?" Leira put her hands on her hips looking back and forth between Correk and Yumfuck. "All the time you two spend together."

"Only as folklore. Unlike you, most people on Oriceran avoid bonding with them. Yumfuck has been an entirely new adventure for me."

"Nana, how did you know? You didn't seem surprised." She narrowed her eyes.

"We should be going," said Mara, arching an eyebrow. "Save some stories for when you visit. Besides the moving truck with all our things from storage will be at the apartment soon."

"I'm not going to forget."

"I have no doubt of that." Mara kissed Leira on her cheek and smiled at her. "Yumfuck," she said, nodding at the troll.

"Motherfucker," chirped Yumfuck, solemnly nodding.

Mara let out a whoop of laughter and walked out the door. Eireka smiled and followed her, hugging Leira one last time. "I suppose this is the new family goodbye." She nodded to the troll. "Motherfucker," she said, smiling before shutting the door behind her. Mara's laughter could be heard all the way across the patio.

Correk stared at the door and then shook his head.

"You didn't think that all that swearing started with me, did you?" Leira shrugged and put out her hands. "Nana has a potty mouth. She said I told someone in a grocery store to fuck off when I was only two."

"Like hearing a beloved bedtime story."

"You played me," said Leira looking at the troll.

"Followed the leader," said the troll, letting out a soft trill. "A little mystery is good." He pulled a pair of underwear up under his chin and curled up into a ball, shutting his eyes.

"Could it be that a five-inch hairy troll is the cagiest one in the room?"

"Size doesn't count when it comes to outmaneuvering someone." Correk went into the kitchen and put the bag on the table. "I got enough tacos at the truck for everyone."

"Good, I'm starving! I'll get the plates." Leira took two plates out of the cabinet and turned around to find the troll lifting a taco over his head, jumping from the table to the chair and down to the floor. "Hey, no one invited you."

The troll blew her a raspberry and smiled as he disappeared into the living room.

"It's like he has a plan and we're all in it."

"Then it involves junk food, cable TV and underwear. I can live with that." Correk sat down heavily in a chair and pulled a plate closer to him while reaching for a taco.

"How long have you known that the symbols on my arm read like a ticker tape?" Leira sat down across the table from Correk. The small guest house already seemed a little empty even though it was filled to overflowing for only a few days.

Correk took a big bite of a taco and chewed slowly, thinking over his answer. He finally swallowed and said, "Since I was three years old and was taught how to read them." He took another bite waiting for the next question.

"Were you ever planning to tell me?"

"Of course. I knew it would come up, but you weren't ready to know all the information spilling out of the symbols."

"Do your arms say so much?"

"No, not nearly as much." He bit into another taco, glad to have something to talk about and take his mind off Rhazdon. *That snake that followed me to the store.* He shook his head, willing it away and let out a sigh. "Good taco."

"What's the difference between the symbols on your body and on mine?"

He put down the taco and brushed his hands. "I can see that you're not going to eat a thing till we get this over and done. My symbols are more immediate. They tell me about danger directly to me. Normal and average for a Light Elf. Your symbols on the other hand..." He hesitated.

Leira cocked her head to the side and gave him a dead fish look. *First one who talks loses.*

"Sometimes I forget what a good detective you are and how patiently you'll wait for an answer. The truth is I can't always read your symbols fast enough. They roll out onto your skin and change just as fast telling about dangers near *and* far. It's like your very core, your energy is connected to something bigger. I've never seen or heard about anything like it. It was amazing from the start and I knew it was far more powerful than I could imagine. That only emphasized for me how important it was for you to learn to harness some of it at least before trying to figure out a puzzle that reached around an entire world. There. That's all I know."

"You have ideas about how much energy I can harness. I can tell."

"I only have theories. But I do know that you've only used a small portion of your magical abilities."

"I want a mentor."

"Splendid. Good luck with that." Correk picked his taco back up and took a bite. "I know what you're thinking," he said, still chewing. "It's not a bad idea. If there's anyone who knows about the reach of your magic it would be Turner Underwood. Frankly, it's not a surprise he showed up when he did."

"I suspected as much."

"Do you know why they call him the Fixer? He doesn't fix problems as much as he reconstitutes people. Magical people. He shows up when a magical is in danger. Sometimes he helps Elves or Witches or even a Gnome master their magic to the point where they're maximizing their potential. Seems to be able to feel how much more someone can do. I imagine the moment you came within range of him he was intrigued."

"This would have been useful to know before I faced off with the black mist."

"No, it wouldn't have, or he would have told you what you needed to know. He's not a cruel or foolish old Elf. If he didn't, he has his reasons."

"But, how do I find him?"

"Put the word out in the magical community. Tell Toni and Larry and the others. He'll find you. There is a very good chance he's been waiting for your call."

"I'm doing it." Leira slid three tacos over to her plate.

"Amazing how much you can eat."

"This is the appetizer."

Correk laughed, and some of the tension left his shoulders. "Turner Underwood will be good for you. Call Toni and tell her tonight." He smiled and looked in the bag to see what was left. "You know you want to."

Leira put the taco down and wiped her hands on a napkin. She studied Correk. "Would it be safer for everyone if I took care of this sooner rather than later?"

Correk looked at the table. "There are things I can't share with you out of loyalty to others, and because I don't know enough but, yes, it would be better if we all did whatever we could to get ready." He looked at Leira directly into her eyes. "Trust me, just this once."

"There's a lot more to this story. It's okay. You've trusted me more than once, and I'm going to try something different and trust you even though you're keeping information from me. You'll tell me when you're ready."

"I only have my suspicions…"

"And if they're right?"

"Then you should learn as much about what you can do from Turner Underwood as soon as you can. For all our sakes, before the symbols on your skin spell something out none of us can handle." *Rhazdon may be alive.*

Correk shuddered and rested his head in his hands.

Leira put her hand on his arm, sending him energy as she picked up her cell phone and dialed. "Hello, Toni, it's Leira. I'm doing fine. I'm looking for Turner Underwood…"

CHAPTER EIGHT

Leira stood in the grassy courtyard of a large stone house at the northern end of Lake Travis. Turner Underwood stood just behind her in a suit and tie, leaning on his cane giving instructions. It only took an hour to hear back from him and all he said on the phone was a time and place for the next day before he hung up. Leira made sure she was early and dressed in running clothes. She had no idea what to expect but wanted to be ready.

"This is good Texas earth here. Draw up the energy and let it flow straight through you without direction. Let the energy go where it wants. You take your hands off the steering wheel. Surrender to it."

Leira focused but the splashing from the nearby pool was distracting her. The troll floated by on a blowup of a turtle, one arm behind his head as he laid back. "Surrender to it," he chirped.

Turner smiled and said, "Part of this exercise is to take in all the noises around you and let them pass through. Yumfuck is helping you with the process."

"Did you know Trolls could speak?"

"Of course, so did you. He's been talking from the beginning."

"I thought it was random."

"What has that damn troll ever done that was random? You chose to assume that all you saw and heard was all there could be."

The troll cackled and rolled off the turtle, falling into the water with a yelp. He gulped water and sputtered, going underwater twice and came up coughing. Leira went to scoop him out of the pool, but he was already dog paddling his way to the edge. He pulled himself out, giving a good shake. "Rat bastard!" He shook his tiny fist at the floatie.

Leira went back to her place in front of Turner. "I didn't teach him that one. Classic though."

Turner nodded. "Focus. Let the furry munchkin do his thing. You do yours. Draw up the energy. Become one with it."

"Wax on, wax off."

"Movie hoo-ha. The exact opposite of what I'm asking of you. If you're working at it, you're doing it wrong. Relax into it." He tapped his cane against the ground.

Leira shook out her arms. "What have I been doing all along if I wasn't relaxing into it?"

"You were taking on the role of creator, acting as if you controlled the energy. You are not the creator of anything, only the hollow bone."

"Now, I'm confused." She put her arms down. "Correk said not understanding how to use magic, this energy that flows through me is dangerous. You're telling me I'm overstepping if I try to control it."

"What I said and what you heard are not lining up. Correk is right. I'm right."

Leira turned around to face him. "This word jumble is getting me nowhere."

"Control is a way to get started at something new but eventually it always fails. True success comes where control ends and we step out into thin air. Correk was explaining to you the same thing I am right now. If you don't gain an understanding of how to trust the source of energy from within you, from within the ground you stand on then you will try to control it, limit it."

"I had to learn how to shoot a gun."

"A gun has very real and obvious limits and is always a weapon. Its definition is brief and with a distinct purpose."

"Magic is bigger…" She said it with hesitation. "I don't get it."

"Clearly, and normal. You are a novice with a lot of power. A unique place to be. You are under the impression that the magic has no ability to understand and is waiting for instructions from you. That would limit the ability of magic to whatever you already know but you've already seen it do things that teach you. How is that possible if you're right about your assumption?"

"Well that just blew my fucking mind." Leira took in a deep breath and let it out slowly. "Hang on." She kept breathing in deeply, letting it out.

"Every Light Elf has symbols that appear on their arm. You call it a ticker. Not quite. Those annoying streams of television junk mail along the bottom of the screen are meant to tease the masses. Everyone has to fit into the one square hole. But these symbols are designed specifically for you. The magic gives each user the information they need and no more than they can handle."

"It fucking knows me…" Leira let out a small gasp.

Turner smiled. "I've noticed you swear more when you're surprised. This is going to be a fucking, wild-ass goddamn ride for you." He snorted with laughter.

"I thought gurus were supposed to be of a higher mind."

"More dumbass movie hoo-ha mostly written by my cousin Irving. Bought him a nice beach house in Malibu but confused a lot of humans and apparently a few Elves. Whatever. It is what it is."

"That was Zen of you."

"It was Elven of me. Not much of a difference. We'll get in

there and fight, make mistakes, say we're sorry, eat too much crap, swear, smoke a good cigar, not make it so much about us, trust the energy and marry a good woman. Basically, have an ordinary life. That's right, ordinary. Ordinary is a little bit of everything. But for us, it includes magic. For you, a helluva lot more magic. Your type of ordinary is a lot of magic."

"How much does the energy know about me?"

"Absolutely everything. More than you know but without the useless judgie parts. Nature doesn't know right or wrong, only consequences. The magic blends with you even as you resist getting out of the way. Your part is to make a choice about using magic in the first place. Magic doesn't intervene without being invited into the party."

"But then it takes over."

"With as much permission as you allow. Some might call that trust."

"In this thing I can't see… I can only feel it." She tapped the scar under her shirt. "My gun was more direct. Aim it and shoot. Hit the target and end the threat."

Turner's face grew serious. "Like I said, a gun has a very defined use and once you run up against dark magic it's as useful as a tissue in a rainstorm." He pointed at her chest. "I imagine that stream of energy you pulled off in the hotel room left a nice mark behind. A spiritual tattoo. Never seen anything like that."

"I trusted the energy in that moment."

"Mostly, but there was resistance and that's what caused the scar. Yes, I knew it left a mark. You pulled in massive amounts of magic and let it flow through you while fighting it at the same time. I wondered if you would survive it and was pleasantly surprised. That's what showed me you are nowhere near your potential yet. A fire hydrant of magic and you lived to tell about it!"

"Everyone can pull in vast amounts of energy but most die trying…"

"Correk again, I take it. He's right but there's some wiggle room." Turner lifted a hand off his cane and waggled his fingers, squinting. "Resistance can cause harm to the user. Usually comes from insisting on a particular outcome out of fear. I've seen Elves blow off a finger or two. Oh, it happens." He sighed and waved his hand. "Feeling is everything in magic and attachment gets in the way. But sometimes the user can overcome their fear and completely surrender to the magic and strange things happen. It's rare. It takes a moment of blank mind and complete presence in the moment. Even humans can succeed when they get hold of an artifact under those conditions. It's true."

"It feels like the top of my fucking head is floating away."

Turner laughed. "Then enough talking for today. Draw up the energy and let it flow through you. Let go of the steering wheel. The magic knows what you need. It's literally telling you in the symbols on your arm and looking for agreement."

Leira turned back around and shut her eyes. She breathed in deeply, slowly letting out the air as she pulled in magic from the ground.

"Quit trying to pull it in. Just make space for it." Turner's gruff voice echoed in her head.

Make space for it. No fucking clue. I can make it okay for it to be here...You are officially invited in. I want you here. Wait! "What?" A sudden rush of magic filled every corner of Leira's being as a low-level musical hum played in her ears. It rolled through her in increasing waves but this time, instead of sending it out in front of her she felt herself let it pass through. She opened her eyes, wide with amazement. "The same thing is happening but without my limited idea of what the magic needs to do."

"Ah, a small kernel of understanding begins. Look down at your arms and take in what's happening."

Leira slowly looked down, feeling the flow of magic coming up through her feet and out through her chest as a shimmering swath curling and turning off into the distance. Symbols were appearing on her arms, reshaping themselves in a constant motion as the energy continued to swirl inside of her.

"Breathe," said Turner.

Leira realized she was holding her breath and took in oxygen in a gulp.

"Drop your shoulders. Relax. Become part of the magic."

Leira looked at Turner and felt the calm strand of magic he was releasing, guiding her into it. She smiled and let herself go with the magical stream, getting pulled along to a destination. Images appeared inside of her head just like before when she sought out the answers to a crime. But this time she was along for the ride.

The magic raced out ahead of her and just as suddenly she felt herself give in and spin around, flowing at the tip of the energy.

"You've surrendered!" Turner marveled at the symbols flowing across her arms and neck as he did his best to steady her with his own magic.

Leira felt the magic slowing down and growing more cautious as it approached a thick forest. *That looks familiar.* "Oriceran..." she muttered. "The Dark Forest..."

"You've crossed the divide! How is that possible?" Turner flinched sending a bubble of hesitation into the stream but Leira's curiosity distracted her just enough to let it pass through.

The magic rolled across the forest floor, slowing to a crawl as it approached a small thatched cabin deep in the woods, surrounded by a dense stand of trees. *I would have never noticed this without help.* The stream stopped yards away and patiently waited. *For what?* Leira focused her attention. *Let the magic tell me.*

Turner watched the symbols along her skin and his eyes widened as they appeared more slowly. "What is that? That's impossible..." He read it again and again. "Eight hundred years," he whispered hoarsely. "How could someone have duplicated Rhazdon's magic?"

Leira finally saw what the magic was seeking out and why it

stopped. A dense circle of shimmering black and the deepest sparkling blue shrouded the bottom of the cabin just at the place where it met the ground, pulsing with energy like a heartbeat. The details of the cabin shimmered above the rim of the circle of dark energy. More energy than Leira had ever seen before even in the world in between.

"It's beautiful," she whispered, reaching out with her energy with an intention to touch the stream.

Turner saw the symbols change and slapped his hand tight around Leira's forearm. "No!" he barked, reeling her in like a fishing line. She snapped back into her body in a rush, the air pouring out of her lungs as she hit the ground hard. The troll ran to her side, growing with each step as he let out a roar bearing his claws at Turner.

Turner took a cautious step backward and let go of Leira, holding up his hands. "She's okay." He was still reeling from what he saw.

Leira sat up, gulping in air, making herself take in ever deeper breaths, fighting off the dizzy feeling from crossing over the threshold to Oriceran and back again so quickly without a portal or a body.

The troll slowly shrunk back down and jumped onto her chest putting its hands on her chin and looking her in the eye.

"I'm okay." She patted the top of the troll's head. "That was some kind of trip. I can't imagine shrooms could do as much."

"Overrated," said Turner, still staring at Leira's arms but the symbols were already fading. He shook his head to clear his mind. "Tell me exactly what you saw. Leave out no details."

"Tell me why you so abruptly killed the vibe." She pulled herself back off the ground. "Feels like the fucking bends."

"You were reacting instead of responding. You stepped outside of the intention of the magic. You wanted to alert a very, very powerful dark magic of your presence. Your own magic would have let you do it. You always have choice. I'm more interested in your survival and put a stop to it. What did you see?"

"Not much. A small cabin in the middle of the Dark Forest. It's protected by a layer of magic around the bottom. It felt like it was drawing me in. I wanted to go inside."

"Part of the spell. It's not meant to repel you but get you to announce yourself."

Leira shuddered. "I assume the end to that story is not pretty. Wait, did I hear you say a name?"

"Rhazdon...The darkest practitioner of magic Oriceran ever knew and wiped from the planet about eight hundred years ago."

"Isn't that the guy whose artifacts are all piled in the Gnomes' vault?"

"One and the same. Whoever created that spell appears to be as powerful as Rhazdon. If that's true it's very bad news." Turner looked grim as he slowly shook his head. "Took everything we had to defeat Rhazdon and even then, there were a lot of casualties."

"Like the old king of Oriceran. Your friend I understand."

"Very bad shit sometimes happens. Come on, that's more than enough for today. I'll make you a sandwich. Magical energy pulls on resources. Good idea to put them back."

"You know I'm going to do something about what I saw, right?" *Go in first, ask questions if I really have to.*

"Understood. Come back here for lessons every morning. The magic feels you have a chance to take on whomever this is, but you will need to be absolutely sure of that before you come face to face."

"You're thinking a confrontation is a done deal."

"The magic inside of you is certain of it."

"Then I'll get ready."

"Okay, don't screw it up this time, Mara. No more rips in a portal." Mara flexed her fingers and shook them at her sides. She was more nervous than she was willing to admit. "Has to be done. I have to go back and finish what I started. Make sure the network is still intact."

Mara stood in the middle of her new living room and conjured a glowing ball of light between her hands as her eyes began to glow. Eireka was out at the grocery store and wouldn't be back for a couple of hours. "No time like the present."

Mara said a spell she remembered from four years ago and thought about ever since the world in between sucked her inside. "Ramanna."

The light expanded and let out a sharp electrical snap, opening up a portal big enough for Mara to cross through to Oriceran. She stepped into the royal gardens behind the Light Castle and breathed a sigh of relief. "I still have it." She set out quickly for the main road to head into town and the cottages that lined the center of town.

"He has to still be there," she muttered, picking up her pace. "I didn't sacrifice all of this crap to fail now."

The smell of the flowers brought tears to her eyes and memories flooded back to her. "Not now old girl." Still, she reached out a hand as she passed a vine growing through a low fence and sang to it, watching it sway with each note, opening its flowers. "I've missed all of this."

A horse drawn cart passed her and the driver slowed, looking down to see if Mara wanted a ride. "Sure! Why the hell not?" She handed the driver an old gold coin she fished out of her belongings from storage. *Thank goodness my granddaughter didn't go through everything.*

It didn't take long for her to get settled into a seat and the driver to get gently moving again. *Finally, I will see you again.*

Mara got off at the center of the village and waved to the driver. She peered at the thatch roofs and tightly packed shops, turning in a circle. "Everything looks almost the same."

A merchant standing outside her shop offered Mara a warm roll. "No need to fix it if it's working fine."

"Damn tourist," muttered a passing Dwarf, curling his lip at Mara.

The merchant waved her hand at the Dwarf. "Pay no attention. Oricerans are growing anxious about the gates slowly opening. Too many rumors." The Witch tilted her head, studying Mara. "You weren't raised here, were you? You could almost pass."

"Not entirely. Is the tavern still in the same spot?"

"There will always be a need for a place to get a drink and swap lies. Stinson is still there behind the bar. A word to the wise, though. Stop looking around at an ordinary street like it's something peculiar. Opening portals is still illegal, and not everyone will stop at calling you a tourist."

"Of course." Mara offered the Witch a coin, but the magical waved it away.

"Enjoy your roll, and welcome home."

"Welcome home," whispered Mara, a catch in her throat.

She made her way down the crooked street, coming to the third bend beside the grocer's. "Right where I left it." She smiled and crossed the street, stopping at the sound of a fight. The doors burst open, and a Wizard was shoved into the street by a large Kilomea. "Don't come back, Arkin, till you can pay your tab."

The Wizard landed on his hands and knees, looking at Mara's shoes. He glanced up at her, shading his eyes, a smile growing across his face. "Can it be? Has my day turned around so quickly? As I live and still breathe, it is you!"

"Hello, Arkin. I was hoping you would have found a few new tricks by now."

"I most certainly have. How do you think I've lasted this

long?" He stood, brushing off his pants. "I made the mistake of comparing that oaf's mother to a buffalo. Just as hairy and about the same girth. I really meant it as a kind of compliment. The woman is sturdy." He gave a whistle, looking at the tavern. "He should learn to take a compliment."

Mara let out a snort. "Can you tell me where I can find Rivers?" She held her breath, hoping the wizard was still alive.

Arkin's smile faded and his brow furrowed. "Rivers... Now who's looking for trouble? He's long gone from these parts. He got caught helping some wanted magicals." Arkin put his hand up beside his mouth, leaning toward Mara. "I heard he was supposed to be headed to Trevilsom Prison, but he made some kind of deal. You better go ask the trees if you want to find Rivers."

Mara held out a pinta and dropped it into Arkin's palm. "Thanks for your help. Nice to see you again, Arkin."

The Wizard bit down on the pinta, and his smile returned. "Same to you." He walked back into the tavern, waving the pinta. "I'm back and I can pay! Put your fur down. I've got no beef with your mother..."

The door swung shut. Mara stood there. "Go ask the trees. Not a bad idea."

She made her way back to the edge of the Dark Forest and walked in far enough till the only light was from the sun breaking through the tall trees over her head.

She centered herself and focused, letting the energy glide up through her feet, swimming around in her belly. Her long, dark hair swayed across her shoulders as she gave the magic an intention. *Find Rivers.*

The magic searched through her memories, pulling what it needed as it set out through the forest, curling around the trees, searching for a trail. Mara followed, waiting for a sign the energy was connecting to something. She bit her bottom lip as the swirl of glittering light crossed into the areas where most magicals never dared cross. She hesitated as the energy continued on. "Buck up, what would Leira do? Hell, what would Yumfuck do? They'd be trying to run ahead of the energy! You can do this."

She hurried to catch up, the darkness closing in as the trees grew closer together. The growls and yelps and loud clicking noises and sounds of tweeting and cawing picked up all around. "You escaped the world in between. This is just an overgrown park, kiddo."

Her foot slid on wet moss, and she put her hand on a nearby tree. Large ants skittered across her skin, leaving a slimy trail. She jerked but pressed her hand against the tree. The darkness around her lit up with trails of magicals who had passed through recently. "Three trails. Now you're talking. Of course, the trees carry a memory of it. Everything is connected."

Two trails traveled over top each other. "They were walking together. It appears the Gardener has found a friend. But this other one." She reached for it, her hand passing through the glittering maroon color. "Rivers. I'd know you anywhere."

The tips of her fingers sparked, and she pulled her hand back, looking at the newly forming blisters. Her other hand was still against the tree. "What the fuck was that?" She leaned forward, peering into the maroon stream and was barely able to make out a hidden ribbon just beneath that had crossed under not long ago. "No light at all. Pure darkness."

Mara pressed her back against the tree, taking deep breaths as she looked around. "What the fuck is out here?"

Her intention began to fade. The energy was circling back, returning to her. "*Portasus*," she whispered, the blisters disappearing from her hand. She shook her head and stood straight, letting go of the tree. "You didn't come this far to turn back." She took a deep breath and steadied herself, reinforcing the intention. The trail lit up again. She stepped gingerly over the space where she had seen the blackness cross. She glanced to the right but kept moving until she came to a small clearing. Mara watched as the trail circled around and around, not going any further. "Rivers, it's me. Show yourself."

A Wizard appeared out of the darkness, coming close to Mara's face. He peered into her eyes.

"A little personal space. It's me, Rivers, I swear." She smelled an earthy dampness about him.

"I heard you were dead." The Wizard stepped back. Moss grew over most of his clothes, and a squirrel perched on his shoulder, nibbling at an acorn.

"There's a lot of that going around. I hear you've been exiled."

"It's only exile if they make you." He arched an eyebrow, looking around. "This is my choice."

Something screeched overhead, and there was a loud rustling as something took off through the tops of the trees, followed by another creature that sounded like it was gaining ground on its prey.

Mara shuddered and stood up straighter. The light still bobbed just above their heads, casting shadows across their faces. "What about the work? What about the magicals they wanted to send to Trevilsom…"

"For breaking the rules about experimenting with magic. I remember. What work?" He threw up his hands, the squirrel chirping loudly, holding on to his tunic. The moss hung from his arms, making him appear bigger than he really was. "It ended when you disappeared. Frankly, it was over the day you tried to get that Light Elf through a portal."

"Harkin. I remember what happened."

"Times have changed. Harkin's dead, and dark magic has forged ahead. They're the ones experimenting with magic. Powerful magic has moved into the territory, making deals with the other side. Makes me wonder if everyone was right."

"They weren't right! Not about Trevilsom."

"Go back to where you came from, Mara. Live your life. Too much has been taken already." Rivers waved his hand over his head, squelching the light and leaving Mara alone in the darkness.

"Not the end of the story, Rivers," she yelled into the darkness.

"We shall see." His voice came back, already from a distance.

"What deals?" she called out, but this time, there was no answer.

Mara listened to the sounds of the forest growing quiet and wondered what could make every creature hold still. A chill ran across her neck, and she chanced opening a portal where she stood. Sparks flew, illuminating the small clearing. On the other side of the opening was Leira's living room. Yumfuck stood on the couch, his fur bristling and baring his teeth.

"Yeah, I sense it too." Mara stepped through quickly, snapping the portal shut behind her without looking back.

The Gnome appeared moments later in the clearing still wearing the prophet robe. He raised his nose in the air, taking a whiff. "New animals in the forest. I'll need to set more traps."

The boardroom was on the top floor of one of the taller buildings in New York City, down in the financial district. Charlie Monaghan had flown in the attendees who saw the portal open for an unexpected opportunity. The group was gathered on a rented-out floor of the Mark Hotel on the east side of Central Park near 5th Avenue till it was time for the meeting. They were whisked out the back in dark Lincolns and taken to the private entrance with its own elevator. It was essential that no one in the media catch wind of the gathering. The gossip on social media would have started immediately. That would have been fine, but they couldn't risk the wrong people making the right connections and speculating about the agenda.

Not a chance someone figures this one out. Charlie was still having some trouble believing all of it himself. *A second fucking portal opened!*

A portal opened in his house in Virginia, unbidden, and a tall frozen beast stepped out of nowhere followed by a woman in a flowing gown holding out a thin wooden stick. The woman explained she was a Witch and the beast was a Crystal man. Both of them were part of a larger group, and they wanted to make a deal. That much he understood.

He was instructed to gather his tribe and set a location at a certain date and time. The prophets would find the location on their own and come with the proposal. No, he wasn't going to learn the details beforehand. A tough negotiation only got Charlie more interested in looking for the angles.

Charlie watched the door and glanced back at the open space in the room, not sure where the prophets would make their entrance. He looked at his watch. One minute to go.

The fifteen men and women sat around a large mahogany table, some nervously shifting in their seats or tapping on the table. They all knew what was supposed to happen next and weren't sure if they believed it. *This is my tribe.* Charlie let out a 'tsk' but said nothing. *Whatever it takes to get a good deal.*

At the appointed time, sparks crackled in the air and lightning flashed in the open space. Charlie sat back in amazement, gasping as he smiled broadly. "Here we go!"

A portal opened and a delegation of five prophets stepped through into the boardroom, all wearing their dark blue robes. Earth's constellations immediately appeared across their backs in perfect alignment with where they stood.

The people seated around the table gasped as they stared at the pixie, the Crystal, the Kilomea, the Light Elf and the Gnome prophets. At the last moment, the Witch stepped through, pulling out her wand as she landed on the thick carpet.

"You half expect one of them to say, we come in peace," snickered one of the men. The Kilomea grunted and glared at the man as his face lost all expression and he turned ashen. Another man's hand trembled as he picked up his coffee cup, sloshing the coffee as he maneuvered the cup to his lips.

The group remained in the spot where they entered the room except for the Witch, who went over to the door. She murmured something under her breath, casting a spell that caused anyone approaching the door to lose interest and wander off aimlessly.

"Get it out of your system," said the Gnome. "We understand this is a lot to take in. Nanoo, nanoo, anyone?" There was a ripple of laughter as the Gnome smiled. "That's better. We're here to make a deal. An exercise you're already very familiar with, and we want everyone to walk away feeling like they got something for their time. Let me start by saying, we already know you're well aware of our existence. But we've known about all of you for millennia." The Gnome stood silently, his hands clasped behind his back, waiting for the murmur to die down in the room. Charlie hushed the few remaining whispers.

"We won't be staying long so we ask that you listen and save your questions. We won't be answering them at this time." The Gnome glanced sideways at the table. "We're here to offer you knowledge about magic and how it works. We know you're hunting artifacts and relics. It's a good idea. The gates will start to open and when they do the magic will increase. Practitioners will find it tempting to rely on it more and more, despite any rules. That's right, there are rules. But I'm sure some of you have broken a few rules for the greater good. Whatever that is. Of course, we want something in return..."

Here we go, thought Charlie. *Our side of the bargain.*

A woman closest to the Crystal prophet watched in amazement as snowflakes scattered to the ground with every breath the Crystal let out.

"We want assistance helping our people emigrate to this world. Let me be clear. It's happening one way or another. Either you get something out of the deal and welcome us, making for a smoother transition. Or you get to know your new neighbors over time and watch us perform magic while you're completely in the dark. Either way, we both go on with our lives, but a little knowledge might go a long way for your side and a basket of muffins, and a smile will ease concerns our people may have."

"People? Those are people?" someone whispered. The Witch by the door raised her wand in the general direction of the table but Charlie grimaced and patted the air.

"Seems reasonable," he said, getting out of his chair. The Kilomea let out a low grumble. "I'll stay right here." Charlie's smile was strained but still in place. "Make a list of the areas you're most interested in, and we'll do everything we can to accommodate you. Do you have an idea of how many Oricerans plan to immigrate to Earth?"

"Not at this time," said the Gnome, giving away nothing. He nodded to the Witch, who swirled her wand in the air producing an arch of papers cascading down to the boardroom table, neatly landing in one pile in front of Charlie. "Our list... and our first lesson about magic. It's all there. Think of that as a taste of what's to come and a goodwill gesture to all of you. A primer on how to successfully use an artifact without turning yourself to ash."

Charlie's eyebrows shot up as he realized what could have happened in his library with Langston. He placed a hand on top of the pile of papers and did his best to keep smiling.

"That will come in handy as you gather artifacts. Oh, and one more bonus. There's the longitude and latitude for an artifact in there as well. A present from us to you. I thought that would lift your spirits." The Gnome nodded to the Witch, and she moved back to the group as the Kilomea opened the portal. Moments later, they were gone in a shower of sparks.

Charlie greedily rifled through the papers looking for the directions to the artifact. He glanced at the passing pages noting the steps the prophets wanted to help humans adjust to the new populations of magical people. It covered a wide variety of areas. *To be expected.*

At last, he found them toward the bottom of the stack. *Wyoming. Unexpected but so much the better. Practically local.* He looked up at the woman peering over his shoulder. "We should send a team with one of the professors we hired. Where there's one, there will probably be others. The race is on, but we now have some juice."

"Do you think they're going to tell us much?" It was the ashen CEO who flew in from England.

"Hell, no. They're probably giving us the kindergarten edition. Not the good stuff."

"Everyone wants to get their shovel in the sand. They're just using a different kind of shovel."

"Well said, it's time we got to digging first and faster."

And figure out how to keep Wolfstan at bay.

"Did you get all that? That was some crazy ass shit! Prophets from another planet!" The PDF agent ripped the headphones off, leaning back against the inside of the white van. It was parked across the street, listening to the meeting. The bug Lois managed to plant was paying off. They were starting to learn all the players.

"Who are the prophets? What the hell was that about?" asked the driver, turning in his seat. "They had a full-on encounter of the fourth kind in downtown Manhattan. Who does that?"

Alan Cohen looked at the two men and sat back, pondering what to do next. *Magical beings want to emigrate to this world.* Alan rubbed the day-old growth on his chin. *Time to tell Leira Berens before this grows much bigger.*

Wolfstan Humphrey sat at the bar, waiting for his mole to settle on his stool. "How was the meeting at Axiom?"

The older man sat down, his wool overcoat still buttoned. "It went just like you expected. The humans were trying to play it cool without succeeding. That Elf you spotted the last time, Pearson. He wasn't there either, just like you said. The Oricerans have no idea any magicals are involved. I don't know who's more naïve."

"What did the Oricerans want?"

"To team up gathering artifacts. Charlie Monaghan gathered a who's who of CEOs."

"Perfect. That will make merging all our efforts even easier." He slid a thick envelope between them.

"Thank you. Nice doing business with you, as usual. You know where to find me if you need me again."

Wolfstan nodded, pulling out his phone. *Time to call Charlie Monaghan and make sure he sticks to our deal, and then some.*

CHAPTER NINE

Leira stood in front of the virtual screen pointing at the different symbols and reading off the information for the people standing around her. "There's another young Wizard who's gone missing from Ohio. Fifteen years old, heading home from a game of basketball. Gone for three days."

The lessons with Turner Underwood were paying off. She was getting a better understanding of how magic worked as well as growing more confident. Magic was simple but not easy. Letting go without knowing where things were headed was not Leira's usual way of doing business.

She was surrounded by the other members of the federal task force, including Hagan and Alan Cohen.

"The common thread all eleven Witches and Wizards have in common is they're young and involved in dark magic."

Hagan flipped through a file. "According to the case file, the dalliance with dark magic goes back generations. They're legacy stupid."

Alan Cohen made a note on his smart phone to look into the background of the latest missing kid. "That's something when dark Wizards and Witches are willing to come to us for help."

"Being a parent overrides even darkness," said Hagan.

"Most of the time." Leira pointed at the symbols and walked over to the map on the wall. "Anyone notice another fun fact? They're in clusters. Phoenix, Arizona has three. Two were in Santa Monica. Two in Austin, and three more outside Richmond, Virginia. Now this one in Ohio. Something about those locations." Her eyes narrowed as she put the pieces together. "Kemanas," she whispered.

"What?" Hagan shook his head.

"Kemanas! They've all got big ass kemanas. Large sources of magical powers. Of course they do. They draw magical communities of every kind. Light and dark. Could be someone is targeting them."

"Are we sure they're victims of a crime? I'm not convinced they're all connected yet. Can I see that?" He held out his hand for the file.

"The parents have a way of tracking their magical children at all times. It's like a trail that none of those kids are smart enough to be able to hide. It takes really advanced magic. But the trails are gone. Nothing there." Leira paced in front of the screen. Something was adding up, but she didn't like the answer. Even for practitioners of dark magic. They were still kids.

"They may have gotten taken into the world in between." She saw the confused faces on the newer team members Mark and Gail. "It's like a netherworld between Earth and Oriceran. Magical people and the dead can get trapped there but it's not really a destination. There's no real there, there, and getting out is just this side of impossible."

"Till a couple weeks ago it was considered completely impossible." Hagan hitched up his pants, grimacing.

"If it is this thing how do we stop it? Doesn't look like there's anything for us to do here." Gail's dark brown ponytail bobbed with each word. "I want to help," she said in a determined tone, "but I don't know how to battle that thing."

"You heard about what happened with the dark mist, didn't you? By now, the story must be pretty hairy, and it doesn't help that it probably doesn't even do it justice. Says a lot of good things about the two of you that you still agreed to sign on to this task force. Humans add a lot to the equation." Leira glanced over at Hagan.

"We've managed to keep our planet spinning on our own all this time and created a few cool gadgets along the way." Cohen pointed at the virtual screen. "That's mostly us with a little magical help but less than you think."

Hagan interrupted, clearing his throat. "We haven't relied on magic all these years. We all became detectives because even among humans we have this weird talent to put pieces together from random places and make up a plausible storyline." He shrugged. "Valuable."

Leira gave him a crooked smile and looked at the screen for more information. "All that being said, there's plenty we can do," she said, without turning back to the group. "We don't know for sure who or what is taking them, so we keep digging till we are. Magical or non-magical, they're citizens and they're kids, and their well-being is our responsibility."

"Mark and I will head to Ohio, interview some parents and work on getting them to lend a hand or a wand. Maybe we can get ahead of this thing." Alan nodded at Mark. "Leira, can you get a complete list of the kemanas in America? Gives us a place to start."

"I can do that. Looks like we have a starting place. Hagan and Gail and I will monitor the different groups all trying to find the necklace and every other magical knickknack out there."

"This job finally has a little heat." Hagan pulled up his pants, his voice excited.

"I'm buying you a belt for Christmas. Better yet a new pair of pants." Leira took the file back from Alan. He seemed to want to say something. Leira waited, but he just nodded and turned to go, quickly crossing the warehouse to catch up with Mark.

"That was weird."

"Only if you're blind. He's got a thing for you." Gail smiled. "You were right, Hagan. Our skills do come in handy." She gave a smirk, her hands on her hips. "He's the hottest catch to come along in a while, too."

"Not on my list of priorities." Leira could feel her face warming. "First one is stop a magical hoarding war, second one is to get back the biggest artifact out there and third is a bunch of missing magical kids. No room to even put anything else in there." She tapped the side of her head.

"Okay, I get it. No worries over here. Dropping the subject. Going to go monitor the corporate Indiana Jones wannabes the old-fashioned way on my computer. At my desk. Way over there." She arched an eyebrow and smiled with one side of her mouth before heading to her desk.

"You know, he's not half bad. Even I noticed, which is saying something. Normally for me to notice a guy he's got to be carrying a football or a doughnut. Either one'll do. I'm just sayin'." Hagan headed back to his desk across the open warehouse.

"Stop saying. I don't pee where I swim." Leira shook her head.

"Never liked that saying, Berens."

Leira let out a sigh and sat down on one of the couches. "Singleness of purpose. Catch magical bad guys and learn more magic before big badass shows up. Sunday dinners with family. My dance card is full," she muttered.

She looked back up at the screen and had an idea. She centered herself and invited in the magic letting it spill out of her onto the screen, speeding up the information.

"Plenty about artifacts, nothing about those kids." Her eyes tracked the symbols as she read out loud. "There's that business again. Fleeker."

"Maybe we should invest." Hagan took out his white handkerchief and wiped his forehead.

"There's the part I'm looking for. Two young Wizards. Vanished into thin air." She looked at the ground, determined to come up with the start of a plan. "Dammit. Not a good sign. This is bullshit. They have to be somewhere."

CHAPTER TEN

Donald pulled into the parking lot of Forest Creek apartments tucked back from the frontage road near I-35 and found a parking space halfway down. He looked in the rearview mirror and checked his teeth before getting out of the car, smoothing down the front of his shirt. At the last minute, he remembered to reach back into the car for the bouquet of yellow daisies. Eireka's favorite flower.

He walked through the small breezeway under the stairs and watched the numbers on the doors of each apartment till he spotted number 183 near the creek.

There was already a yellow and blue windsail hung over the small patio and two chairs with a few potted plants tucked here and there. He walked around till he found the front door with a holly wreath and gave a good knock.

"Come in!"

He hesitated, not sure what to do.

"Come in!" The voice yelled louder but it wasn't Eireka. He checked the apartment number on the door and was about to open it when it flung open. Mara looked him up and down. "Nice flowers, Donald! Good to see you again. Been a number of years."

She walked to back to her seat on the couch. The troll was on the ottoman with a pair of black lady's underwear wrapped around his head in a turban. In front of him there were six cards face down. He looked up at Donald and trilled.

"Don't mind us. He's reading my aura. He got bored being at home alone all day."

"Does Leira know he's here?" Eireka came barreling down the circular stairs dressed in black pants and a short-sleeved turtleneck.

"Questionable. He won't comment on that topic."

Donald smiled when he saw Eireka, holding out the flowers. "These are for you."

"My favorite, you remembered. Let me put these in water." She went into the galley kitchen ducking down to look through the pass-through. Donald watched the troll, who was rubbing his chin and squinting at his cards.

"Don't mind them. Mom's trying to convince me trolls are psychic. No one can see the future." She smiled and shook her head.

"He doesn't read your future. That's ridiculous. He can tell where I need magical adjustments by reading the cards. Like a mechanic hooking your car up to one of those motherboards! You get that, right Donald?"

"I... I think I do?"

The troll flipped over a card and sat back, his paws on his legs. "Ooooh... Uh oh..." The card showed a troll smelling a yellow flower. "Big Brother," he chirped. He blew a raspberry at Mara, who gave him a look, drawing her mouth into a thin line.

"He's been using the names of reality shows to talk lately. I know you can say whatever you want."

The troll shrugged and made a face as he reached for another card.

"Little shit!"

"Real Housewives..." he squeaked in return. "...of Jersey!"

99

"Oh, that does hurt." The card showed a troll rolling through the grass.

"Huh! Amazing Race!"

Eireka came out of the kitchen carrying the vase and set it down on a side table. "Where'd you get those? Those are new, and that flower is definitely not from this world."

"Oriceran... a while ago. No big deal. You better hurry if you want to see the bats. Dusk is coming." Mara didn't look up at Eireka.

The troll flipped over another card. A troll eating a blue worm. "Bachelor, season eighteen. Bleck!" He frowned, holding his nose and shook his head, looking disappointed at her as the underwear slipped over his face. He pushed them back up with one hand and shook a tiny finger at Mara. "I know what you're up to," he whispered.

Mara arched an eyebrow and sat back.

"You ready?" Don put out his hand as Eireka took it and turned to wave goodbye. "Motherfucker," she said sweetly.

"Motherfucker!" The troll smiled and waved.

"Motherfucker!" said Mara, turning back to give the troll a look.

"Okay, let's go." Eireka had to pull Donald by the hand and out the front door as he stammered.

"Mother what? Who... I..."

"It's a family thing, like aloha. Suitable for a lot of things. Come on, it's almost dusk and I don't want to miss a million bats flying out from a bridge." She pulled a red-faced Donald out the door and closed it behind her.

Mara waited a moment and pointed a finger at the troll. "Repeat what you saw and no extra pizza from me."

The troll opened his mouth and thought better of it, pressing his lips together and pulling an imaginary zipper across his mouth. He held up his hand and solemnly looked at her, holding out his paw.

"Okay, that's fair. You want something in return. I tell you what, I'll draw you a map and show you how to get to our new place. You and I both know you're taking side trips all the time. That way you don't have to wait for me to pick you up." She looked at Yumfuck, but he kept his lips pressed together. "Is it a deal?"

She gently shook his little paw as he trilled. "Don't rat me out if they find you with the map!"

The troll harrumphed, crossing his arms in front of his chest.

"I wasn't calling you a rat. Next card!" She pointed at the remaining cards in front of him.

He flipped over a troll curled up in a ball, sleeping on an orange leaf. "Naked and Afraid. Booooo, *thbpft!* Hell's Kitchen!"

"That's enough out of you!" Mara scooped up all but one of the cards and put them back in the leather pouch. "One small trinket from where we were born. Not so much to ask. You keep that between us. I gave my word."

The troll flipped the last card. An oversized troll was roaring at some unseen danger against a red background. The troll shook his head. "American Ninja Warrior. You will need help."

"Are you offering?"

"If you need me."

She gave the troll a stern look. "You're going to have to talk at some point in actual English and complete sentences all the time, you know."

"Meh." He shrugged his shoulders as he hopped into her lap and handed her the remote.

"Fine but only an hour. You're getting a little addicted."

"This is The Voice!" he chirped as he leaned back and sighed.

Lois and Patsy were happily ensconced back in their old PDF office in Alexandria, Virginia. A middle-aged Wizard in a short sleeve dress shirt and brown pants waved as he passed by their door. A late-model willow wand was sticking out of his pants pocket. He was brushing his sparse comb-over back into place atop his bald head with the other hand.

"Hey Ira, how's it going? How was Disney World?"

He teeter-tottered a hand, shrugging his shoulders. "It was okay. Kids had a good time, but they kept asking the characters about Oriceran and how old were they really. Had to stop the teenager from pulling out her wand to shorten the lines. The wife told the kids no wands, no phones but of course the kids heard, *smuggle them in by any means necessary.* My oldest did get everyone to scatter at the hotdog stand with a few harmless mice. Have to say that was sweet. Glad to be back at work where I can relax."

"Maybe next year you try Hogwarts. More of our kind are working there already, anyway."

"Next year is my turn and we're going to the beach!" Ira waved again and kept walking.

Lois pulled her sweater around her as she pulled out her wand, waving it in a V pattern creating a virtual fire right next to her desk. "That's better. Feels like an icebox in here. Remember those days? They used to deliver that big block of ice through the little cubbie in the wall? Of course, we made our own most of the time."

"I make a point not to talk about the old days. I slipped once and asked a mechanic about a crank shaft. I'm pretty sure he was about to check and see if there was a silver alert out matching my description. I'm not even old enough in human years for one of those! I had to make up a whole story about being into antique cars."

Lois let out a laugh and lifted her hands to warm them by the faux flames. "That's a good one! Not the first time something like that's happened to one of our kind. And just when Agent Berens managed to get everybody out of the institutions and back on the street. Don't need you taking anyone's place."

Patsy shivered just thinking about the prospect. "That was a nice little piece of work you did, Lois, putting that bug in under those big shots' noses. Wasn't sure you had that much left in you."

Patsy ducked as the inevitable pea-sized fireball flew over her head, ricocheting off the far wall and hitting the filing cabinet before sizzling into ash. She was used to Lois taking everything to heart and just as quickly changing her mind.

"Come on! You know what I mean! That was a decent-sized stunt you pulled off. Getting in that building without a care. Not sure I could have done it." Patsy waved her wand over her head, styling her hair into an updo. "What do you think?"

"It suits you! Sorry I bopped off at you like that. I've been so keyed up ever since I glamoured my way into that fancy high rise. Couldn't be absolutely sure there wasn't a magical being working somewhere in there that might catch on to what I was doing. I'm a little rusty."

"You were seamless! Even rusty, there's a lot of magical folk who don't match up to you. Made me proud to be a PDA in the PDF!"

"Not a single strand of magic in the building. I was shocked! All human, all the time. Earl said it was no surprise. He says, why spend so much time working your way to the top if you already have a wand?"

Patsy opened her desk drawer and rifled through the peanut M&Ms in the plastic tray where pens normally sat. She pulled out an orange one and a yellow, admiring how well the colors went together before popping both of them into her mouth. "Oh, dang it, there goes another one!"

Patsy swiveled her chair and looked up at the screen. Symbols poured across, spelling out the destruction of another old, historical site in a small corner of Nigeria. "That makes the second one this week. New players too."

"Will you look at that! China is getting into the race. You'd think they'd figure out they have a treasure trove already in their own backyard."

"You think they've already marked all those places?"

"Not a chance. They would have tested some of it, somehow and we'd know. Very interesting times. Lots of border crossings. I've said it before, and I'll say it again…"

"Humans are weird. I know." Lois pushed off with her foot, sliding to the right just far enough to miss the inevitable pea-sized fireball. "Better make a report for the general and Agent Berens."

"PDQ for the PDA in the PDF!"

"Also a repeat. I know what I'm getting you for your birthday. The *Witching World's Book of Magical Records and Other Fun Facts.* The new edition. Give you something new to talk about for once." Patsy zipped her wand out in front of her. She batted the small fireball right back at Lois, who ducked to the side at the last second with a wide-eyed look of surprise.

"You've been waiting to do that." Lois was frowning but she was still impressed. "All this falderol, there'll be a few new things to mention. Like that Hannah Beecham sending up a call for help. What do you think that's about?"

Patsy shook her head, scowling. "Hard to say. I'm leaving that one to the Silver Griffins. Lacey will know what to do with the betrayal. Do we mention Fleeker?"

Lois looked up at the screen. "No, there's nothing up there. Must have been a glitch. Whoop! There goes another one. It's picking up. The corporate types have scored an artifact! Very interesting times, Lois."

"More will be revealed."

General Anderson showed up at the Chicago Water Tower without any aides, as requested by the Silver Griffins. He told no one where he was going and left his phone in his hotel room to make sure no one could track him. He gave his word to Lacey Trader and he planned to keep it. "Death, taxes and a man or woman's word should be the three things you can count on from anyone," he was fond of saying.

He wore a long overcoat over his uniform and left his peaked military cap back at the hotel, opting instead for a black wool hat lined in sheepskin with ear flaps. It was a typical winter day in Chicago with bright blue skies and a wind chill dipping well below zero. It made it easier for the general to go unnoticed by all the passersby who were tucked down into their scarves, scurrying toward their destinations as fast as their feet could carry them.

He went in the entrance to the Water Tower and waited by the will call booth for the theater, doing his best not to pace. It helped to grasp his hands behind his back and walk around slowly, reading all the posters for upcoming shows. "Hmph, Oz. Little on the nose."

"Still a good musical." Lacey Trader put out her hand and smiled to put the general more at ease. "Although, I've yet to see a green Witch unless it's from some bad sushi."

The general didn't hesitate and walked over briskly, pulling off his leather glove to grasp Lacey's hand. "Thank you for agreeing to meet with me."

"You said it was a matter of national security. I checked you out. You're not one to use hyperbole. Thank you for agreeing to our conditions."

The general smiled but spoke the truth. "I didn't have much choice, did I?"

Lacey smiled and arched an eyebrow. "No, I suppose you didn't. Follow me." She led the way into the theater where the council for the Silver Griffins waited.

The general took a look around at the ordinary people sitting in folding chairs and wondered if he was doing the right thing.

"I've seen that look more than once. People underestimate us all the time. I blame the Brothers Grimm. Bunch of Gnomes with an axe to grind. Made us all into some hook-nosed evil creature who only wears black. I love wearing colors and yoga pants. Don't wear the yoga pants in public, yet. Got a good look at the backside in the mirror. That put the kibosh on that one. Take a seat." Lacey took the last seat in the semi-circle, leaving the general with the chair facing the group.

"I don't mean to put anyone off." He pulled off the thick hat, resting it on his knee. His cheeks were still red from the cold. "I don't have time to make a lot of mistakes, even small ones and I have to trust my instincts on this one. I don't mind but I prefer to mix in verification."

"Magic makes that more difficult. I understand, especially with us. We cover our tracks rather well, even among our own kind. Take comfort in the idea that our organization is much older than this country and has managed to keep a pretty good lid on magic all this time. That should tell you something."

"Indeed, it does. I'm going to go ahead and assume if it involves magic you already have the background on things."

"I appreciate the show of respect. Good first impression."

The general gave a nod and a tight smile. He was determined to have this go well. There weren't many other options if this mission failed. "I'm going to speak plainly. I need magical allies in larger numbers who are already trained in calmly holding back a magical arms race. There are a lot of different players messing around with magic who have no background on how to contain or use it properly. That's not including the decimation to some pretty important historical sites." He spit out the last words, letting anger rise up in him.

"We've noticed, and we are already taking steps to turn back the tide."

The general shifted in his seat, excited and relieved. "Good news! But there's a catch that I can only manage and not control."

"The Federal government wants their share of the artifacts," said Lacey, pursing her lips. Several of the members stared blankly at the general, waiting for his response.

"To the point, I like that. Well, yes, that is the situation. I'm here outside of orders. A new twist for me but then, there's a lot of new things happening that don't exactly fall into what has ever been known by human beings."

"Not exactly true. Your kind knew us rather well a very long time ago. Your history has been rewritten to exclude any mention of us. Probably for the best."

A Wizard cleared his throat and shifted in his chair, crossing his ankle over his knee.

The general rubbed a hand through his brush cut. "I know our history with things we don't understand is very mixed. But I'm here to say we want to work with you as allies. You have all chosen to be citizens of this great country, and that means something to me. You live among us, paying taxes, raising your children, and going to work. The only difference is a slight change in DNA and an ability to bend physics in ways I'm not used to seeing." He shook his head, holding out his hands. "Just means I now have more in common with the first man who tried a bicycle and went down a street faster than any human had ever traveled before that day. A simple device we take for granted that must have seemed like magic at the time."

A Witch rolled her eyes, and another smiled broadly. The general caught on. "I take it there was some magic involved?"

"Just an old idea we reintroduced," said Lacey. "Ask us what you came to ask."

The general sat up straighter. "Help us identify and protect as many sites around the world as possible. In exchange, we'll negotiate with you fairly and openly to leave many of them untouched."

"Most..."

"It would be naive of me to assume our senior leaders in

government will not want to stockpile a few as insurance against foreign threats."

"Including us."

"Change can breed fear, it's true. I'll do what I can to inform others. I have it on good authority a few magical beings already serve as Senators and Congressmen. Explains a lot, both good and bad." He smiled to break the tension. "This will be something we all work on together. As good a place as any for us to start and, at the same time, stop another side with less honorable intentions to acquire too much power."

"Our Witches and Wizards remain under our command. That is a non-starter," Lacey said.

"Of course. I understand you operate as your own form of government. As I said, I'm doing this outside of normal channels. That doesn't mean there isn't infrastructure in place."

"You're talking about the PDF."

The general grimaced, hoping he had some secrets left. "That's correct. It's a black-op funded off the books and without oversight by anyone but me and a very select few. If you are willing to help, your Silver Griffins will coordinate with them."

Lacey clapped her hands and stood, surprising the general. "I was hoping that would be the case. We will work with Lois and Patsy." She held her hand up to stop him from interrupting. "I'm not negotiating. I'm telling. You're lucky to have them, especially Lois." She narrowed her eyes. "I know Leira Berens is an agent with you as well. She's very special to all of us and, as you know, very powerful. A word of unasked for advice. Don't treat her as a useful tool but as a magical being with a life."

The general stood and extended his hand to each council member, who up to this point had let Lacey do the talking. The general knew the mistrust with humans and the government still ran high. *Give me time.*

"We'll be in touch with a list and coordinate our efforts." Lacey directed him toward the exit.

The general turned at the last second, clearing his throat. "One more thing. More of a heads-up at this point. There's a rumor someone is looking to mix your magic with our technology to enhance plants or animals. I'm sure you know even good intentions can lead to disaster." He noticed a few of them fidget, and he looked down, pressing his lips together. "I was hoping this would be old news to you." He waved his large hat in a salute. "It's a lot to ask, but if you can share information…"

Lacey didn't bother answering him, gently giving his shoulder a nudge.

Once they were gone, a murmur arose among the other members of the council.

"Do you think we can trust him?" asked a Wizard who was still recovering from injuries taken when protecting the vault.

"More than most, I suspect. This will be a good time to get field practice for some of the younger ones, like Ernie. He's already battle-tested after getting thrown into the world in between. A few others could stand to be out there using their skills." The Witch stood and stretched her arms over her head. "We really need some better chairs." She took out her wand and wove a quilted seat, testing it out.

"That's against the rules, using magic in here like that," said another Witch, eyeing her own wand with the same idea.

"Apparently the rules are changing."

The other Witch looked around and with a quick wave of her wand made an overstuffed cushion for her chair. She sighed after she settled on top of it.

CHAPTER ELEVEN

Leira stood in her living room looking down at the black cowboy hat in the box. "Mom's been shopping again, I take it."

Correk picked up his dark brown suede hat and tried it on. "Remarkable. It fits perfectly."

"That long hair and those jeans, you look like every guy I went to high school with."

"Is that a good thing."

"For the most part."

Correk waited for a longer explanation but Leira shook her head. "Nope. Those memories are in the vault."

"Challenge accepted. Don't glow your eyes at me. I can do the same, Cousin. It's inevitable. Another sudden jolt of too much magic when you're not expecting it and out come the memories." He laughed as Leira put her hands on her hips, giving him a dead fish look.

"Not gonna happen. Turner has taught me how to be one with the magic."

"It's true, you've come a long way in a short amount of time but there's still some surprises ahead." He held out his hands. "I don't know what they are, of course or I'd tell you."

"Like you told me everything else."

"Point taken."

Leira narrowed her eyes, studying him. "You'll tell me whatever is making you toss and turn at night sooner rather than later?"

"That is my hope, but I need to button up a few things first, gather more information. Otherwise, all I can do is speculate."

"It's what I do for a living. Helps to do that with someone, you know." She could see he wanted to tell her something.

"Not yet." His face grew tense. *If I tell you, you'll be out that door, everything else forgotten, running right into a danger you can't handle. Last time it took every ounce of strength of seven armies, and then some. You need more time.* "It will have to wait."

Leira nodded and gave him a crooked smile. "Then it waits." She took the hat out of the box and an invitation fluttered down to the floor. "The intrigue grows. I forgot this about my mother." Leira bent over to pick up the card. "Did I ever tell you my mother used to create elaborate scavenger hunts for me when I was little? To get another clue I had to perform a song or recite a poem or run as fast as I could. At the end were chocolate coins in gold foil."

"What is today's adventure?"

Leira's eyebrows shot up and she looked amused. "Austin Rodeo!" She looked down at the troll.

Yumfuck was standing next to the box, wearing an identical tiny version of Leira's new hat along with his red cowboy boots. "You pull those off well."

Yumfuck trilled and tipped his hat.

"I take it, you knew all along."

The troll blew a raspberry at her. "Motherfucker!"

Correk shook his head. "It actually sounds like he's saying yes."

"I liked it better when you said Yumfuck all the time," Leira said. The troll cackled and wiggled his butt, twirling around in a circle.

"This invitation is for tonight and it includes dinner, sort of. Well, what you two will think of as food porn. There's a carnival attached to the rodeo and rides and fried food out the wazoo."

"What's a wazoo?"

"Need to know. Just trust me, we may actually fill up Yumfuck. I guess we're going to a rodeo." Leira's phone buzzed and she pulled it out. "Not work. It's Mom. She wants to know if we've left yet. Apparently, everyone is overly excited. Are you ready?"

Correk tilted his hat back on his head. "As much as I know how to be, considering I have no idea what we're heading into."

"Typical operating procedure lately. You're about to watch a bunch of humans play with much larger animals in ways that could get them hurt for a really cool buckle and money. Throw in some fried Twinkies, fried doughnuts, fried Milky Ways, and a corndog. Then throw it all up on a ride that spins you around."

"Wooooooohooooooo!" squealed the troll, showing all his sharp little teeth as he circled his hand in the air like he was holding onto a lasso.

"Sounds like fun. Let's go." Correk scooped up Yumfuck and helped him settle in the pocket of his jacket. "You're going to have to take the hat off till we get there. It won't fit. You'll crush it."

The troll hissed at him but finally took it off and handed it over.

"I'll keep it in my other pocket and give it back the moment we get in the car. You have a Light Elf's word."

They got out to the patio and noticed all the regulars sitting at three tables all bunched up together. There was silverware at every place and a glass of water sitting next to the usual beer.

"That's different," said Leira. "I don't think I've ever seen them eat food here before. Nachos, yes."

"Leira!" The chorus went up. "Correk!" yelled Mike and Mitzi.

Leira looked at the gate but curiosity got the better of her. "What's with the formal eating?"

"We never got around to celebrating winning the bowling tournament. You should join us! You two were a big help." Kimberly looked around to see what table they could add on the end.

"They're heading out to the rodeo, aren't you? Lots of firsts going on tonight. Never seen you in actual cowboy gear before, Leira." Scott gave her a thumbs up. "Didn't know you had it in you."

Estelle came tromping out of the restaurant carrying a large tray loaded down with hot food balanced on one shoulder with a folded stand in the other hand, the cigarette dangling on the edge of her lip. She crossed the patio without effort and unfolded the stand, resting the tray in one fluid movement.

"Why I don't talk back to her," said Craig. "She could take one of us down while slapping another."

Estelle harrumphed and stood back, one hand on her hip while she took a long drag on her cigarette. "Food won't serve itself!" she finally said as Mike and Janice hopped up to help sort out who got what.

"This is where we go," said Leira. "You guys have a good time."

"We'll have to do this again," said Paul. "Maybe after we win the softball tournament. What? I'm feeling optimistic."

Leira looked up and noticed a man lift his glass to her and wink. She turned away, doing her best to ignore him but she saw him getting up out of the corner of her eye. Just as he got close to the table, a cluster of women dressed for a night out sidled up to Correk.

"My friends bet me I couldn't get a kiss out of you," said a tall brunette, tilting her head to the side. "Help me take their money and I'll give you half."

"Go back to your minivans," snarled Estelle, idly blowing

smoke in their direction. "Take it on down the street. We don't do to-go orders here." Estelle glared at them through the haze of smoke.

"Excuse me, I couldn't help noticing you and was wondering if I could buy you a drink." The man from the bar was smiling at Leira, waiting for a response.

Everyone at the table rose to their feet and started shooing the table crashers away. Leira shook her head, smiling at Mitzi waving her napkin at the man. He retreated to the bar with a smile and a shrug. The women took a little longer, taking a few steps back, still giggling and waving at Correk till Mitzi turned her napkin on them and they wandered inside to look for a table.

"You know I can handle myself. Federal agent and everything." Leira hooked her fingers in the belt loops of her pants.

"Sugar, it's not about whether you can do it alone. You don't have to, and besides, it makes us feel useful. Frankly, I'm surprised it doesn't happen more often to either one of you." Mitzi smiled at Correk as she sat down.

"Okay, down girl," said Kimberly. "There is something fetching about you, Correk. Damn, now I've got it!" Kimberly took a long drink from her water.

"Now, we really have to go. Thank you again for the block."

"Bring us back something!"

"Have a good time!"

"Take a ride on the Tilt-o-Whirl for me!"

Correk started to say goodbye but Leira squeezed his arm, cutting him off. She was careful not to say anything till she got to the gate and held it open. "Bye, everyone!"

A muffled "Motherfucker!" sang out from Correk's pocket, making him flinch as he waved. "Goodnight!" he said in a booming voice, turning heads, muffling the second small, "motherfucker."

Once they were safely in the car, Correk handed back the

cowboy hat to the troll. "That signature goodbye you have going is not as funny as you think."

The troll cackled loudly and sat down on Correk's leg. "Aloha!"

Leira startled and looked at him, laughing.

Correk looked puzzled. "What was that? Some new way to swear?"

"I think that was a compromise."

CHAPTER TWELVE

They met up with Eireka, Mara and Donald by the fairgrounds. Yumfuck sat on Correk's shoulder and was an instant hit with everyone, especially the children.

"Look at the gerbil in the cowboy outfit!" A boy pointed and jumped up and down. "Can I get a picture with him?"

Yumfuck smiled and stood up, leaning a hand against Correk's neck, one cowboy boot crossed over the other. The boy came and stood next to Correk, not even waiting for an answer as his father took out his cell phone, snapping the pictures.

"Got it!" The boy ran over to his father to look at the pictures, laughing. He turned and yelled, "Bye, gerbil!"

"Mother..." The rest of the word was lost as he found himself suddenly jerked up into the air.

Leira grabbed him by the scruff of his neck, plucking him off Correk's shoulder and holding him up in front of her face, inches from her nose. "Don't even think about it, little pardner." She lowered her voice and whispered, "One little motherfucker out of you and I take you back to the car, and you never find out what a roasted turkey leg tastes like."

The troll gasped, holding his hands over his mouth in horror.

"Do we have an understanding?" Leira leaned close till the troll was brushing against her nose. He nodded his head hard, dangling in front of her face.

She put him back on Correk's shoulder and brushed her hands together, still giving him a stern look. He turned his back to her and watched the lights on the rides. A man walked by and nodded at Leira, giving her a smile. She ignored him and kept an eye on the troll.

"You're going to make a great parent someday," said Eireka, smiling.

"Not even a little funny, Mom."

Eireka let out a snort as Donald took her hand and whispered something.

"We're going to go take in a few rides by ourselves."

"Make sure you don't have to be a great parent again someday," said Mara.

"Boom, karma kicks you back," said Leira laughing.

Eireka smiled and rested her head on Donald's shoulder for a moment as they turned and strolled away, chattering away to each other.

Leira took a step back, jostling a man in jeans and a t-shirt. "Sorry," she said, righting the cowboy hat.

"I'm not," he retorted, smiling, the creases deepening around his eyes. He kept walking but turned back to look, smiling again at Leira.

"That could be you, if you wanted it to be." Correk nodded his head in the direction of Eireka and Donald. "You're part Light Elf. We have a natural charisma and now that you're learning how to work with your feelings it's attracting the local male human population."

"It's not real. They're attracted to magic, not me."

"Not gonna go with you on this one, Cousin. I believe in your world they say, you're starting to blossom."

"Oh my God, you've turned into an after school special. Please shut the fuck up as fast as possible."

"There you go. The swearing should act as a decent birth control for a while."

"Let's get a turkey leg to stuff in your pie hole."

"Turkey leg!" The troll jumped up and down on Correk's shoulder, finally willing to look at Leira.

"Much better."

"Hey, that's the talking mouse! Hi Yumfuck!" A little girl waved at the troll as her mother pulled her away. The troll waved and squeaked, "ET phone home," pointing his finger at her. She pointed back, smiling as they disappeared into the crowd.

"You're a regular ambassador of fun," said Correk as they walked up to an empty table.

"I'll get the food. Maybe it's better if you guys wait here. Turkey legs all around. You too, Nana?" Leira put an arm around her grandmother.

"I've been looking forward to this all day!"

Correk opened his mouth to say something but Leira cut him off. "Yes, I'll get my own. You don't share food. I get it."

It took a while to move up in the line but Leira finally brought back four turkey legs and found Yumfuck posing for pictures in the center of the table. Cell phones were waving in the air all around him as Correk stood off to the side out of camera range. Leira put the tray down on the table and pulled Correk over by her side. "Aren't we a little worried about the world asking about our dressed-up rodent?"

"Humans are remarkably willing to absorb most anything into their world and make it quickly normal. They think he's a clever rodent, that's it. No one is wondering anything other than what sort of tricks he can do."

"Shoo them away. Now."

"As you wish." Correk rolled his hand down in front of him, bowing slightly.

"Princess Bride, isn't it? That's not an Elven thing."

"I beg to differ. Just a retelling of tales from Oriceran. It's obvious. Okay, okay, I'll get them all to go. Even take care of the videos." Correk shielded his eyes with his hat as they started to glow, whispering, "*Troll invisibilia.*"

Instantly people spun around, filming the rides as if there was something exciting happening off in the distance. "Do you see it?" someone shouted, convinced there had to be something there. The crowd moved in that direction.

The troll harrumphed and pouted for a moment but changed his mind when he saw the turkey legs. He grabbed a leg and bit down, burying his face in it.

"I'm always amazed he can still breathe when he does that." Leira drew her brows together. "Why is no one paying attention to that? He's swearing like a sailor tearing apart a turkey leg."

"They won't see or hear him for the next few hours."

"Another one of those temporary spells."

"Making anything invisible takes a lot of energy. It's not worth making it permanent, even on Oriceran," said Mara.

"Wait, repeat what you just said."

"It takes a lot of energy to make something invisible."

Leira sat down next to Correk and pulled a turkey leg closer to her, leaning close enough to whisper to Correk. "I saw something on Oriceran." She shook her head, annoyed with herself for not seeing it sooner. "The first day I was learning from Turner. The energy pulled me over to Oriceran. I know, Turner had the same look of amazement on his face that you do. Not the important part, believe it or not. I got close to this large amount of dark magic. Turner pulled me back from it. He actually looked worried, which I cannot imagine is something he does often. It was surrounding a cabin deep in the woods. But I missed something when I saw it. My magic could see it, but I couldn't, not on my own. I was able to raise enough magic to make it visible. To everyone and everything else around it..."

"It was invisible." Correk's smile dropped.

Mara looked at him, and his smile returned as he bit into his turkey leg, hiding the truth from her.

"That must have been a tremendous amount of energy." Leira put a napkin in her lap.

"Do you know where in the woods it was located?"

"No, I don't know enough about Oriceran to recognize anything and it just looked like dense woods. This is tied to your secret, I can tell. I can ask Turner to help me do it again."

"No, not yet. There's too much risk involved. You may trigger some sort of alarm or let whoever created the spell know you're on to them."

"That's basically what Turner said. Oh, wait and he mentioned that name. Rhazdon. He said the power was just as impressive as something Rhazdon could have pulled off."

Correk felt the truth settle into his bones. Oriceran was living inside of a dark fairytale that was eight hundred years old. Rhazdon was still alive and biding his time. *But what is his end game? I need to warn the king and queen.*

"Does this help you at all?"

"It does. I have a friend, Perrom and I can ask him for help. Thank you." Correk kept his voice as even and friendly as he could manage.

"You never talk much about your friends or family back on Oriceran. You've helped me to literally put my family back together again. I want to know more about…"

Leira turned in time to see the troll reaching across the table for her plate, his claws outstretched. "Not so fast, dancing rodent!"

Correk smiled and whispered to her, "There's time to tell you all about my life back on Oriceran. We should enjoy this night." *And leave Harkin where he is in my memories.*

"You mean before the shit hits the fan," whispered Leira.

"Whatever you two have your heads together about, either tell me or drop it. We're here to have a good time tonight."

"And to see grownups wrestle large animals," said Correk, taking another bite. *It can't be him. Eight hundred years.*

"That's one way to put it."

Two men walked past in cowboy boots and chaps, their spurs jangling on their boots. They tipped their hats at Leira and smiled.

"I do not know what to do with all of this," she said, exasperated.

"We know, dear, but you've faced tougher challenges." Mara turned and winked back at the men, laughing. They smiled and said, "Ma'am," as they walked in the direction of the rodeo ring.

"Finish up, boys and girls. I want to watch some hunky men throw down!" Mara wiped the grease off her hands and fixed her lipstick.

"Berens' women run hot," said Correk.

"Only way to go." Leira took her grandmother's arm as the troll sat down on Correk's shoulder, and they walked across the fairgrounds while taking in the sights.

They found a few seats near the top of the metal bleachers that encircled two sides of the large open ring filled with a powdery dirt that made for softer landings. The Mutton Bustin' contest was well underway with a ten-year-old boy riding a sheep, holding on for all he was worth for six seconds. Mara crowed and cheered as if she knew the kid, shaking her fist in the air. Leira gave her a crooked smile and took a deep breath, letting it out slowly. This is life, I suppose. *You stick to the moment you're in whether it's good or bad.*

Next up were the bullfighters and rodeo clowns. The clowns were in full makeup and wearing their version of Western wear. One had a tutu over his jeans and was throwing t-shirts into the crowd.

"Kind of reminds me of your idea of what a cowboy looks like." Leira smiled at Correk who let out a laugh.

"It wasn't that bad..."

The clowns dragged out tall blue plastic containers, half filled with sand and ran near the bleachers, waving at the kids. The announcer came over the loudspeaker, "First out of the chute... Kyle Elliott riding Steamroller!" The metal gate lifted and a grey and white five-year-old bull weighing sixteen hundred pounds charged out of the chute, whipsawing a man back and forth as the seconds ticked by. His hat flew backward, landing in the dirt as a clown saw his chance and retrieved it, ducking behind one of the blue containers.

"Eight seconds to glory!" Leira yelled.

The announcer boomed out of the loudspeakers, "Six seconds! Too bad, almost had it. Ol' Steamroller got another one," just as Kyle rolled off the side, narrowly avoiding the sharp hooves. Two clowns ran in front of Steamroller just far enough away to give themselves time to roll over the top of the wooden wall as Steamroller bore down on them, horns lowered. The cowboy got up and ran for the fence, easily climbing over it, leaving Steamroller to slow to a walk as he trotted around the ring.

"That was amazing!" Correk was on his feet, eyes wide watching two riders come out on horseback to corral Steamroller back toward the pen. Another rider was getting ready, but the announcer was sputtering, confused. "Seems we have a change up, folks!"

Leira looked back at Correk. "Where's Yumfuck?" She whipped her head around, looking at Mara and under the seats.

"He was just here..." Correk checked his pockets and looked down toward the front of the bleachers.

"Famous last words with the tiny troll."

"Here we go, folks! A late entry riding Beaufort!"

"You go on, if you need to. I'm staying here to watch the

riders. That troll will be fine," Mara pronounced firmly. She wasn't going anywhere.

Leira scrambled down the bleachers to head toward the row of food stands over by the rides, Correk close behind her.

"That's a hairy son of a bitch," said an old man with a leathery face wearing a beat-up white cowboy hat.

"What's that he's wearing? Are those assless chaps?" A man was standing with his hand shading his eyes, straining to get a better look.

Leira stopped and slowly turned, sure she knew what she was about to see. Correk was already moving closer to the fencing.

Yumfuck was twelve times his size and wearing a borrowed cowboy hat, holding on to the thick rope with one hand, the other in the air as Beaufort did all he could to buck off the over-sized troll.

"My money's on the troll. He's all muscle." Correk stood by the fence, his hands on his hips.

"You're proud of him? You're missing the point. There are phones here."

"He'll shrink down again, disappear into the crowd. Your internet will rave about a yeti showing up at a rodeo and some yahoo will claim it was him in a costume. Everyone will move on to the next stupid video. I'm not worried."

"The Silver Griffins are no longer a worry?"

"That's not magic. That's a troll riding a bull. That's entertainment! Besides, they all know how hard a troll is to keep contained."

Leira stopped arguing long enough to take a good look at Correk. He was doing his best to enjoy this night. *It's that bad. What's coming. He thinks it's that bad.* She cocked her head to the side. *He's trying to protect me. Okay, for today, Cousin, but only today. You're going to have to learn how to let me take my chances, even if we are family.*

"Twenty-five seconds! A new Austin Rodeo record! Someone

get that hairy son of a bitch's name!" The announcer's voice cracked with excitement.

"Come on, he's off the bull and running for the fence. We need to be over there to scoop him up."

Yumfuck ran for the wall, turning at the last second as Beaufort rammed the wall with his horns. The troll dodged around a blue barrel as the clowns distracted the bull. Yumfuck ran back toward the wall, sliding around the back as he shrank back down to his normal size of five inches, getting lost under the cowboy hat and rolling in the dust.

"Where'd the feller go?"

"He was just here! What the hell was he wearing? A cow onesie?"

Yumfuck scurried along the backside of the wall, making his way between the moving feet while everyone looked around for the missing rider. Correk found him just as he got to the side of the announcer's booth slipping back into his cowboy boots and hat. He scooped him up and put him into his shirt pocket where he could lean out of the top, holding onto the shirt.

"Did you think we wouldn't notice you riding a bull?" Correk looked over at the crowd, still buzzing about the mysterious rider even as someone else took their turn.

"America's Got Talent!"

"That's enough for one day. Nesturnium." The troll blew a raspberry at Leira and she blew one back. "We'll still ride a few rides, but you're doing it from the comfort of Correk's pocket. No more growing into something bigger."

"That was pretty cool, though." Correk shrugged at Leira, holding up his hand near his pocket so the troll could high-five him with his tiny paw. "I'd actually try that if we had more time."

"Yeah, time is what's stopping you."

"I could do it. I've told you. Light Elves are gifted athletes."

"Big difference between bowling and riding an angry ton of beef. Come on, let's go see if we can pull Nana away from the human beefcake long enough to ride the Ferris wheel. I've always loved that view, and it's been years since I've seen it."

Correk caught himself and grew thoughtful. "Fifteen years, isn't it? Well, it's about time. Will make me feel like I'm back in my room in the castle."

They stayed till dark, riding every ride, including the rollercoaster, holding the troll tight over their heads as he screamed with delight and the Gravitron that spun so fast they were all pinned against the thick pads behind them. By the time they finally found Eireka and Donald and got back to the Mustang, the troll was asleep in Correk's pocket, and Leira and Correk were laughing over the troll's jowls shaking in the wind on the swings.

"Thank you for teaching me how to do this, Cousin." Leira slid into the driver's seat as Correk got in, making sure he didn't wake the troll. "It's a rare thing to learn how to be happy in the moment no matter what's going on around you."

"I suspect Turner Underwood has a little to do with your new skill as well."

"He tells me to do it and you show me how it's done. Tonight was a lot of fun, even if tomorrow you tell me the truth and we fight the bogeyman."

"It will take more than the two of us or even what can fill a hotel room this time. We will need serious help."

"I'm going with you to Oriceran. I know that's where you're headed. Don't slip out without me. I'm going with you."

"You're right, it's your home as well, and your power is going to be needed. But heed my warning, be very careful when we're there. Give nothing away about what we suspect, or that we're even worried about anything when we're out in public. Surprise at this moment is all we have on our side. Before we go, we need time to gather more information if we are to prevent another widespread war. And you need to get even better at harnessing all of your power."

"A war… Let's start with Turner Underwood. I have a feeling he knows more than he's telling us, anyway.

CHAPTER THIRTEEN

The plan was simple. The celebrity Penny Ryan was going to be eating lunch outside on the patio at the current hot spot, Il Pastaio in Beverly Hills. Her publicist made a point of alerting the paparazzi on the sly, and a Gnome photographer passed the word back to the prophets.

By the time Penny arrived, there was a large gathering of tourists and photographers all vying for a spot on the sidewalk being held back by a small crew of overgrown bodyguards. Penny pulled up in her trademark cream-colored Cadillac and got out, handing her keys to the valet, a Light Elf placed there by the prophets.

A Wizard posing as a hipster in a man bun, turned into a crazed stalker when he got close enough to Penny to start ranting and lunge at her with a sharp knife. The damage was done before anyone understood what was happening. Two Kilomeas posing as bodyguards and glamoured to look human shoved the tourists aside, jumping on top of the Wizard. One of them stood on the Wizard's hand till the bodyguard could pick up the knife and hold it out in front of himself between two fingers.

Smart phones came out of pockets from every angle as people

recorded the mayhem. Whispers could be heard in the background, and only a couple of people thought to use their phone to call for an ambulance.

Suddenly, gold and silver sparks started spitting out of the air from under the stiff white awning. A portal opened, hanging in the air between the entrance and the crowd on the sidewalk. All the phones immediately swung toward the opening, recording the sudden appearance of a lush forest in the middle of North Canon Drive, as the large Crystal prophet climbed over the edge of the portal and onto the sidewalk.

"It's a stunt. They're doing some Marvel movie. Is she even hurt?" The Witch prophet followed quickly and waved her wand, lifting the man into the air several feet as he shrieked. She gently put him back down again and went to the wounded celebrity, kneeling by her side and comforting her. The Crystal helped the Gnome prophet through the portal, and he made his way to Penny, pulling a small leather pouch out of his robe. There was already a pool of darkening blood around her, and her breath was getting shallow and raspy.

"Give me space!" he shouted, waving his arms at the crowd. The two bodyguards pushed the crowd back, giving a much better view of the girl on the sidewalk and the strange creatures huddled around her. The Witch made sure not to block the cameras as the Gnome knelt, exposing the gash while Penny screamed out in pain. There was a murmur through the crowd as the wound oozed blood. The Gnome pulled out some of the powder in the pouch and rubbed it into the wound. *"Experialis, dragonus."* Only the first part of the spell was needed to activate the powder. The powder sizzled and sank into her skin as the wound slowly disappeared.

The rest was for the cameras to ensure no one missed the point. Magic had landed on Earth.

The second part of the spell caused a small dragon to appear in the air, beating its wings, rustling the bushes that ran along the outside of the tables and blowing everyone's hair around in a whirl. The dragon let out a high-pitched screech and flew into the portal, disappearing as it flew higher above the trees. The Gnome knew how much the humans loved a plot twist and some drama.

Penny Ryan finally came around just as the ambulance arrived and was helped onto the gurney as the Gnome raised his hands to get everyone's attention.

"Who are you?" someone shouted from the push of people still trying to get a better look. The attacker was all but forgotten. Wizards posing as police hustled him off to cheers from the crowd. They drove away, lights wailing.

The plan is working, thought the Gnome. He smiled at the crowd as he got into position in front of the open portal. The chatter in the crowd grew as more people came rushing over to see.

"What the hell just happened?"

"There are fucking aliens in Beverly Hills! I am not surprised."

"Is this for real? You guys casting? I have a head shot here somewhere."

"Hey, you guys get out of my way! I'm late for a meeting in there!"

"Those robes are amazing! The stars on them move every time one of them turns around! Can I get a picture with you?"

He nodded to the Witch, who gave a wave of her wand, silencing the crowd. He waited a moment, giving everyone a chance to settle down, take it all in, and catch on that an actual hole was torn in the ozone.

"We are from Oriceran, your sister planet just on the other side of the veil." He pointed to the portal, passing his hand through and jostling a nearby plant. He hummed a song as the plant leaned toward him, opening large pale pink bulbs. A sleeping Pixie woke up startled and flew into the woods.

"Tinkerbell!" someone gasped.

"We saw what was happening and heard that young woman's cry. We had to do something even if it meant risking everything and telling you of our existence."

"How did you fix her? What was that stuff?"

Play to their ego. Tell them they've got one on us. "You see, where you are more advanced technologically than we are, we have something you have only dreamed of in movies and books." The Gnome muttered a spell and lifted a foot off the ground as a glowing haze of purple surrounded him. "Magic. We're here to help and we want to get to know you. Tell your friends, share this story. Magic is real." He ended with a flourish, throwing his cape over his shoulder and climbing through the portal. The others quickly followed until the Witch climbed through and closed the portal with a spectacular display of sparks.

"Damn! They just beamed themselves up!"

A waiter quickly arrived with a bucket of water, washing away the blood on the street as the crowd dispersed, already posting, snapchatting, reddit and tweeting. Within the hour the story went viral and trucks with large satellites on top were parked outside the restaurant broadcasting live even though by then there was nothing left to see.

"Aliens emerged from what was called a portal today in posh Beverly Hills." An anchor from a cable entertainment show did her best serious and concerned face as she told the story. The world was on the edge of their seats, wondering if it could be true.

There was an entire planet on the other side of the veil.

"What did they call it? Oriceran?"

Katie Toler sat in the folding chair, happy to be able to shed the glamour and let her tentacles unfurl down her shoulders, gently massaging her neck. She knew Lacey Trader wasn't happy that the necklace was still out there, but she also knew she had given it everything she had. *Hell, May Sage got herself injured trying to retrieve the damn thing.*

Katie sat back, waiting for the Silver Griffins to finally make their way into the theater and hit her with a barrage of questions. She looked at her phone. "Two minutes late. Not like this bunch?" She got up and walked into the hallway. "Hello? Did I get the day wrong?"

A young Witch appeared on the stairs coming up from the vault.

"I was told to give you a message. The meeting's been cancelled. Lacey Trader will get in touch with you to reschedule."

"Now, what could be so damned important they'd drag me all the way here just to cancel? Is this the punishment? Mild annoyances?"

"The prophets appeared in Beverly Hills today and saved Penny Ryan's life before announcing to the world about Oriceran and that magic is real."

"What, no fucking way!" For once, Katie was speechless.

"I'm sorry, I have to go. Things are blowing up, some of it literally. People are breaking the rules about magic left and right. Reports of someone growing a taller fence right in front of their neighbors and someone else using a wand to get their waiter to come back to the table. Small stuff now..."

"But it'll grow into something bigger."

"I heard that someone stole a parking place using magic. The human got out and ran away, leaving their car. That one's not substantiated yet, but it doesn't look good. The Silver Griffins are out stamping it all down, handing out fines. In the light of what the prophets did, they're giving everyone one pass, as long as no one was harmed."

Katie let out a breath. "That was a lot of information in one blast? Well, then, I'll be on my way. Please tell Lacey I will be continuing my mission and will report in as soon as I have made progress, which I hope to be soon?"

Katie pulled out her wand and waved it around her head, changing the tentacles back into long, blonde tresses. "I was half-tempted to leave them, but I suppose even after everything the humans have seen, it would freak out one or two of them? Medusa ruined it for Atlanteans with the whole snake thing. Not even the same," she said, "but try telling someone while they're passing out."

The Witch blinked, not sure what to say. "Okay, well, then we'll be in touch. No, you'll be in touch. Right, okay. So, I've got to go." She backed away till she got to the stairs and turned, taking them as quickly as she could, disappearing at the bottom into the vault, closing it behind her, the tumblers turning to lock it.

"Good idea," whispered Katie. "If magic is breaking out all over, there will be some who look to take advantage of an opportunity or two. Best they not get any more assistance. That damn necklace is enough of a problem child."

The dark mist seeped through the world in between, sliding down wormholes and gliding into different places overlooking the two worlds where it could feel the dark, shimmering trails of a twisted spell or a dark push of energy. It was in search of dark magic to absorb, greedily seeking out the practitioners and dragging them inside. Gathering dark energy any way it could was the only thing it knew. The only mission it had.

There was no thought that ran through the dense knots and pulsing mist. Only a swirling desire to have more dark energy.

So far, it had found eight young practitioners who answered the call, listened to the whispers. The black mist knew how to beckon those who played with dark magic, soothing them into coming closer to where the veil was thin in the world till the shroud could gather round them.

Its energy was growing slowly, too slowly but there was not much that could be done about that. More powerful practitioners were strong and could resist the urge, brushing it aside. It was alright. The dark mist never knew time and was patient, even now to gather what it could. Time was on its side anyway in the world in between, even if it was because it never passed.

May Sage stood next to Lacey Trader, her hip jutting out and a smile on her face. Her long black leather jacket hanging open. "Well done, old girl. Couldn't have done that one better myself." They were standing in Lincoln Square in Chicago watching as a group of local magical beings pulled themselves off the ground. Their clothes were still smoldering from where Lacey managed to lasso them all with a winding bolt of low-level lightning. "Next time, I up the amps!" Lacey shouted.

She stood there whacking her wand in the palm of her hand, daring anyone to try something else. The magical creatures were there to show any humans who passed by a thing or two about magic. They said it was like a show. Lacey was not amused. She waved her wand high in the air in an arc sending out a shower of sparks as she said in a bellowing voice, "Never was, never will be!"

All the humans froze where they were as the assortment of Elves, Witches, Wizards, and other magical creatures hurried off to their homes.

"You have to do this. We can't leave Hannah there." Lacey didn't look at May. She wanted to make sure no one doubled back. She was ready to make an example of someone. Her temper was growing shorter by the moment.

"Can't do it. You know I'm right. I'm needed elsewhere. Let

those two older birds do it. Those friends of yours, Patsy and Lois. I imagine the government is spinning its wheels right now trying to figure out exactly what to do. It'll be a day or two before they figure things out. Take advantage of it. Leave me in the shadows where I'm useful."

CHAPTER FOURTEEN

Patsy was well into her second big bag of peanut M&Ms, crunching them so fast she was barely tasting them. All hell was breaking loose. The virtual screens were spitting out symbols the two Witches had never seen before, making loud noises like metal gears grinding against each other.

"How is that even possible?" squawked Lois, her hands clamped over her ears. "The damn thing is magical!" She aimed her wand at the board, waving it in every direction but nothing changed.

"You've already tried that several times. It's not going to work!" Patsy's mouth was so full of candy she sounded like she was talking through marbles.

"Slow down on that stuff, girl. You're going to make yourself sick, and then you won't be any use at all just when we need you the most. We're about to earn our keep, and then some!"

"I'm just so damned on edge, and this noise is not helping," Patsy shouted.

Lois held up her wand again and aimed the tip straight at the board as she focused all her energy, shooting out a blast of light that pulsed into the board, vibrating it till the symbols scattered everywhere, disappearing into shimmering beads of light. Silence fell over the room as the board stopped working.

"Well at least the racket died down. Don't worry, I'll figure out how to fix it later. It was no damned good the way it was going on, anyway. Couldn't think either!" Lois pushed her glasses up her nose and put her hands on her hips, her wand still clasped in her hand. "This is not good. Those damned prophets showing up like that. You'd think they'd give somebody a heads up or something. I mean, it's great what they did, saving that celebrity and everything."

"I love Penny Ryan. Have you seen her videos on YouTube? I've tried a few of those makeup tips. They really work."

Lois thought about zinging Patsy back onto the subject with a little fireball, but she was finally slowing down on the candy. She settled for a scowl and sat down at her desk. "Somebody needs to figure out a way to make this all into a big hoax. A mass hallucination or a giant marketing something or other."

"The general said we are not to do a thing without his express instructions. He showed up here in person and said each word slowly like he was biting them off." Patsy shook her head. "Amazing how frightening that little man can be, and without magic!"

"You know how I hate to sit on the sidelines at times like this." Patsy scowled.

"You love sitting on the sidelines! We both do, well, normally. We like watching everybody else scurry around like rats and reading off the information. Of course, that part's gone kablooey." She glanced over at the sizzling screen. A triangle symbol fell off a corner and went skidding across the floor burning out in a bzzzzt and breaking apart.

"There's my damn phone. Buried in my purse again. It's been blowing up with relatives from every corner. A lot of them I never even knew I had. Suddenly, everybody knows I work for the government, and they want to know if something bad is going to happen. Another incident like what happened in Area 42 a while back. You remember when they conducted those so-called paranormal tests. Thank goodness we had the good sense to throw them off the scent by failing every one of them." Lois finally found the phone. "Oh, wait, it's Lacey. She never calls me during working hours. Things really are loosie goosie. Lacey, what are you doing? No one's supposed to know we still talk! I know, I know, we saw! Boy, did we see! Rescue who? You're kidding!"

Lois held the phone to her chest to muffle the sound. "You'll never guess in the lifetime of a Witch who they want us to rescue. Hannah Beecham!"

"No! Rescue her from what? She's a traitor to her kind. Isn't she parked right where she wants to be in the first place?"

Lois put the phone back to her ear. "Huh, really? Well, you don't say. You still got it, Lacey. Even I didn't see that one coming. Uh huh, uh huh, well when you put it that way how can we say no? She's a regular hero! Send me the details, what you have. Sure, I still remember the old spell. I'll retrieve the information from the Silver Griffins channel. I kept my old password just in case. Well, that is one helluva tale, Lacey Trader. You and I will have to catch up soon. Sure, I don't suppose that'll be anytime soon. World's being exposed and all. Okay, better go and get started. Right-o."

"What did she say?" Patsy blurted. She held it in for as long as she could.

"That Hannah Beecham is a hero! She was undercover looking for the mastermind of all this trouble."

"No! Isn't she a little young to be out in the field like that? Do her parents know?"

Lois shook her head in amazement. "No one knew but Lacey. Boy, that's gonna cause a tickle or two." Lois got up, gathering her sweater and purse. "Come on, you and I have to go get her out of that mess she's in. She sent up a flare for help and no one else can answer it. It's up to you and me, it seems."

Patsy got up, pulling what was left of the bag out of the drawer and stuffing it in her purse. "Might as well. Nothing left to do here. The general can reach us no matter where we go. Where are we going?"

"Just across the river. Hannah is in D.C.!"

"You think the necklace is with her?"

"That would really be something, wouldn't it? If we were the ones who finally got it back! Come on Patsy, times a wastin! I feel the old juices flowing. Let's go show them how it's done and rescue that young witch."

Patsy was already halfway down the hall as Lois got the lights, jogging to catch up to her. "What are you going to tell Earl about all this?"

"Oh, everything! I always do! Hell, we may even need him before this is all over. You drove today, right? Let's take your car. I'm low on gas. Tell me you brought more than that candy. Road trip!"

"Do it because we're paying you." Lacey Trader gave Katie a cold stare. They were meeting at a diner on the corner of Western Avenue in Lincoln Square just by Welles park that served a better cup of coffee than expected given its shabby interior. Lacey took a sip of the hot coffee, her mind wandering to one of an increasing number of magical problems. *This one is worse.*

Another report of a missing teenage Witch came in just before Katie arrived. Lacey was well aware of the family's long history of dabbling in dark magic, but it didn't matter to her. The Silver Griffins were sworn to protect all magical beings, even if some of them were part of a larger problem most days. She was tired, and her muscles ached from a day of tamping down magic, and she had no patience left for the Atlantean. "Bring Hannah Beecham back safely or consider your services no longer needed."

"I do like a clear message, I have to admit."

"You're doing this one without your sidekick." Lacey watched the awareness come over Katie's face. "That's right, May was talking to us without telling you. Apparently, trust doesn't run deep in your relationship. I've sent two other Witches to help get Hannah out with as little fuss as possible. I don't need any more public shows of magic... None," she said, icily. *No trace of any of the missing teenagers, anywhere. Not even a residue of a magic trail.*

Katie held up her hands in mock protest. "I have no intention of alerting the media. I've managed to keep under the radar so far, and it shouldn't be a problem?"

Lacey held up her wand, the tip glowing, and she tapped Katie's phone. "Those are the coordinates Hannah was able to send to us."

"I would have rescued her off that damn Camelback Mountain if you'd trusted me with this information earlier. Just saying..."

"Don't try what little patience I have left, Katie. You let the necklace slip through your fingers there, too. Go be of some help and earn your keep. Be a team player this time."

"Not my strong suit but I'll do my best? At the least, I'll get your little Witch home safe and sound."

"Do a better job than you've managed with the necklace."

"Ouch, no need to turn bitchy?" Katie tilted her head to the side, her magical silky tresses cascading off her shoulder. She lifted her chin, irritated. "That necklace is more popular than the last condom on the last night of an Amish *rumspringa*. Dark forces are moving it around from place to place? Doesn't help that the good guys can't all work together. I've run into Leira Berens more than once. Not useful."

"That many justifications usually means someone is beginning to recognize they can't do the job. Do you want to just part ways tonight? I'm not risking Hannah's life if you're unsure about your abilities."

A cold smile came across Katie's face. "No need? You're right. All of this talk is a distraction. I have my marching orders and a road map to D.C.? Enough said?"

Lacey gave her a cold stare as she waved to the waitress for the check. "I'll take care of this. You have a flight to catch."

Katie Toler stood at the main entrance to the Virginia Seminary in Alexandria lit only by the two tall streetlights. She gently pulled out a tentacle and ran a finger along it, whispering to it before she put it on the ground. She watched the long black tentacle slither to the grass and quickly head west down Deanery Drive toward the small post office carved out of the campus hundreds of years ago. Deanery Drive ran parallel to the main public road, Seminary Road and curved by the small white two-room post office built in the late 1700s. The Seminary was conceived a generation later by a group looking to forge a place of peace in the middle of growing unrest.

Every dean since its inception was informed of the Seminary's other function as an ally to magic.

Katie was familiar with the old post office and remembered stories from her childhood. The magical community in the area was protective of the site. It was used as an outpost by Witches and Wizards to safely get messages back and forth during the last big scare about magic. The Seminary had long been a refuge for all kinds of creatures and was surrounded by a light spell performed by the Silver Griffins well over a hundred years ago.

The tentacle turned suddenly by the refectory as Katie jogged easily in her leather boots to keep up. Her camel-haired coat cinched around her waist, the bottom flapping in the wind.

The tentacles on her head still keeping watch in every direction as she ran by Johns Hall dorm. The campus was tucked in for the night, and only a couple of lights shone behind windows.

The coordinates from Lacey Trader included a residue of Hannah's magic giving Katie a way to track her more quickly. Katie had already crossed out of Georgetown over Key Bridge and through Arlington tracking Hannah, finally coming to a stop on the campus in Alexandria. Her trail was a bright mix of yellow and green, mixing in with several others. Her trail was even showing signs of darkness just around the edges.

"It's definitely time for you to come home, dearie. This would be a lot more fun if the necklace were with you." The artifact's powerful trail was nowhere to be seen. Katie came around the dorm, still following the tentacle, and ran up to the aging red brick gym built like a solid square. "Unimaginative but useful?" She could hear the sound of rummaging inside the building and tried the door. *Locked.* She tapped it with her finger, letting out a small burst of magic, moving the tumblers and pulled open the door.

Inside in the darkness, several young Witches and Wizards were digging holes in the gym floor.

"It's here, and we need to find it tonight." A silver-haired Wizard in a long black coat was barking orders, distracted as he felt about with magic for an artifact. "We don't leave till it's in our possession."

My advantage so far. Katie saw Hannah on the far side of the room digging in a hole with another Witch, not looking up at anyone. Katie sensed the Wizard's strong magic and kept the door to her back, just in case. She created a fireball behind her back and sent out the first volley, slamming the Wizard hard against the wall and knocking the wind out of him. He righted himself, angry he missed her entrance.

Hannah clambered out of the hole along with the other Witch, who took her hand and pulled Hannah close to the wall.

"Let the grownups fight this one out," the young Witch whispered.

The Wizard pulled out a retractable wand, snapping it easily into place.

"Unusual for you tall, handsome and very dark types to not go for whatever's old. Family heirlooms and all." Katie snapped her fingers, sending two young Wizards into the nearest hole. She formed another fireball, ducking as the Wizard sent out a pulse of energy. "Not so fast, grandpa." She returned fire, sending out another volley that exploded at mid-point over the floor of the gym, lighting everything as it met with the Wizard's energy. Katie startled, surprised at the Wizard's power but quickly recovered.

The Wizard kept up the steady wide stream of pulsing energy as Katie ducked, sending out fireballs to ward it off, as the Wizard mumbled a spell too low for anyone to hear, and in the darkness not possible for Katie to see.

She was working on a spell of her own as a crushing weight suddenly pushed against her chest, drawing the breath out of her. She choked for air, managing to form two more fireballs before she became too lightheaded to think clearly. The pulse of energy finally threw her hard enough against the glass doors behind her to shatter them, leaving her lying in the broken glass, gasping for small bits of air. The Wizard advanced on her, still pushing the energy toward her, his wand raised, ready to do away with the intruder, unconcerned about the wreckage. "This place has been a thorn in dark magic's side long enough, anyway," he yelled quickly crossing over the gym.

As he got closer to the alcove that separated the gym from the front doors, he felt his feet growing heavier, and it was taking more effort to lift each foot. He looked down and saw hundreds of small silver spiders quickly weaving a web of iron ore, shining black in the glow from the shimmering black stream of magic. He twisted around to see who was behind him.

"Well, will you look at that Patsy. The dumbass finally noticed we were here. Told you I remembered that cloaking spell. Like the back of my hand." Lois nodded to Patsy who moved to the far side of the gym, her wand raised.

Lois lifted her new government-issued wand and made ever-larger circles as the spiders climbed up the Wizard's legs, still weaving, crossing over each other. The weight started to compress his bones, and he cried out, refocusing his magic as he lessened the pulse of energy aimed at Katie. He raised his head and roared, waving his wand, straining as he turned the webbing to thick black ooze, running off him and into the floor.

"Well, dammit, that's not good," said Patsy. "Time for Plan B. Not to worry, mister. Our plans run all the way through Z." Patsy swiped her wand as a long gold line of light whipped out the back with small green thorns lining it. She whipped her wand forward just as Lois pulsed energy at him. "Yep, I know that spell too. Oldie but a goodie," said Lois.

Patsy's gold vine caught him in the face tearing open his cheek and drawing blood. It wrapped around his arm, the thorns digging into his cashmere coat and tearing the fabric as it went deeper, ripping his shirt and scraping at his skin. His wand wobbled in his hand sending the pulse out in a wavy, uncontrolled flight, crashing around the room. The young Wizards and Witches all ducked, falling to the floor except for a Witch across the gym who raised her wand, pointing it at Lois.

Hannah saw what the Witch was doing and turned to the girl next to her. "If you ever change your mind…," she said, a puzzled look on the witch's face.

"No, don't. You'll get hurt," the girl said.

"A Silver Griffin never backs down from a fight." Hannah stood up straight and pulled out her wand, aiming it at the witch across the gym, spinning the girl like a top till she fell over, pinning her arms and legs to the floor.

"Wooohoooo! That's my girl! Keep an eye on the junior hood-lums and we'll take care of the big bad wolf." Lois held up her wand to her mouth, blowing in one end. A small twister appeared out the other, growing as it sped across the gym, ripping up the floor, sending pieces of debris through the air.

The twister picked up the Wizard, spinning him and lifting him off the floor, whipping his wand from his hand. He shut his eyes, giving into the howling wind, concentrating on speaking the words to an ancient family spell even as pieces of sharp wood slammed his body. The wind died, resting him on the gym floor, and he held his hand up, the wand flying to his open palm.

Katie stirred and attempted to sit upright amid the glass. It was hard to take a breath, and a gash in her forehead bled into her eye and stained the pale tan of her coat.

The Wizard sent out a series of rapid fireballs at Lois who dodged each one, hitting some of them back with the energy from her wand. Several of them turned, seeking out Patsy who stood her ground, casting a spell to turn them into one large fireball that roared at the Wizard. He opened his mouth yelling, "Freesia," just in time but not before the tips of his eyelashes were singed and his wand was left smoking. He dropped the useless wand to the floor and pulled out another.

"Dang! A backup wand. I appreciate a thoughtful man." Patsy sent out a stream of light-filled chiggers that crawled up the pant leg of the Wizard, the small bugs wailing in a high-pitched siren. The Wizard cried and ran from the large room and out the alcove, raising his wand at Katie, who covered her head with her arms.

"I will take some revenge!" he growled.

"Not today." Hannah Beecham ran between Katie and the Wizard and held out her wand shaking with nerves as she shouted, "*Capreasious formus.*" She held steady as best she could, focusing the magic.

Her magic didn't hold in the face of the Wizard's experience and strength.

The Wizard sent out a blue flame from his wand that encircled his body ending the wailing and dissolving the chiggers. The anger was getting the better of him. He wasn't used to being bested by anyone, especially two aging witches and a young girl. He raised his arms as the ground trembled, ready to bring the building down and bury them all.

"This isn't good, Lois!" Patsy and Lois did their best to hold the structure together as the young Witches and Wizards ran for the door at the back of the gym and out into the night.

"Hang on, Patsy! This isn't the way we're going out!"

The building trembled and bricks fell from the top of an outer wall. The blue flame from the Wizard spread out slowly surrounding the building, creeping up the walls.

"If we don't make a run for it right now, we won't be able to once that fire closes in." Lois nodded at Patsy. "You go first and I'm right behind you."

"Not that stupid, my friend. We go together! Earl would kill me if I left you behind." The building shook again, and the floor opened up in the center creating a wide crack right down the middle.

Hannah did her best to hold back the Wizard from getting any closer, but she was losing the battle. Still, she didn't move, standing her ground in front of the dazed Katie.

Something tapped at the Wizard's shoulder, drawing his attention, sliding around his waist and gliding up to his shoulders. "What?"

"You really know how to make an entrance, kid." Hagan stepped out of the darkness beside Leira, the troll sitting on his shoulder. He waved at the Wizard. "Hello sir. Your worst nightmare has arrived you son of a bitch and in a variety pack. You're fucked."

Leira stood yards away, her eyes glowing letting an intention loose and following behind the magic as it sought out the Wizard, putting out the blue flame and enveloping him in light.

The troll dropped to the ground, growing to the size of a

German shepherd taking his place by her side, teeth bared, growling, pawing at the ground. Hagan pulled his gun and ran toward the gym as students poured out of the nearby dorm and faculty in pajamas and robes came running down the road from nearby houses. "I got this," yelled Hagan as he ran inside.

Leira looked down at the troll. "Go with Hagan." The troll nodded and dropped to all fours, easily running to catch up with him.

The shaking in the building started to subside as Lois and Patsy finally lowered their wands. "We're the good guys!" Lois saw Hagan, gun raised running inside in the dim light. She lit the end of her wand to illuminate the room.

"Hagan! It's you! You brought a troll! Follow this-a-way! There's some little twerps we still need to round up." Patsy ran for the back door as the building let out a loud moan and started to list to one side. "It's like trying to get off the Titanic!"

The teenage Witches and Wizards could be seen running in the distance. "That's who we need to grab. They know where that damned necklace is!" Patsy took off at a trot in her Clarke's, glad she wore comfortable shoes.

"Oh geez," said Lois. "Not sure magic covers running that fast."

"This is where all that dieting pays off." Hagan took off at a clip, running after the teenagers as the troll galloped on ahead, his growl a low rumble. Hagan started to close the gap. "Thank you, Rose, for all your lectures!"

The troll ran past some of the teenagers and turned around, snarling and raising up, claws bared, sending them running back toward Hagan and Lois.

"Drop the wands and put up your hands. Nice work, Yumfuck." Hagan held his gun steady as Lois caught her breath.

Lois waved her wand, creating handcuffs out of light, snapping them shut on each of them. Hagan pointed in the direction of the small crowd that was gathering in front of the destroyed gym. "Start moving. Don't make me ask you twice. I've been off sugar for a while and I'm not as easy going."

"Hagan, this is where we leave you. It's best if we don't stay around for too many introductions. Part of our usefulness is that not too many see us coming." Lois gave him a short hug.

"What, okay, I guess we're hugging." Hagan patted Lois on the back as Patsy waited her turn. "Come on Patsy, let's get going. If I hurry, I can catch Earl before he's asleep. He will never believe this story."

"Let stop for Taco Bell. I'm starving. All that magic and running really takes it out of you."

"Taco Bell," Hagan grumbled. "Eyes front!" He shoved a Wizard who tried to look back at Patsy and Lois as they walked away.

Around front, Leira closed her eyes, trusting the flow of energy and opened her hands wide as the symbols sped up along her arms and neck, spitting out information. It sensed another powerful presence even as it sought out the Wizard in an increasing urgency, silencing his dark magic.

Something shoved against Leira, pushing her backward. Something familiar. Her eyes popped open. "The fucking dark mist. It can't be." It shoved her again, pushing her back further as a large rip opened behind the Wizard who was starting to regain his senses and was smiling menacingly at Leira.

He raised his wand to blast her with energy just as the dark mist enveloped him, sucking him backward with a whoosh as the tear in the veil snapped shut. A silence came over the street as Hannah let her arms drop and knelt down to check on Katie. The glow in Leira's eyes faded as the dean approached her.

"It didn't want me this time." *It's gathering more power. I have to tell Turner.*

The gym gave out another loud creak and the north wall collapsed in a cloud of dust, sending bricks tumbling outward.

The dean surveyed what remained. "We were thinking of remodeling anyway. Is everyone alright?"

"You don't have a million questions?" Leira looked at him, amazed.

The dean leaned closer and his eyes glowed momentarily. "No explanations necessary. Just glad to see the cavalry arrive. Don't worry, every student who's accepted here is sworn to secrecy. We understand quite well the battle between light and dark," he said with a wink. He looked at the demolished gym, his hands on his hips. "An unfortunate gas leak, wouldn't you say? Thank goodness it was in the middle of the night. We'll start a capital campaign to rebuild at once."

"Is there an artifact buried under all that rubble?"

"Better we keep some of our secrets," said the dean. "We've kept it this long."

Hagan came around the side of the building leading three teenagers as the troll nipped at their heels, corralling them toward Leira. "Caught these three, at least."

A fireball came out of the dark aimed at the back of Hagan's head from a Wizard trying to set his friends loose. The troll jumped in the way at the last moment, batting the fireball back at the Wizard, catching him in the gut and rolling him backward. Hagan ran over and grabbed the kid by his arm, taking away his wand and slapping him hard in the head. "Does it ever occur to you to stop being such a general dumbass?" He marched the kid over with the others and shoved him. "Okay, now we have four." He peered into the darkness behind him. "Anyone else out there want to make it five?"

The troll sat on his back legs by the teenagers still growling and occasionally showing his teeth. They clung to each other, trembling looking back at the oversized troll.

"Yumfuck, I take it all back," said Hagan as he hitched up his pants, putting his gun away. "You're worth every penny of that forty bucks. Hell, dinner's on me."

"What forty bucks? Never mind." Leira knelt beside Hannah and looked at Katie. "You got your ass kicked and good. Can you get up?" She held out her hand, and Katie reluctantly took it. "Drop the act, Katie. You're lucky Hannah was here, or you'd be dead by now. You can show a little gratitude."

"It's okay, it's part of my oath to the Order. We do what's right even when no one appreciates it."

Katie pressed her other hand against her head and let out a sigh. "I appreciate it. It's new territory for me, losing like this. I think I may be out of a job, temporarily."

"Maybe use it to rest up. Come on, Hannah. We were sent to make sure you got out okay. Turns out Lacey and the general are old friends and Lacey wasn't taking any chances."

"Looks like you're a hero, witchling. You were impressive standing in front of me like that." Katie smiled, wincing from pain.

"We'll take care of these teenagers and lecture them till they regret ever showing up on our grounds." The dean smiled, waving to a few of the faculty members who rounded up the Witches and Wizards, marching them off. "By the time we're done with them, they'll know church history by heart and be able to recite it."

The troll shrunk back down to five inches as Hagan held out his hand and put the troll on his shoulder. "Good job, kid."

"Shark Tank!" The troll let out a soft trill.

"It's a thing he's doing." Leira shrugged as she let out a sigh of relief. *The dark mist pushed me out of the way. This time.*

The dean smiled warmly and put out his hand to Hannah to shake. "Good show. Sometimes the most powerful magic is an act of courage like yours, standing up to something more powerful than you are and challenging the odds."

"Did anyone let my parents know...that I'm not a traitor?" There were tears in Hannah's eyes.

Leira took her by the hand. "Already taken care of, and in fact

I have it on good authority you've been promoted in the Silver Griffins. You have quite a career in front of you Hannah Beecham and a couple of parents who are anxious to see you."

"Let's stop for dinner. I'm even gonna take a short break and eat real food. I've earned it! Don't anyone tell Rose! Yumfuck, you ever had a hotdog? You're gonna love it. Tube of hot meat in a bun."

"Yumfuck!"

"We need to get it to go. Hannah's parents want to see her and Correk and I have something we need to do. You can buy as many as you want. We'll take them on the plane."

Hannah laughed, tears on her cheeks. *Going home, at last.*

"Yumfuck! Hotdog!"

"Definitely making sure you get a few. Pile on the toppings, too. You saved my ass out there today." Hagan rubbed the back of his head. "Thanks, little buddy." The troll let out a soft trill.

"Do you know what he was having you look for in the gym?" Leira put an arm around Hannah as they headed to the rental car.

"He only said it was a powerful artifact. A backup plan. There's a problem. Some of the old families who deal in dark magic have taken over the necklace and are refusing to give it back to the new Rhazdon followers. A war is brewing among the different dark sides."

"How many sides want that damn thing now? It's hard to keep up." Hagan counted them up. "That makes, what, I think five."

"That Wizard wasn't with the families, I take it. Do you know who was giving him orders?"

"An old Gnome wearing a dark blue robe. It's all I know."

A prophet. Not possible, thought Leira. *Rhazdon turned a prophet. Things are getting worse.* Leira felt a pull in the soles of her feet, the magic nudging her. She stepped away from the crowd and street-lights and let the energy settle in, her eyes glowing. There was another trail of magic, ropey and thick with a deep navy color verging on black.

"Who are you?" she called out.

A portal opened in the distance, and a Light Elf stepped into it. The ropey trail swirled around him as he pulled his cloak tighter over his head, disappearing into the portal, leaving behind sparks in the dark night.

"Wolfstan! Not this time!"

Leira turned her head in the direction of the shouting.

A second portal was opening just as quickly, the sparks mingling. A broad-shouldered Elf pulled it open further, gazing at her, his eyes glowing. He grimaced and stepped through in a swift motion, closing the portal, the sparks skidding across the grass, leaving thin burn lines.

Leira had caught the resemblance immediately. "Harkin. That's not possible."

The dean came running, breathing heavily, with a few students in tow. "What was that? Were there more of them than we realized?" He pointed to the students and signaled them to spread out and search for others.

"I'm not sure, but I intend to find out."

CHAPTER FIFTEEN

Charlie Monaghan was whistling as he drove down the long winding road to the manufacturing plant nestled in the farmlands of Linn County, Missouri. He loved this part of the drive. Nothing to see but open farmland for miles and miles and most of it belonged to his company. There were only a few family farms still dotting the landscape here and there, and Charlie knew every one of them. He sent the people cards at Christmas along with a gift basket and a reminder of his generous offer. In the spring, he sent daffodils and the offer of help relocating at no cost to them.

Soon enough, we'll pick those up too. That one.... And then that one...

A farmer walked across the land, watching the Lexus cruise past. He knew the car well. Charlie Monaghan was back in the area. "Hmph, another basket of pumpkin spice everything should be on its way soon. The wife will love that." He snorted to himself, bending down to run the dark, rich soil through his hands. *Family farm for the past hundred and thirty-two years. Not quite done with it yet, Monaghan.* The offer was tempting. None of his children were interested in staying on the land, especially since so many of the families had already sold and moved on, cutting down on all the social activities the farmer remembered from his childhood. *Tempting but not quite yet.*

The wind picked up, blowing the seeds across his fields. The seeds had started riding the current from miles away till they came to settle on his acreage. Nothing magical involved. Just basic weather. It wasn't the first time. More and more the seeds were blowing in and taking root in even rows as if they knew what to do with themselves once they landed in dirt.

They settled into the small farmer's ground and soon enough began to sprout into seedlings even though it was winter. Even the short rainfalls didn't deter them. They moved gently in the breeze, leaning toward the sound of the chimes that hung from the house across the way and played constantly, especially when the wind was blowing. Magic was gaining root on Earth, even in the soil.

The farmer came out every day to watch the plants, amazed at his luck. *How was this possible?* He saw the videos online with Penny Ryan and the prophets and wondered, but just for a moment. *Not all the way out here. That's ridiculous! Just having an unusually good year a little early, that's all.*

Charlie drove by the last farm that wasn't part of the family of Axiom companies that made up the conglomerate, as he liked to think of them. He noticed the rows of green heads budding. He saw them all leaning in the same direction, waving their tiny leaves as if they were dancing to music.

He hit the brakes, the tires squealing and got out to take a closer look. Sweat quickly gathered on his brow and he turned in a circle wondering what to do next.

He took pictures with his phone and made himself get back in the car. "If anyone finds out what we did. Where we got those plants!" He hit the steering wheel with his fists. "Now wait a minute. Wait a minute." He took in a deep breath and let it out slowly. "Maybe it's not so bad. The word is already out about

Oriceran. People will understand. This is a good thing. Yeah, a good thing." The panic started to settle, and his feeling of control returned. *This will be good for everyone. Feed more people. Make the economy grow right along with it.*

Charlie started the car back up and drove off, convinced the next step was an easy one he'd done a hundred times before. *Sue the bastard. Hell, maybe I can even keep the rest under wraps. Skip the damn FDA and all their red tape and delays.* No one needed to know he had Langston open the portal a few times to let his team venture over into Oriceran on fact-finding missions. The prophets were all too eager to accommodate his request to receive larger supplies of a variety of seeds.

It didn't take Charlie long to realize there was a profit to be made if he moved fast. He knew what a good idea it was to transplant the seeds from Oriceran to Earth and that every other company would see it too. He needed to make the first footprint and get to the market first. *Hell, if I'm going to let some stubborn farmer take it away from me.*

He hit the gas, speeding past the company farms, already lost in thought, planning his next move, tapping his finger on the steering wheel, humming a song.

"What are we doing in America's heartland?" Correk sat on the passenger side of the rental car as Leira navigated their way to the large corporate campus in Linn County, Missouri. He looked over at Leira, who was stealing glances at him, puzzled. "I read it on a cereal box. Most of your food source comes from a place called the heartland."

"I'm going to show you a library as soon as we get back. No Gnomes, by the way. You can check out almost anything and no one cares. We're here because General Anderson thinks someone has made a deal with the prophets and is growing food on Earth that came from Oriceran. Is that bad? I mean humans can eat the same things, right? We're not talking about a mass poisoning?"

"No, more like a mass indigestion and noxious fumes. We've learned over the years that some of the food on Oriceran doesn't go down so easily with humans. The humans who live on Oriceran all know what to avoid, but even if someone eats a purple carvet or a red bart the worst that can happen is gastric distress. Most of it, anyone can eat just fine. That hairy limeola you loved so much is suitable for anyone."

"Then, this is more of a problem with diplomatic relations. Good to know. Makes it easier to negotiate."

"Slow down a little." They were passing by the large open fields with tall plants poking their heads out of the ground despite the frost. Correk opened his window and formed a ball of light in his hands, singing into it and holding it out the window, letting the wind take it. The blue ball of light danced over the fields, releasing the song as the plants all moved in time to the music. "Bingo, we have a winner. They're not even doing a good job of hiding what they're doing."

"I doubt they anticipated a site visit from Light Elves who worked for the U.S. government. I suspect this is one of those times a corporation hoped to ask for forgiveness rather than permission. And that's after they showed all of us a cheaper kind of food."

"You think they'd make Oriceran food into some kind of snack like Cheetos?"

"I think it's second nature to us, and they're probably already trying. Oriceran plants grow faster and their love of music over light and water even, makes them a cash crop for Earth. But no testing is making the Feds nervous. These things have a way of biting us in the ass in ways we can't predict."

"Like turning people a pale shade of purple."

Leira looked over at Correk, her eyes widening.

"Never mind. Forget I said that. It was from a long time ago and the plant is quite rare. I'm sure those aren't part of the bargain they made with the prophets. I suspect the prophets made the deal to help ease the opening of the gates. If humans start to see Oricerans as a positive, then it'll be easier for us to emigrate here."

"Don't underestimate how fast we can change our minds. Takes us about an hour of tweeting and things could go sour and back to welcoming and then onto a travel ban, just like that." Leira snapped her fingers. "Of course, how we'd enforce a travel ban against a bunch of magical beings would be interesting to watch."

"Especially since there are already so many of us here."

"Yeah, let's keep that to ourselves for as long as possible, if we can. There's the Axiom headquarters."

Leira pulled onto the long driveway that circled around a campus of three-story brick buildings, green lawns, benches and modern sculpture with walking paths across the entire ten acres. Leira pulled into a parking space right near the main entrance.

"Looks rather friendly." Correk got out of the Mustang and pulled the jacket closed against the cold, biting wind. "The heartland feels more like the land of the Crystals."

"Looks can be deceiving and this isn't cold for here. It can get cold enough for spit to freeze."

"Something to look forward to."

They were met in the lobby by an intern smiling broadly and talking non-stop as she handed badges to Correk and Leira and asked if they wanted a long list of possibilities to drink or something to eat. Leira answered no to both quickly before Correk could ponder trying yet another new snack food. "Singleness of purpose," she whispered to him.

"No photographs of any kind while you're on the premises," said the intern, still smiling. "I'll need your phones, of course." She held out a plastic bag. Leira dropped in the burner phone she had ready, and watched the woman label the bag and cinch it shut. She held out another bag for Correk, and he dropped in the second burner phone, repeating the process.

"I can eat and focus at the same time," he quietly retorted after the woman turned to give the phones to a security officer. "That young woman is very shiny and precise. She isn't magical..."

"She's human. She's just young and optimistic with no pets, no spouse, no kids." Leira smiled as the intern handed her a site map pointing out the various special attractions to the campus.

Correk waited till she started walking again to say anything else. "You can tell all of that from looking at her."

Leira was walking along quickly studying the map. "Very basic detective skills. Come on, let's get lost in this building for a little while." Leira waited till the intern's back was turned, pointing out a famous painting by a Midwestern artist, to pull off her badge and ditch it in a potted plant.

Correk followed her lead and did the same as they ducked down a side hall to a door that had a sign that read, Building B with a punch code lock on it. "This is it. Their research and development are behind this door. If we're going to find out anything, we need to get in here."

"You know what to do. Or do you need me to take over?"

Leira rolled her eyes. "Very funny, I think I got it." She pulled in magic, her eyes glowing as she touched the lock and felt the magic seep into the lock, opening the door.

"Not like when we first met anymore. You've come a long way." Correk pulled the door behind them till it locked.

They hurried down the corridor looking through the long glass windows that lined both sides showing the different operations in each room. Music was coming from one of the labs further down the hallway. On a hunch, Correk headed straight for the window, stopping at the edge.

"There," hissed Correk. Researchers in white hazmat suits were dissecting and studying seeds and plants. There was a line of potted plants listening to old Beatles songs swaying to the beat. "Lennon is always a favorite. Especially off Abbey Road."

Leira pulled out her phone from her boot and filmed the lab. One of the researchers turned around and noticed the glint from the light on her camera bouncing off a microscope and followed the light back to the window. "Hey! That's not allowed! Security!" He hit an alarm on the wall, tapping in a code.

"Fuck me. Time to go," said Leira, putting the phone back in her boot. "There's no signal in here. We'll have to send the video once we get clear of the campus."

They headed back the way they came just as the door burst open behind them and security guards hustled toward them. Charlie Monaghan was behind them, waving his arms. "Take them into custody for trespassing! Unlawful visiting!"

Leira looked at Correk and gave him a sly smile.

"Do it," said Correk. "This'll be fun."

Leira put out her arms and focused, taking in a slow deep breath. The guards ran closer just as the symbols lit up on her arms and neck and her eyes glowed. "Come and get it mother-fuckers!" She looked over at Correk. "That's my version of abra-cadabra."

She let the magic pass through her and out into a wide stream of glittering light shoving the guards and Charlie back against a wall, pinning them just above the ground. Their feet dangled in the air.

"Come on," said Leira. "That'll hold for a little while."

"You got the idea from the Gravitron, didn't you?"

"You know it."

"We had a deal!" Charlie was screaming at the top of his lungs. He squirmed like a bug pinned in a middle schooler's science experiment as his underwear quickly rode higher and higher.

Correk and Leira ran for the lobby, bumping into the intern who looked startled and confused. "There you are! The tour's not over!"

Correk brushed his hand along her arm and shrugged as they kept moving. "Very life-like," he muttered.

Guards came running at them from the far side of the large lobby and Leira pulled in more magic, letting it ride through her and pinning the guards. They ran to the Mustang as Correk slid over the top and got in the front seat. Leira backed out, tires squealing and peeled out of the parking lot and down the road, away from the campus.

"Nice slide across the hood. You've been saving that one."

"I saw my moment. That was actually a lot of fun. We made a good team. I'm Batman to your Robin."

"Don't go there. I'll be my version of a superhero."

"Fair enough, it's a new day after all."

"And all hell is breaking loose in it. What other options do we have besides reporting back to the general? Not sure humans policing humans over magic is a winning plan."

"I take it you mean on Oriceran. Maybe it's time that company met my friend, Perrom and found out how well a Wood Elf can look like a wall. He can slide in and dismantle their labs right under their noses."

"We need to find their source for the seeds. At least, if we take this supply they'll go hunting for more."

"Given the prophets latest actions, I suspect they might be the ones. No one else has the resources."

"If that's the case, the prophets will be happy to give them more."

"Not if we let the prophets talk directly to the government. It may be what they've really wanted all along. Most of them anyway."

"We'll need to be sure. Cover our bases." Leira's phone rang with the number from the burner phone. "Right on time. Hello?"

"You had no right to film anything on my property!" Charlie Monaghan was yelling so loud it was making the sound crackle.

"What'd we film, sir? Care to fill in the empty spaces?"

There was dead silence on the phone as Charlie's mind raced. Wolfstan Humphrey would expect him to do something.

Leira filled in the space talking first this time. She had something to say. "I'll bet the average American would love to know what you were about to feed them. Wonder what the label would have read. Some long, complicated word with almost no vowels that was a code name for Oriceran."

"There are bigger forces at work here than you can see. Deals had to be made..."

Leira cut him off. "Listen up. We have our proof. The good news is, we're not 60 Minutes. The bad news is we are the Feds, and we'll be coming back in larger numbers. Get ready, but don't try to hide. I'll find you." She pushed the button on the steering wheel and hung up.

"Impressive. You think he'll cooperate."

"He'll negotiate. Corporate world's idea of cooperation. It's a start."

"Good job, superhero Leira. The troll would have been proud of you."

CHAPTER SIXTEEN

By the time Correk and Leira got home, it was already late at night. They could both feel the press of time. Leira filled out the report for the general but she wanted to do something more. "I have an idea and you're going to have to get comfortable with it. I want to go see the Jersey Willen."

Correk narrowed his eyes but only responded with, "Take the troll. He'll come in handy. Magical people know not to mess with anybody who's bonded with a troll. He could take their head off with a swipe. You've seen him do it."

"Time to head back to Oriceran? It's a good idea. I know I said I wanted to go with you, but we need to divide and conquer this time." She risked it and pushed further. "You can find out more about your father."

Correk flinched, but he recovered and nodded. "Harkin's not alive. That was someone trying to distract me from the real problem."

"Rhazdon."

"Yes, all day long. I'm going to find Perrom and get a few answers if I can." He held up his hands in protest. "I won't do anything foolish like look for the cabin, you have my word. I'm just going to see if I can bring back Perrom for a short visit to Missouri and see what he knows. I'll have him back in Oriceran before you even get home."

Leira parked the car and put the troll on her shoulder as she navigated across the rocky terrain using magic to guide her way. She made it to the hidden passageway and pushed on the infinity sign opening the door to the underground world of Hilldale. She hurried down the steps, the troll sliding into her jacket pocket as she moved. She put out her hand when she got to the bottom and put him back on her shoulder. "Where everyone can see you." He put out his paw and she reached in her other pocket and pulled out the cowboy hat. "Here you go."

She hung a left and headed for the small grocery store in the square. The grocer remembered her and called out a hearty, "Hello! You're home again! This time you brought a troll! You must be a very patient Elf. What can I do for you this time? Here to do a little grocery shopping?"

"I'm here to exchange some cash. I'll give you forty dollars for twelve pintas." She waited, watching him try to size her up. Correk had already warned her to ask for a little more or he'd see her as a novice and haggle her down.

"Fine!" He blurted it out, letting out a breath in a gush, slamming his hands on the counter. He counted out the diamond-shaped pieces of metal quickly and routinely, letting them drop with a plink on the counter. Leira waited till he was done before showing her money, sliding the pintas off the counter at the same moment she dropped the cash. A deal was never over at an exchange until both parties had their money.

She was going to need the pintas to negotiate with the Jersey Willen. He promised her a favor, but she was hedging that with some cash. She figured his obligation would make him agree but the pintas would make him more agreeable, especially after his injuries on the last mission he did at their bidding.

She hurried down the cobble-stoned street, nodding at a passing Light Elf couple on a date. The troll tipped his hat and cheerfully called out "Yumfuck!" as they passed.

"The classic. I like it," said Leira.

He held out his balled-up fist to Leira for a bump and she reached up and obliged.

The colorfully painted cottages grew shabbier and plain as she picked up her pace until she got to the block where the Jersey Willen lived. The troll looked around at the broken-down homes. "Fixer Upper."

The Jersey Willen's light was still on and Leira could see Willens scurrying back and forth behind the lacy curtain in the front room.

She remembered to watch herself on the wooden steps, picking her way carefully across the porch and pounded on the door. The curtain in the front window pulled back a few inches as whiskers and a nose peeked out.

Heavy footsteps approached the door and it pulled open with a loud squeak. *That's new. The house has gone downhill even since I was here last.*

"You're back for the favor so soon. That can't be good news." The Jersey Willen looked around the edge of the door and saw Yumfuck, letting out a frightened squeal.

Yumfuck obliged by hissing at the Willen, his teeth bared.

"No idea what that's about, but that's not why I'm here. You cool it." She slid Yumfuck into her pocket, purposely setting him on top of the bag of pintas. "Nesturnium."

The Willen gave a shudder but held the door open so Leira could step inside. He was wearing a worn blue jacket with gold trim. *That actually looks made for him.*

The foyer was at one time grand with a solid oak staircase in the center, a library on one side and a dining room on the other. But everywhere she looked something was chipped or cracked or had a water stain. Nothing was in its original glory.

"Leira! You're here! Are you staying?" The grandmother came and gave her a hug. Leira could feel her rummaging through her pockets but she waited for Yumfuck to do the inevitable, knowing that would take care of it. He bit down on her paw just enough to warn her, sending her reeling backward and letting out a high-pitched whine.

"She has a troll with her."

"Would have been nice if you'd warned your grandmother. Either one of you!"

"Nobody asked you to feel me up." Leira arched an eyebrow and waited.

"You need something," said the Jersey Willen, ignoring his pouting grandmother. "Nobody comes here for a social call. It's alright, I get it."

Great. A sensitive Willen. "Information."

"Of course it is. You're not the thieving type. But no more Gnomes. That's off the table." The Willen absent-mindedly whipped his tail around and held it gently in his hands. There was still a crick in the middle where it was broken getting information the last time.

"No Gnomes. I need to know how a human corporation is getting seeds from Oriceran. I want you to be there the next time they get in a shipment and tell me exactly who does the delivery. Follow him back to the source."

"A much easier task. Child's play."

"I thought you'd think so. Do it, and the favor is done. And, since you were injured the last time, something to help you on your trip." Leira held out the bag of pintas, emptying them into the Willen's hand. His eyes shined and grew wide.

"If you don't find the source back on Oriceran and bring me a

164

name, you can keep the money, but the favor is unfulfilled. Do we have a deal?"

"Deal!" The grandmother rubbed her paws together.

"I need to hear it from you."

The Willen looked at Leira suspiciously. "Deal. This is harder than it appears. I can tell you suspect something you don't want to say. No matter."

"I'll say this. Trust no one."

"As usual." He nodded his head.

"More importantly, let no one see you, for your sake," she said, solemnly. *Just in case a dark force has something to do with all of this.*

The Willen raised his brows as his whiskers twitched. "Fair warning for a Willen. I like it."

"I'll meet you back here tomorrow for the information."

"That important? Alright, tomorrow it is." He slid the coins into the folds of his skin before his grandmother could sidle any closer to him.

They steal from each other. Not a surprise. "I'll see myself out." Leira backed out of the door, not taking her eyes off the Willens, pulling the heavy door behind her. She quickly scooped the troll out of her pocket and put him back on her shoulder, releasing him from the nesting spell.

"Good job in there. You didn't even break skin."

The troll let out a trill and tipped his hat. Behind them there was a sizzle and a pop accompanied by a flash of light as the Jersey Willen took off through a portal to Oriceran. *Good,* thought Leira. *Maybe he can find some answers.*

"Hang onto that hat. We're going to take a nice run through Hilldale and get the hell out of here and back home. I want to hear what Correk found out."

The troll sat down on Leira's shoulder and grabbed onto her collar, holding down his cowboy hat as Leira went down the stairs and took off at a run, passing through the old neighborhood quickly. It wasn't long before they were at the square and headed up the stairs to the surface again.

Leira got to the top of the wide stairs and stood on firm ground, breathing in the cool night air. "That was a pretty good run. Maybe even a personal best and with a troll on my shoulder."

The troll stood up and let out a cackle. "Yumfuck!"

Leira smiled and set off across the rocky ground, headed for the car and home.

Perrom stood in the small clearing and waved as Correk stepped back through the portal and into Leira's living room. The portal closed with a small shimmer of sparks, Perrom looking up at the two moons of Oriceran and the night stars. It hadn't taken him long to remove any evidence of Oriceran from the corporate labs and return home, but he knew it was just a temporary reprieve. The humans would get their hands on more seeds.

Correk's suspicions about Rhazdon left Perrom with a feeling of anger. *Once should have been enough.*

He looked down from the sky and peered into the dark woods.

"I know you're there. You may as well show yourself." His pupils moved in different directions, looking for the Gardener of the Dark Forest. "You know it's easier for one Wood Elf to detect another."

The Gardener stepped into the clearing, the scales on his skin quickly flipping back to a smooth tanned skin. The flowers on the vines woven through his long hair were all closed for the night. A hawk sat on his shoulder and his constant companion, the lion with antlers, came up quickly behind him, rubbing against his leg.

"It's a wonder everyone still thinks you're only a legend given the entourage you've got with you everywhere."

The Gardener spoke in a deep baritone as he scratched the lion behind the ears. "Anything that lives in the Dark Forest knows how to blend in when outsiders approach. You're not really an exception to that rule, considering you were born within the forest."

Perrom's skin bristled, strips of skin flipping back and forth, reflecting the night stars and shimmering with light.

"Not to worry. I gave you my word I'd keep your secret. I have no intention of breaking it. That's not what family does. How is your life among the Light Elves?"

"Satisfying and necessary. I came here looking for your help."

"You came here on your way back from Earth with your friend," the Gardener said, pointedly. "Does he even know the truth?" The Gardener crossed his arms over his chest. "I'll let it go, for now. This must be important if you're asking for my help. Tell me quickly. I can't linger here for long in the open. There are a lot of eyes that pass through these woods."

"You'd prefer to remain a myth."

"Fables are more powerful than reality. Everyone tells the story adding their own embellishment. Before long, the forest is dangerous and impenetrable. It's kept the creatures and plants on this part of Oriceran safe for a very long time."

"Till now."

Anger flashed across the Gardener's face as he drew the pupils in his eyes together, glaring at Perrom. The lion let out a low growl.

Perrom was prepared for his reaction and stood his ground. "Not by my hand. Humans from Earth are responsible."

"Your friends led them here?"

"No, they had nothing to do with it. We suspect a false prophet. The Gnome who travels with them. He is the one we believe is stealing from the forest and making deals with the humans. He's giving them seed pods to grow in their world." Perrom watched the Gardener. "You're not surprised. Why is that?"

"I've noticed the patches of destruction in the forest but couldn't be sure who was doing it. Powerful dark magic is behind it if I can't follow a trail. I know about your Gnome. He barters with the Dark Market and oversees the large tent in the back."

Perrom startled and blurted out, "You've been visiting the market. How long has that been going on?"

"Hundreds of years. I told you, the stories about me are more mythical than reality. I'm a Wood Elf after all. I can blend in."

"What do you know about the Gnome?" Perrom felt his heart pound in his chest.

"He's an unusual Gnome, that's all. A dark-hearted one, which is not their usual temperament. He keeps secrets like they all do but the ones he keeps are his own. He travels in and out of these woods all the time, but I always lose his trail. Like I said, very powerful magic. If he's the supplier of the seed pods, stopping him may not be so easy. Are you sure it's him?"

"You suspect someone else?"

"He's not the only dark trail that's passed near these woods lately. There's another presence, but they're using shadow magic. I can only sense them."

"That's not the first time something has tried to hide in the Dark Forest. Why suspect a magical you can't see?"

"The trails always end abruptly."

"Like at a portal."

"Yes. Someone is traveling back and forth." The hawk lifted its wings, shaking its head and settling back down. "Too much intrigue."

"I should go."

"Be careful, Perrom. The animals and birds of the forest are on edge these days. They always know when dark magic is around. I haven't seen them like this since the time of..."

"Rhazdon," whispered Perrom, finishing his sentence, a shudder rippling through his skin. *It can't be him. He can't still be alive.* He didn't want to say it out loud. "You be careful, too." His voice grew softer. "Tell my mother I said hello." He turned to go.

"Tell her yourself someday."

Perrom turned back to say something else, but the Gardener was already gone.

CHAPTER SEVENTEEN

The Gnome prophet moved from floor to floor on the outside of the castle. "Altrea extendia." A shower of bronze sparks went out in front as another short staircase appeared taking the Gnome to the floor of the castle where the library was kept. He walked confidently along the unseen hallway, nodding at a passing Light Elf as he got to the door of the library.

He strode between the shelves, muttering a greeting at a passing Gnome as the poppy on the bowler let out a puzzled squeak. The prophet kept moving, not looking back. The time had come to take back some of what was his before events got much further.

His plans were already in motion on Earth and humming along nicely. Soon, there wouldn't be a need for this squatty old body and then gaining access to the Gnomes' vault would be much harder. *Time to strike.*

He got near the stacks filled with books about horticulture closest to the vault and stopped to take down a book and peruse the inside. The first chapter was on how to clear graveling worms out of a garden. He kept an eye on the Gnomes wandering nearby and waited till there was only the one

Gnome guard standing in front of the iron gate across the front.

The prophet muttered a spell low under his breath, killing the Gnome where he stood, stiffening his body so he stayed perfectly still and upright. His eyes looking straight ahead. The prophet worked quickly conjuring a small fire ball and whispering into it, sending it through the lock in the gate, breaking the eternal spell that surrounded the vault.

He opened the gate just enough to slide through and pressed against the wall as a Gnome passed by the far end of a stack. The poppy on his bowler turned to look back but saw nothing and settled back into place.

He waited till he was sure there would be at least a few seconds before another Gnome appeared. *This will take some doing.* He raised both his arms using a spell that was over a millennium old, passed down among the Atlanteans. The power running through his muscles and out his hands in a flash of light that felt familiar and welcoming. *It's about time.*

The thousands of small tumblers rolled around in the door like marbles rushing to get into place. *Not much longer.*

The sound carried across the library, attracting startled looks as the Gnomes worked to reconcile the noise out of context. The vault was opening at an unscheduled time.

As soon as the thick, large door opened just enough for the round Gnome to squeeze through he pushed his way in, pulling in energy and sending it out, searching for his old artifacts and books and commanding them to come to him. There was a clatter and crash as the artifacts pushed their way out of drawers and off shelves, knocking over anything in their way. Books flew through the air, their pages rustling as they landed in a pile at the prophet's feet. He pulled out a sack and held it open as everything clambered in. At the last moment, he held out his arms and released a temporary glamour, giving the illusion he was a Wood Elf.

He came out of the vault as the Gnomes came running and he pushed their dead friend toward them as he ran, the bag of artifacts magically riding a current of air in front of him.

"Altrea extendia!" he shouted, running down the stairs. The bag easily stayed three paces in front of him as he made his way to the ground and ran across the royal gardens. The Gnomes were just two floors behind him but as the prophet reached the edge of the woods he stopped suddenly and bellowed, "Mortimis linger".

The Gnomes stopped where they were and waved to everyone nearby to get away from the edge of the woods. They knew the spell. They had been holding the secrets of dark magic for longer than anyone else could remember. The thief released a death spell that would claim anyone who followed too closely. The poppies were all hissing and baring their teeth as the Gnomes looked at each other.

No one knew that spell but them and one other. Someone had mastered Rhazdon's old spells and now was in possession of his old artifacts and books.

They scurried back to the library, all of them muttering, "Trouble, trouble, trouble." An inventory would be needed before they reported to the king.

The Gnome prophet hurried to the cabin deep in the Dark Forest, releasing the glamour spell as he ran. He didn't stop until he was safe inside the walls of the small dwelling, his heart pounding with joy and exertion from the long run. He settled the bag in a corner and took off all his clothes, releasing the spell as his bones painfully grew back into place, stretching and growing. The top of his head sprouted tentacles and his body took on more curves as Rhazdon emerged, standing naked in the center of the room.

"At last," she yelled, stretching her arms overhead. The tentacles on her head writhed and twisted until they were in a loose bun at the back of her head. She pulled on a dark silk robe, excited to open the bag. "At last," she whispered again, "Revenge is sweet, even after all these years."

She pulled out an old flute, holding it gently in her hands. Old Atlantean magic was encased in the wooden instrument and when the right notes were played in the right order by someone powerful enough to flow magic through it the flute was able to make others do the bidding of the musician. Rhazdon held it tightly to her chest and shut her eyes. "Good times," she laughed, remembering how she used it to gather her first followers. She picked up an old amulet on the top and held it against her skin feeling the hum of the dark magic resting in it. "Mmmmm, delicious."

She put both artifacts back in the bag and cinched the rope. "I'll be back soon." She patted the bag lovingly. "This has to wait. I need to make an appearance and create an alibi. Not time to reveal who I am just yet. They'll be looking for a thief." She shook her head. "Not a thief if you're taking back what's yours." She smiled and patted the bag again.

Rhazdon dropped the robe and took a last look at the bag, reluctantly casting the powerful spell again, twisting herself back into the old Gnome prophet. "Soon," he muttered, standing there transformed as he picked up the dark blue robe. He hurried out the door to the Dark Market, leaving the circle of dark mist around the bottom of the cabin making it invisible to anyone who might pass nearby.

The Gnome prophet pushed his way into the Dark Market, shoving people aside. He was in no mood to talk to anyone, and he wanted to be sure everyone remembered his entrance.

"Hey! Watch where you're going!" The tall young half wizard, Louie bellowed at the Gnome as he passed, steadying a stack of electronic components as they teetered to one side. "This four by eight space is my castle," he said, waving his large muscular arms around the tight space. "Yeah, that's right..." He marched back and forth in the space, stomping his feet.

"Hey, Louie." A Witch wandered by, shoving her wand into her sash around her waist. "How are you doing?"

Louie stopped his frantic waving and put his hands on his hips. "I'm dying, that's how I'm doing. Dying!" He shook his blonde curls, making the Witch laugh. "Hard to get some respect around this place. What are you up to, Ramona?"

The young Witch laughed again. "That's a good one. Respect at the Dark Market. No one respects anyone here. Fears maybe. And I don't know how far you're going to get selling used parts from the last century in a tiny booth."

"Don't insult the size of a man's booth! This is a perfectly respectable size. Okay, I'll give you the one about the parts. They're a little old, but that's just the stuff to get people to come closer."

"I don't know that you understand marketing."

"I'm half human. Marketing is our own brand of magic. My kind has convinced people to buy crap they don't need that's not even good for them for generations. Time-honored practice!"

"So, what's the good stuff?" Ramona walked closer to the booth while Louie dug around under a wooden table pulling out a large crate. He dug through the hay and lifted a tray of polished stones. "Huh? Yeah?" Louie held out his arms, tilting his head to the side, smiling.

"You have more charm than most Light Elves, Louie."

Louie smiled, the dimples deepening in his cheeks. "What can I say?"

Ramona drew closer to peer at the stones.

"Artifacts. Shhhhh." Louie put his finger to his lips. "Not supposed to have these."

"I really think you're missing the whole point of a dark market there, Louie. We're not supposed to have any of this stuff." She stepped closer and ran a finger over one of the blue stones with a silver streak through the middle.

It sparked as she yelped pulling her hand back and sticking her finger in her mouth to cool it off. "What the hell, Louie!" She took out her finger and looked at the blister. "Even your good stuff is crap. You're lucky you're not bad looking. Only thing you have going for you." Ramona picked up the edge of her robe and marched off in a huff.

Perrom saw the spark as he was coming out of the market and looked down at the stones. *Ancient and powerful.* "Where did you get these?"

"Everybody knows an artifact is only as good as the person holding it!" he yelled to her retreating back. "Hey there, how you doing? Uh, what? Oh these! Found them near the Concha. Probably dropped by a Nicht." He whistled, pointing to the sky. "Bat wings are not always good for deliveries." He held his arms out to the side, bent at the elbows and flapping his hands. "Wind thrust not the best."

Perrom knew he was lying but let it go. "How much?"

"For you, a bargain! Five pieces of gold. What do you say?" Louie picked one up and held it against his skin making his heart race. "Good stuff. Better than weed, I hear."

Perrom narrowed his eyes and looked at the artifacts again. *No spark when the half-wizard handles it. Interesting.* He walked away without answering Louie.

He needed to keep up with the Gnome, but he looked back over his shoulder. *There's more to that wizard. He's covering a lot of ground if he can find anything that good. What else do you know?* The skin along his neck fluttered. Perrom turned back and saw the Gnome in the distance turn a corner in the bazaar. *Another time.*

A Kilomea grunted as he passed by Louie. The two were at eye level with each other. "Interest you in a Walkman, big guy? Still has all its parts."

The Kilomea smiled and gave Louie a shove as he went deeper into the market. Wolfstan Humphrey slid by unnoticed behind the beast, turning his head away as he followed the Gnome a few paces behind.

"All you need to say is no, thank you. Not that hard." Louie carefully put the tray of stones back in the crate and hid them back under the table. "These babies are by appointment only and a show of cash." He stood and wiped the sweat off his face with an old rag. "Good looking and charming are not the only things I have going for me," he muttered. "First thing but not the only thing. Not bad with a wrench and a wand. Don't see any other Wizards who can say that…"

A trail of Pixies fluttered around a pile of crystals. "Can I interest you ladies in a nice green amethyst? Very rare!"

CHAPTER EIGHTEEN

Turner tapped his chin, his elbow resting on his arm held across his waist. He was sitting in a green Adirondack chair on the thick grass with a view of the lake. "There is a way you could venture a little closer magically to the cabin."

Leira was standing in front of him practicing as Correk stood off to the side watching grackles take flight off the roof of Turner's large house and fly out over Lake Travis. He looked back at Turner. "It's too dangerous," he said firmly, fully expecting a glare from Leira. He wasn't disappointed. "You've made up your mind, I see. Fine, what's the idea, Turner?"

"It would take an artifact from the ages of the old king. Something that has the magic layered into it over time."

"You mean like that damn necklace." Correk scowled. "Right back where we started."

"Not necessarily. The necklace is imbued with magic over generations. It's what made it so powerful. A family tradition. The Oriceran royal family are not the only ones who have that tradition. There were others, which means there are other artifacts out there. Almost all of them are an adornment such as a bracelet or an armband or a simple ring. They may not look like much. That was done on purpose to hide their true value. But touch one in any way, and they will give themselves away."

Correk remembered the buzz in his fingertips. "I think I know where we can find one. I saw something like that in the dark market. More like right in front of it."

"Then I suggest you retrieve it. It will act as an amplifier for Leira's magic and more importantly disguise her identity. The artifact will be full of so many different users' magic it will be more difficult for whomever it is that you're pursuing to quickly identify her. If it is who we all suspect it is, the sooner you retrieve the armband the better. Time is not on our side."

Turner shut his eyes and felt Leira's magic riding out over the current of air, curious and open. *A good sign.* "Send out an intention Leira," he said, without opening his eyes. "Do it without attachment and let the magic respond. You must learn to recognize that feeling and lean into it."

Leira thought of her mother's new apartment and sent out an intention to let them know she cared. Turner felt the energy quickly change, the slow swirling motion take on direction and coast outward, seeking its destination.

Eireka felt the thick flow of energy wrap around her, filling her with a loving warmth. "Hmmmm, Leira is getting better at magic." The tired flowers in the vase on the counter from Donald perked back up and the air around Eireka shimmered in light. "It's a new day," she said, smiling.

"What dear?" Mara called out from the other room.

"Nothing, Mom. Leira called to say she misses us and is doing fine."

Leira stepped onto the firm ground of Oriceran just inside the forest and breathed in the scent from the lilies nearby.

"Try singing to them and see what happens." Correk nodded. "Go ahead."

Leira sang one of her favorite songs she'd heard in Antone's Nightclub in Austin.

"Home is made for coming from, for dreams of going to, which with any luck will never come true. I was born under a wandering star. I was born under a wandering star..."

The flowers bent their heavy heads toward Leira and released a puff of perfume that filled her head and left her with a feeling of peace. "What a wonderful trick!"

"Not a trick. Basic botany on Oriceran. What an appropriate song for you."

"Not really. I was born and raised in Austin. Haven't wandered far at all."

"Strange how it seems like it."

"When you met me, I wasn't really connected to anyone. I was eternally restless. Felt like I was barely tethered to the Earth. Turns out I was right. Part of me is from this planet."

"Come on, are you up for walking? It's a few miles to the Dark Market but it's a beautiful day. You can see more of the area walking than you can bouncing on the wooden seat of a wagon."

"You're really selling it. Sure, let's walk."

They passed by the royal gardens, and Leira looked up to where she knew the Light Elves castle was hanging in the air, even if she couldn't see it. "Still strange to know there are tons of rock and furniture and Light Elves up there and only magic is holding it there."

"Magic is more powerful than nuts and bolts, but you don't question their ability to make a skyscraper."

Bronze sparks spilled out into the air and a staircase appeared quickly followed by a line of schoolchildren running down them toward the ground with a ball in their hands.

"You have recess here!" Leira watched them kick the ball back and forth. "Just like Earth...no...wait..." A boy pulled a ball out of his pocket and spun it in the air, releasing it as it raced ahead of the larger ball, pulling it along as the children ran after them both. "Okay, that seems more like it."

Correk laughed and pointed out the woman draped in what looked like a coat but was really a swarm of purple bees in constant flight wrapping themselves around her. "That's common on Oriceran. They feed on anxiety or grief. Those bees will do wonders for your day."

They walked down the wide boulevard between the ancient trees. Trolls played among the roots, occasionally peeking out and blowing raspberries at Leira and Correk. Leira laughed but when she saw the startled look on Correk's face, she held up her hands. "I swear, no rescuing any more Trolls. One is enough! Didn't even know you could bond with more than one."

"It's rare to find someone foolish enough to rescue more than one, but it's happened."

"You have to admit, Yumfuck grows on you."

"He told me *Top Chef* this morning. Not sure if that means he liked what I gave him to eat or he wanted me to up my game."

"Yeah, I've tried to get him to talk to me again, but he keeps shaking his furry butt at me. Did trolls invent twerking?"

"Look over there!" Correk grabbed Leira's arm pulling her closer to his side. "Don't move," he whispered. He could feel the muscles in Leira's arm tense.

"Look at the treeline over there." Correk pointed to the tall spruce just ahead of them. "Do you see it? Just behind them."

At first, Leira couldn't tell what was moving just behind the trees. At last, a large white elk emerged out of the stand of trees and stood in the clearing. "The rack on his head must be easily five feet across," said Leira in a hushed voice. "He's got to be well over seven feet tall. I've never seen anything like that. His fur is glowing."

"The Gardener must be nearby. That is a very rare beast and an omen."

The elk pawed the ground, snorting as it raised its head and let out a loud bleat.

"A good or a bad omen?" Leira was captivated at the beauty of the animal as he easily maneuvered his antlers through the branches. It raised its head again and let out another bleat. It bent a front leg and lowered its rack toward Leira.

"Omens aren't always about a good or bad event. It's more like it's a sign of something new and powerful. I think the new power he's heralding is you."

Leira watched the elk rise to his full height, looking her in the eye, holding her gaze. She nodded her head and said, "thank you." The elk turned back into the woods, picking up his pace to a trot and vanishing among the dense trees.

"Even the stream of magic knows you're powerful. You've learned a lot from Turner, and you're letting the magic float through you more effortlessly. Everything around you is becoming aware of you."

"That could be a bad thing if Rhazdon figures out I'm here before we find an artifact."

"We'll take care of that at the market."

"No, you're a flaming asshole!" Louie hollered cheerfully at a customer who stomped off, his fingers singed from handling an artifact. "Separates the beasts from the boys!" Louie picked up a stone and tossed it into the air. "See folks? No problem here. Want to see if you've got what it takes? Prove you got a little juice!" He held out a small stone to a young Wood Elf. "I'll cut you a deal on this one. It's puny."

Correk walked to the table and scanned the items piled on top, searching for the armband he saw last time. It wasn't there.

"Who's the Harrison Ford guy?" Leira stole a sideways look at the tall blonde dressed in leather boots and a grey tunic over tight leather pants.

Correk glanced up at Leira. "Down girl. It's not like you to be drawn to the love them and run like hell kind."

Leira kept glancing over at Louie. "I'm not dead, Correk. I can look at the merchandise without wanting to take everything home."

Louie finally noticed them lingering over his table and came over, a big grin on his face. "Well, hello." He leaned in closer to Leira. "You think you got the juice to take the ride?"

"Smooth." Correk rolled his eyes. "Do you still have any armbands?"

"Sure, sure pops. Hang on. What's your story? You looking to buy an artifact?" Louie picked up an azure blue stone and held it out for Leira. It bounced around in his palm under its own power.

Leira slowly picked up the stone, not sure what would happen and held it out in her open palm. The stone gave off a low vibration and took on a lacy glow showing the interior of the stone. "That's beautiful." Leira stared at the stone, entranced at its beauty.

"That's fucking amazing! I didn't even know it could do that!" Louie looked at the stone and up at Leira. "You're hotter than I realized…" He was grinning from ear to ear, his blue eyes shining in the sunlight.

Correk cleared his throat. "The armband? Hello?"

"What? Oh yeah, right, right." Louie stood up straight. "Gotta make a living, am I right? Okay! You want an armband." He clapped his hands together. "May still have that thing here somewhere." He rooted around under the table occasionally taking a look back up at Leira.

"You're not sure of your inventory. Great." Correk drummed his fingers on the table. "If I'd known this was going to be more of a date for you, I'd have come alone," he whispered to Leira.

"Put your fur down. It's just flirting. It's in the Berens' women DNA. We're regular Amazons."

"You're a little small for an Amazon, trust me. I've met them on my travels to the other side of Oriceran. Big gals. Could snap you like a dry twig."

"Here it is!" Louie emerged from under the table, his curls pushed back off his sweaty forehead, holding the metallic armband in his hands. Set in the middle was a deep green emerald. "Want to try it on?" He held it out to Leira but Correk pulled out a handkerchief and scooped it out of Louie's hands before Leira could touch it. He dropped ten gold coins on the table.

"We didn't do any bargaining yet." Louie was still smiling but his face was tighter, and the smile didn't reach his eyes. "Not a McDonald's buddy. No set menu."

"We bargained the last time I was here. There's your money," Correk said with some menace. He wasn't in the mood for one of Louie's scenes. "Worse than theater in the round."

"This armband for you?" Louie switched tactics, taking Leira's hand and stepping closer. Leira gave a crooked smile and waited to see what he was planning to do.

"Ten gold coins," she said, not answering his question. She put the blue stone back on the table. "A deal's a deal." She pulled her hand back and smiled at him.

"Okay, I'll tell you what. Keep your money." He slid the coins back across the table. "Instead, I want this recharged." He pulled out an old scepter, two feet long with a round red glass bulb at one end. "I know you need that armband." The smile dropped from his face. "We're cool, no worries. We're going to do some business, but I need something too." He slapped his hand on the metal shaft of the scepter. "I'm gonna have to insist and you're going to have to come back for that armband. You see it takes about ten Wizards to recharge this baby. One Light Elf and one half Light Elf aren't going to cut it."

"We don't have time for this. Give it to me." Leira held out her hand. "Come on, hand it over."

"Alright but I'm telling you…"

Correk stood back, his arms crossed as Leira held the scepter and set an intention, letting the magic flow through her, lighting up the symbols on her arms as it sought out the scepter and recharging it within seconds. The red glass bulb on the end glowed brightly.

"Holy fuck! What did you say you are? Never seen a Light Elf do that before!"

Leira felt the magic recede and the glow fade from her eyes. She handed back the scepter. "We have a deal now, bitch?"

"Okay, okay, no need to get personal. Damn, girl! We have a deal and to show you what a great time I've had you can keep the stone. On the house." He scooped it up and placed it in Leira's hand, folding her fingers over top. The stone glowed through her fingers.

"That is still fucking cool." He felt the warmth through her fingers. "You're an open channel, baby." He shook his head in amazement. "Never met anyone like you," he whispered.

"Okay, enough. I've reached my limits. Cousin, we're done here." Correk folded the cloth over the armband and stowed it in his satchel.

"Cousin, huh? Light Elf but not all Elf. You must be like me, half human." The creases deepened around his eyes.

Leira slipped the stone in her pocket. "Thanks for the stone." She gave him another crooked smile and a nod and turned to go.

"Come again! Here every day!" Louie shouted as Correk and Leira headed back toward the castle.

"Good grief. It's a wonder someone doesn't shoot him clean through with an arrow." Correk shook his head.

"Noticed you made a point not to handle the armband. What was that about?"

"It's ancient and powerful. I didn't want to find out in front of your boyfriend that it was more than I could handle."

"You didn't want him to know your magic was smaller than his magic. I get it."

"Juvenile."

Leira laughed. "Fucking amazing!" she said, imitating Louie. "Let's get back to Turner and try that baby out."

***

Queen Saria paced the large ballroom in the castle throwing out her arm making walls appear and disappear out of frustration. Her long silver gown swished behind her. She stopped at one of the tall windows, clenching her fists.

"Something bothering you?" King Oriceran stood in the doorway calmly watching his wife.

"I was distracted..." She looked away for a moment, pain in her voice. "I took my eyes off what matters in the kingdom. Now, we are not that many years away from when the gates start to open again, and we've done nothing to get ready. Nothing."

"There's still time." He went and stood by his wife at the window.

"Not as much as I'd like. There's a lot to do and you've seen what the prophets are doing. They're jumping out ahead of all of us. Earth needs protecting just as much as Oriceran, but we haven't forged any alliances. Our ancestors were way ahead of us at this point."

"Not true. We have made unexpected alliances on Earth. Leira Berens is on our side and grows more powerful every day. She's even taken on a role in her country's government." The king looked down on the gardens below.

"I want to speak with her. Directly." The queen gently waved her arms making all the walls vanish. She took in a deep breath and let it out slowly. "Time to negotiate with Earth on behalf of our people. Stop letting the prophets run the show."

"I know you don't agree with all of the prophesies."

"I don't agree with the way they're interpreted. But it's more than that, my love. I don't trust the prophets. They meet in secret, they tell no one of their plans and yet we all give them free reign. I tell you, someone let that human into our walls, and he killed our son."

"Surely, you can't suspect a prophet."

"I suspect almost everyone and if I find out who it was…" Her eyes glowed brightly, and the symbols ran up her arms and covered her chest and neck. The king didn't need to read them to know what intention she was putting into her magic.

"Trust me," hissed the queen, "their death is one prophesy that I will make sure comes to pass." She slowly curled her hand into a fist, holding it up in front of her before letting her hand drop. "I will protect my people the same way. They will learn to listen to Queen Bitch. I know that's what Leira Berens called me." She lifted her chin. "I've heard the way that woman swears. I think it was meant as flattery. So be it, we understand each other. We will see if there is a way to forge a relationship with Earth."

"While there's still time."

CHAPTER NINETEEN

The troll slipped out the door of the guest cottage early in the morning before Correk or Leira were awake, dressed in his cowboy hat and boots, determined to visit Eireka and Mara in their new apartment again. He was armed with the map Mara drew for him and a small bag of Cheetos for the road.

It took him an hour just to get to the bridge at South Congress overlooking the Colorado River. He took a break, crawling under the bridge and onto the steel rafters where he could sit down and have a view of the river, away from any humans.

A million bats lined the entire underside of the bridge, their wings folded. They had all returned just a few hours before to sleep off the day. A bat lazily opened one eye and looked at Yumfuck.

"Yumfuck!" He waved and pulled out a Cheetos, taking a bite. The bat stirred, resettling its wings and went back to sleep.

The sun was fully in the sky, and people were out in kayaks in the river below, runners sprinting along the paths.

The troll swung his tiny legs over the river quickly eating his way through the bag, letting out a loud belch at the end, disturbing the bats closest to him. A few fluttered, taking flight briefly or crawling away. Yumfuck shrugged and got up, trilling softly as he petted the one sleeping bat that remained near him. "Survivor," he chirped.

He climbed back onto the bridge, being careful to stay close to the railing and away from the quickly moving feet of the tourists. He made his way to the other side, crossing over Riverside Drive as he looked for another place to take a short break. Preferably someplace with food.

The small troll put his nose in the air, sniffing around for a scent. Nothing. He kept moving, wandering by the small businesses that lined the street, tripping over a small pile of cigarette butts. "Son of a bitch!"

He picked himself up and brushed the ashes carefully off his boots. "Hmph! Wha?" The smell of bacon hit his nose. He turned around and around, but the wind was changing direction making it difficult to tell where the smell was coming from.

The troll moved closer to the buildings, running through the short front yards of sparse grass, the occasional palm tree or clusters of cacti, stopping briefly in intervals to take a good whiff again. "Bacon!"

At a long, red brick building with a sign outside that read Ladybird Assisted Living the troll smelled the air. The bacon scent was stronger. He trilled, clapping his hands and made his way toward the front entrance. A middle-aged woman in colorful pink scrubs rushed right by the troll without noticing him, headed for the double glass doors.

Almost late for work again. Second time this week. She clutched her blue lunch bag tighter, picking up the pace as the automatic doors opened up in front of her and she rushed inside, headed for the time clock.

"Oooooh." The troll walked up to the doors, waiting for them to open but nothing happened. He jumped up and down and waved his hat, frustrated.

He went back to sit on a bench in the front, the smell of bacon still in the air when a man walked briskly toward the entrance and the doors opened again.

The troll got there just as the doors closed. "Motherfucker!" he chirped, waving his fist. He leaned his head against the glass and watched an orderly wheel a cart down the hall with trays of food. "Rat bastard!" he yelled through the tiny opening between the doors, but no one heard him.

Yumfuck stepped away from the doors and squinted up at the cameras, waving his hands. He looked back at the doors. Nothing. The orderly came out of one room and went in another one further down the hall. The troll stuck out his tongue and blew a raspberry, marching back toward the bench just as a large dog ran in front of the doors, triggering the sensors, opening the doors.

Yumfuck scrambled as the doors closed. He looked at the dog trotting away in the distance, looked at the doors, and looked at the dog as Yumfuck smiled.

He stood back and let out a roar, growing to the size of a large dog, waving his arms as the doors opened and he ran in, already shrinking back down to size. The orderly came wheeling out of a room as Yumfuck slid on his belly toward the wheels, grabbing on as the cart turned a corner.

"Morning Mrs. Toler, how are you doing today? Let me set this up for you." The orderly pulled out a tray with a menu sticking out of the side and put it on the table over Mrs. Toler's bed.

The troll peeked out from the wheels he was clinging to and swung himself over to the bottom shelf, quietly lifting the cover off a tray and carefully taking off his hat. He put his head underneath, burying his face in scrambled eggs, letting out a tiny muffled 'yumfuck'.

The orderly looked up, confused at Mrs. Toler who smiled

sweetly and said, "Yumfuck". It was the first word she had said all week.

"That's an auspicious word, Mrs. Toler. Not sure how your family is going to take it. Wonder if I should even report it." He scratched his head. "Maybe I should just put down yum."

"Yumfuck." Mrs. Toler smiled again.

"Okay, have it your way." The orderly carefully wrote down 'spoke today, said yumfuck' in her chart.

Two guards ran by the door on their way to the entrance looking for the large furry animal that waved at the cameras by the front door.

"Nothing yet, Bob," one of them said into a walkie talkie. "Damndest thing. Kind of a cross between a small bear and a dog."

Yumfuck ate his way through the tray till the food was gone. He pulled his head out, putting his hat back on and slid out of the cart while the orderly's back was turned. The orderly turned around just in time as the troll got to the door.

"Yumfuck!" He waved and lifted his hat before scampering down the hall."

The orderly's eyes grew wide. "Have to stop taking these double shifts. They're gonna find a bed for me in here. Not even forty yet!" The orderly pushed the cart to the next room, muttering the entire way.

Yumfuck made his way down the hall turning into the activities room where several residents were sitting in chairs watching the weather channel.

"Bleh!" The troll spotted the remote in the hands of an elderly man's hands and trilled softly, smiling at the man as he held out his hands.

The man gave a toothless smile and slid the remote toward the troll, chuckling. "I used to put a cowboy hat on my dog." The man put out a finger and rubbed the troll's head as the troll trilled, shutting his eyes for a moment.

Yumfuck picked up the remote and held it over his head, jumping down to get closer to the television. He flipped through the channels till he found a movie channel playing *Dirty Dancing* and squealed with delight.

He put down the remote and lifted his arms over his head, dancing to the music as the residents started to clap in time with the beat. The troll trilled with delight and bent over toward the residents, twerking as he backed up closer to them. Several of the residents were dancing in their chairs, waving their arms.

"Woot! Woot!" The troll watched the girl run toward the man as he lifted her over his head.

"Oooooh, yeah? Yeah!" He nodded as an elderly woman nodded back. The troll raised his arms high over his head and ran toward the woman as she put down her hand scooping up the troll and lifting him over her head.

He arched his back, holding out his arms and legs, smiling so all his sharp, pointy teeth showed. The woman put him gently back down on the floor as the troll turned and took a bow, waving his hat in front of him. "Yumfuck," he said, solemnly.

"Yumfuck," she said, nodding her head graciously.

The troll went and took another bow in front of the group and gave a big wave. "Dancing with the Stars!" he chirped. "Yumfuck!"

"What's all the commotion in here? Who changed the channel?" A large orderly barreled into the room and headed straight for the remote. The troll backed up to the wall, hugging it closely until he got to the door and ran out of the room. He stopped at the front desk and hopped up to take three roses out of a vase before he grew to the size of the large dog, opening the doors. He turned as he got outside and waved at the cameras, smiling. "Yumfuck!"

The guard sitting in front of the monitor spit out his coffee and stood, not sure who to call.

The orderly in the activities room changed the channel back

to the weather as a resident said, "Yumfuck!" pounding his fist on the table. He was soon joined by another, and another, all pounding their fists or tapping their canes. "Yumfuck! Yumfuck!"

"Okay, okay," said the orderly changing the channel back. The other orderly on the floor came in the room, scratching his head again. "Did we miss something? What's with all the yumfucking?"

Yumfuck finally made his way to Eireka and Mara's and knocked politely, standing back as Mara opened the door. "I don't suppose anyone knows you left."

The troll held up the flowers, smiling and nodding, his fingers crossed behind his back.

Mara leaned and took the flowers. "Thank you, and don't kid a kidder. Just so you know, I'm calling Leira to let her know where you are. Come on in, are you hungry?"

"Yumfuck!" He strolled in and settled onto the couch. "Nobody puts baby in a corner," he squeaked.

"One of these days you're going to tell me about your adventures."

"As soon as you tell me about yours." He tilted his head and waited.

"I see you've learned a few tricks from Leira."

She pressed her lips together, wondering what to share.

"Spill it," squeaked the troll. "We were meant to do things together."

"I used to have purpose, helping magicals who were refugees from Oriceran. But the band broke up while I was gone, and I'm not sure what to do."

"Gather the information. It's always the first step." Yumfuck shrugged his tiny shoulders.

"Wow, not even a movie reference. You're not feeling sorry for me, are you?"

"You seem to have that angle covered." He blew her a raspberry. "Just keep swimming."

"And we're back to the movies." Mara shook her head and went into the kitchen to get him some food.

"When you remember how to ask for my help, I'll be right here." The troll sat back and reached for the remote, searching for another movie.

CHAPTER TWENTY

The teenage Light Elf made his way up the rocky slope of Camelback mountain to the Dark Kemana. His sneakers slipped on a rock, the burned rubber tip brushing against the clay, streaking it with dirt. His bright red hair matched the red windbreaker he was wearing. Not enough protection against the wind as he climbed higher in the early morning light, but he didn't notice.

"Keep going, not much further." He repeated the whispers he was hearing. They were drowning out every other thought. The voices overlapped each other, calling to him in his dreams, telling him how important he was. *We need you. You belong with us. Follow us. Hurry now.*

He got to the top and stood in the center watching the sun rise over Phoenix down below. He pulled out his wand and raised it up like he was conducting an orchestra repeating the family spell passed down through generations. Dark magic was not to be used before someone was ready. But the whispers told him. *You're ready. Do it.*

He started the spell as the voices increased, gaining strength. He pulled in the dark magic, feeling it course through him from generations that came before him. "Expellorium…" A black mist crept up around his ankles, the whispering getting louder, enveloping him in the darkness as he finished the spell. The black magic opening a rip in the veil between his world and the world in between.

"It's beautiful." He looked inside the shimmering darkness as it sparked all around him, suddenly sucking him in with a whoosh, lifting him off his feet into the world in between.

Leira made her way back through Hilldale, the troll riding on her shoulder. "That was nice of Nana to bring you home." Leira glanced over at Yumfuck, who smiled and let out a soft trill. "You want to tell me about that reporting of a large furry dog smiling at the cameras at a nursing home? The general called to ask me about it. I covered for you."

"Whew…" The troll wiped his forehead dramatically.

"You need to be a little more careful. Nana wouldn't say how you managed to find your way over to their apartment. I know you two are keeping secrets."

The troll turned his face away from Leira and made a point of watching the small cottages as they walked quickly past them.

"Have it your way, but secrets come out eventually. Might want to plan on a controlled crash."

Yumfuck shrugged and let out a cackle, holding on to Leira's collar.

It wasn't long before they were back at the Jersey Willen's front porch. There was a note stuck on a nail by the door marked, 'Leira'.

"Willens can read. Why does that seem so weird?" Leira pulled down the note and read it.

'I still owe you the favor but per our agreement, I keep the gold.'

Leira started pounding on the door. "Not good enough,

Willen!" she shouted. "Not leaving till I get more of an explanation. Don't mind if I wake the neighbors with an oversized troll, either."

The troll looked at her, ready to go.

"Not yet." Leira pounded on the door again. "I can hear you in there. Thought you guys knew how to move around a little more quietly than that." She pounded again but the door finally creaked open just a crack. The Jersey Willen stood at the door, his son peeking out from behind him.

Leira pushed the door open further, stepping into the opening. *This is too important to get the brush off from a magical rodent.*

The younger Willen stepped back, gasping at the sight of the troll. The troll smirked, annoyed and sat down on Leira's shoulder.

"Tell me what you found out. Sooner you do, sooner I leave. No one will know where I got the information. Now." Her eyes glowed from the anger and annoyance.

"Okay, okay." The Willen held up his paws. "But if you tell anyone it was me, my life will be over. Nowhere to hide! Worse than the Gnomes!"

"I told you to be careful…"

"You didn't tell me you were hunting dark magic like that!"

"What did you see? I'm growing tired of asking."

"You were right, the humans got more seeds from Oriceran. A lot more. Whatever you did only slowed them down temporarily."

"Did you see who was in charge?"

The Willen shuddered and gasped, looking up at the ceiling as he groaned. "Terrible, terrible. Alright, already. It was a prophet. Can you believe it? A prophet! Saw him clear as day!"

"Which one?" Leira needed confirmation the Gnome was responsible.

"The Gnome prophet, yes, the Gnome."

"Did he see you?"

"No, or you wouldn't be seeing me now."

"What did he get in return?"

"All sorts of technology. Boxes and boxes of it." The Willen waved his arms, the jacket shifting over his belly. "Things from Earth flying over to Oriceran, things from Oriceran flying over to Earth. Never seen anything like it, I tell you! But there's something more." He shook his finger at Leira. "Dark magic, the really strong stuff. Nothing like I've ever seen before. Not to be meddled with. Terrible, terrible. A prophet!"

"Thank you, your favor to me is over. You did your part."

"Reluctantly. Please…" The Willen was already shutting the door. "Tell no one. Forget about Hilldale. Forget about the Jersey Willen. Dark magic like that sees through things, goes everywhere." The door shut with a loud click.

"That was a bum's rush, Yumfuck. He was really scared. I don't blame him." Leira went slowly down the front stairs and walked back in the direction of Hilldale's square. "Rhazdon may be posing as a prophet. Now we need to prove it. We better get home."

CHAPTER TWENTY-ONE

The prophets nervously awaited the old Gnome's arrival into their chamber at the back of the meeting room. The vote had already taken place, and the Gnome was out. There was a growing suspicion about him and his dealings with the Dark Market.

Rumors had made their way back to the prophets about the Gnome controlling most of the dealings in the bazaar. An emergency meeting was held without him to discuss their options, particularly given the looming prophesy.

The vote was unanimous. He was fired, and all that was left was to take his robe from him and show him the door. Only hitch was that no prophet had ever been fired before in the long history of their group.

"It needed to be done. Overdue," said the Wood Elf prophet. "Maybe we can ask another Gnome."

"Who knows what he's gotten himself involved in, and by extension us. If it all comes out no one will follow us, and everyone will be doomed." The Arpak fluttered his wings. "He's a thug."

The Pixie fluttered nervously over her seat and the Kilomea

prophet grunted, standing up, the stars shifting on the back of his robe to stay in alignment with the night sky illuminated on the ceiling. The four levels of the gallery went up behind them ringing the room, but they were all gathered down in the well in the front just behind the lit stand in the center that held the worn leather-bound ledger. In the ledger were all the ancient quatrains under a glass dome protected by a spell.

The Gnome stepped inside the room, his eyes widening when he saw all the other prophets crowded together in one long row. A sneer came across his face. "What have we here? There's a sense of gloom in the air."

He stepped in closer, letting the door close behind him. "I just received your message and hurried right over. Why do I get the sense you've all been here just a bit longer?" He walked slowly around the lit stand. The Light Elf nervously tapped his fingers on his leg, ready for anything.

"Someone want to tell me what's going on?" The Gnome stopped beside the ledger, his arms crossed in front of him. *So the day is here, at last.* He waited for someone to find their courage. *I've waited centuries for this moment. Let it take as long as it needs to.*

Kyomi stood, clearing his throat. "The group has asked me to speak for them. It has come to our attention that you are the mastermind behind the Dark Market. You are the one who has been breaking the treaty and opening portals for years now, trafficking in Earth's technology and trading favors. These are just the things we know about."

The Gnome scowled. "Your plot to bring over a human who kills the royal Light Elves' prince and sets a powerful artifact loose in the world. You scheme to harm a human celebrity to put yourselves in a good light and create chaos for the Silver Griffins, and you take responsibility for none of it," he hissed.

"We had good intentions!" The Nicht prophet leaned forward in his seat.

"You've failed at every one of them."

"All of those ideas started with you," insisted the Light Elf prophet. "You came up with them!"

"I never heard any protests, and I wasn't in charge of the execution of them."

"Convenient memory," said the Pixie. "Tell him the rest."

Kyomi stood up straighter. "You're relieved of your duty. As of today, you are no longer a prophet of any standing. Turn over your robe and you can go."

"I can go any time I want to. Was this unanimous?"

"On the first vote."

A smile spread across the Gnome's face. "Very well." He removed the robe but didn't stop there, carefully removing every article of clothing despite the loud and varied protests from the other prophets.

The Gnome ignored their confusion and pleas and spoke the magic words that till then he only dared say in the sanctuary of his small cabin. The transformation began almost immediately.

The sounds of bones stretching and growing filled the chamber, horrifying the other prophets.

"What's going on?"

"Is he dying?"

His body twisted and pulled as he grimaced. The top of his head sprouted tentacles that slowly grew until they covered his head and the skin on his body became smooth. It only took a few minutes but when it was done no prophet could look away.

It was the moment they would all use to mark time. Before they learned the truth… and after.

Before them stood a naked Atlantean woman. There was stunned silence in the room. Rhazdon turned around in a slow circle, finally comfortable in her own skin, appreciating the gaze of onlookers. Finally, she picked up the robe and held it in front of her. "I'm going to borrow this robe for a little longer."

"An Atlantean…" gasped the Light Elf.

"Half Atlantean, actually but thank you. We've never been

formally introduced. My name is Rhazdon, you may have heard of me."

The Light Elf stumbled backward, catching himself as the Kilomea pulled out the knife he always kept in his boot, despite the prophets' rules.

"You can't be! Rhazdon died centuries ago."

"And was a man!"

"Rumors of my gender were greatly exaggerated. And as you can see, I'm very much alive." She slipped into the Gnome's old robe, hanging loosely off her shoulders but barely covering all the necessary parts. "Thank you for this. I was wondering when it would be the right moment, but you found it for me. The necklace may have slipped from my fingers, momentarily and my new following has had some setbacks but no bother. I've had just enough wins to still be ahead."

"I don't believe it." The Pixie flew a little closer but retreated just as fast.

Rhazdon pointed at the Light Elf. "You're with the royal court, are you not?" Rhazdon smiled, her eyes cold and menacing. "You never told the public what happened to the king's father during that last, great battle." She spit out the last words slowly. "You said he died in combat, killing me. Not true. Liar, liar." She waved a finger in the air. "How many years has he been trapped in the world in between?" Rhazdon smiled, satisfied as the Light Elf gasped.

"Is it true?" asked the Crystal prophet. The Light Elf sunk into a chair and nodded, the color draining from his face.

"You see? But no one ever knew I was a female. Dark magic can do so many things in the right hands. Of course, in your cases I never had to use it. Good old fashioned suggestions that fed your egos worked just fine."

"How can you still be alive and look so…"

"Young? Rumors of my power were not exaggerated. I'm a very clever girl."

"You were the one that broke into the vault!"

"Now you're catching on. The bitch is back, and she has her playthings. Careful, careful, boys and girls. I have more than dark magic in my hands now. I have all your secrets. What would Queen Saria do if she knew you were the ones who let Bill Somers into the castle and set all of this into motion. I thought so. You have very convenient integrity. At least everyone always knew what I stood for and what I was willing to do. Don't worry, I'll burn this thing when I'm done with it." She wrapped the robe tighter around her curves.

The tentacles on her head wrapped themselves into a loose braid down her back. "Thanks for everything. I could have done all this without you, but it would have taken more planning." Rhazdon laughed and waved her arm, opening the door to the main hallway and strutting down the middle of the post office, holding up her chin and giving a cool smile to anyone who stole glances in her direction.

The gargoyles flying overhead let out screeches and flew higher, sensing the dark magic as she passed by the mailboxes. Rhazdon threw up her arms, opening all the boxes sending the mail fluttering through the air in a rain of letters.

She stopped at the door and turned around, smiling. "Tell everyone who cares to know, Rhazdon is alive and well." She flung open her robe and stood there with her hands on her hips. "That's right... not a man." She said the words slowly and evenly.

"She's beautiful," whispered a Light Elf. "Perfection."

"That is some bold move!"

"Rhazdon is dead. It's been eight hundred years!"

"To look that good... it would take the darkest kind of magic..."

"Is she the one who broke into the library and killed that Gnome?"

"What's she doing with a prophet's robe?"

She laughed as some looked away while others stood there with their mouths hanging open.

Rhazdon closed the robe again, turned and marched out of the post office, dark magic radiating off her as her bare feet hardly touched the ground. She reached the edge of the forest, turned and waved at the few people brave enough to follow behind her from a distance. Once she was within the treeline she cast a spell she had found in one of her old books.

"Feels good to break out an old favorite." The spell left behind no trace for anyone who dared follow her all the way home to the cabin deep in the Dark Forest.

The Light Elf yelled, "Altrea Extendia," as bronze sparks flew, and a staircase appeared. He took the stairs two at a time, yelling "Altrea Extendia," again, running up the next flight of stairs as fast as he could. He did it over and over again until he reached the royal family's floor and ran, searching from room to room until he could hear the queen singing at the end of a long hall.

He found Queen Saria standing in a large room singing to her plants. Her voice was a rich alto that carried easily.

"Why are you out of breath? What's happened?"

"Queen Saria..." he panted, trying to catch his breath. "I...I..."

"Say it!" she hissed as the plants drew away from her, irritating her more.

"Rhazdon lives."

"I know already." She let out an annoyed sigh. "There are new followers picking up where Rhazdon left off. Ridiculous empty-headed fools."

"No, your Highness." The Light Elf gulped in air. "Rhazdon is alive. The Atlantean. But he's not a he, he's a she. She lives!"

The Queen wrinkled her forehead and narrowed her eyes.

"Who said this? Who's spreading this lie?" *More trouble in the kingdom. It only gets worse.*

The Light Elf sputtered trying to explain. "There...I mean...I saw...lots of us! She walked through the post office! Letters flying everywhere! Took off her robe and no clothes! No clothes! Announced she was Rhazdon! The gargoyles screeching overhead!" The Light Elf was waving his arms around while telling the stories in bits and pieces. The queen grew more thoughtful, piecing it all together.

"The prophets... and then she disappeared into the woods! Poof! No one could see her!"

"Go back..."

"She disappeared into the woods!"

"Right before those words."

"The prophets?"

"What do they have to do with Rhazdon?" The queen turned over the bits of information, each one helping to fill in a hole in a bigger picture. *Is this who I've been looking for?*

"She was wearing an ill-fitting prophet's robe. Walked right out in it. The prophets, well they, I don't know, left by a back door. No one's seen any of them. Ran home I guess."

"Did anyone check to see if there was a dead prophet left behind?" She put out her arm, sending a calming strand of energy through the Light Elf. His breathing slowed down, and he gathered his wits.

"Ossonia ran back there. I didn't even know there was a room back there. I followed her but we didn't find anything. The room was empty except for an old ledger. Everyone was gone. Nothing was out of place."

Allies of some kind... "I see. Does the King know yet?"

"I ran straight to you. It just happened!"

"Find the King and tell him the same story. Tell him where he can find me."

The Light Elf gave a small bow. "Your majesty." He ran out

of the room yelling "Altrea Extendia!" as bronze sparks shot out at the end of the hallway with stairs leading back down a floor.

A thin stem of anger grew inside the queen's heart, spinning itself through her veins as she began to wonder if she had the answer to the one question that bothered her most.

Deep, dark red seeped into the fragrant white flowers on her crown till they were blood red, shimmering against her silver crown. Her jaw set as she clenched her fists.

The prophets are powerful enough to get an inept human in and out of the castle without anyone seeing them. They would never... The inane prophesies! An archaeologist... That stunt they pulled on Earth. It all fits. Her eyes shined with tears as she dug her nails into her palms. "Foolish idiots!"

The rows of plants in front of her shrunk from the sound of her rage. "I need someone I can trust! An ally of my own."

The king came into the room, his eyes wide. It was too late, the queen's mind was made up already. "I'm going to Earth to seek out Leira Berens. We need to hurry our plans along." She bit out every word.

"Why not the Silver Griffins?"

"I need someone I can trust. I may not always like her or her lack of manners, but I trust her. Right now, that's more valuable than anything else I can think of." She turned and shook her head, the pain that was starting to fade was back in her voice. "You understand what this means."

"We don't even know if the stories are true. They seem farfetched. Rhazdon!"

"Did you hear about the gargoyles? Nothing fazes them. Nothing! It takes so much dark magic for them to fly higher, away from the trouble."

Her eyes grew wider as she ran out of the room and down the hall to the library. The king chased after her.

She stopped just short of the stacks as some of the Gnomes

looked up in curiosity. A poppy on a nearby bowler opened and shut.

The queen turned back to her husband. "Rhazdon. It's true. A woman, not a man. She can change her physical structure and hold the spell for centuries! Who else possesses that knowledge and can let that much darkness pass through them without being consumed by it? She stole back her books and her artifacts! She's been gathering followers on here and on Earth!" The queen beat against the king's chest, a wail ripped out of her throat. "She helped kill my son!"

The king let her pound on his chest till she wore herself out, weeping in his arms. *Grief has no ending.* "And condemned my father to the world in between," he said softly.

The queen lifted her head. "That bitch has to die once and for all. I'm going to Earth to ask Leira for help and to end this before we're defending all of Oriceran against that damned changeling!"

CHAPTER TWENTY-TWO

L eira parked the Mustang at the top of the long driveway on the side of Turner Underwood's large house and jumped out, carrying the artifact still wrapped in a cloth. She was following the slate path to the back, halfway around the house before Correk caught up with her.

"We don't even know if he's home." Correk carefully stepped over a garden gnome with a little red hat. He shook his head. "Turner has the strangest sense of humor. I suppose it's what happens when you hang around on Earth for hundreds of years."

"I sent out a stream of magic to check. He's here."

"That's a little invasive, using your magic like a tracking device."

"He didn't shove back. I only asked as my intention. We think Rhazdon is alive and well. The Jersey Willen saw that prophet trading with humans through a portal. It all adds up. You know that's Rhazdon. We have to find him! There's no time to get on people's schedules." Her words came out in a rush.

"Leira! Thanks for the heads up. Gave me a chance to dress for the occasion." Turner Underwood was standing in the middle of his patio leaning on his cane, an unlit cigar in his mouth, wearing a coat and tie. His idea of casual. "I take it your trip home was successful and you found the prized artifact."

Leira stopped short. "Home." She said the word with awe in her voice. It was the first time she took it in. She shook her head. "No time for that. We need to try again and see if I can reach the cabin in Oriceran with the energy stream. Find out if our suspicions are true."

"Right to the point. I like that about you, kid."

There was a loud pop and a blue ball of light rolled across the lawn, changing direction as it sought out Correk, stopping at his feet and dissolving into the ground.

"What was that?" Leira peered more closely at the ground but there were no remnants.

"Another way of locating someone. In our world there's hundreds of little tricks like that. It looks like the royal family is looking for you, Correk." Turner pursed his lips. *This is not good.* "And they found you."

He held his finger up in the wind. "Incoming," he said calmly as a shimmer of sparks appeared and a portal opened up on his lawn. "Busy day for me. Your Majesty, my Queen, what an honor. Your Highness, my King, pleased to see you. You are welcome guests!"

Correk quickly went to the portal and held out his hand for the queen, helping her onto the lawn. "My queen."

"Turner Underwood! Perfect." There was a strain to the queen's voice "I'm glad you're here. I need your counsel as well."

The king nodded but said nothing. He knew enough about his wife after hundreds of years of living side by side that she wasn't going to waste any time. Not over this.

"Rhazdon is alive and has made her presence known in a very public way. Alive and a woman…" The queen stopped short, watching the trio.

Leira's eyes widened and Correk arched an eyebrow as Turner let out a heavy sigh and chewed on his cigar.

The queen's eyes narrowed. "You already knew. All of you." She held back her sudden flash of anger, waiting for an explanation.

"Not for certain, and definitely not a woman." Correk bit his bottom lip. "We were just about to attempt to prove it. Once we had the proof, you were our next stop."

The queen looked weary. "So much intrigue for one day. I long for rigorous honesty."

Leira bristled, pulling her mouth into a thin line.

The queen turned and looked out over the lake. "Such a beautiful spot, Turner. Sometimes I wonder what Earth would be like…but it doesn't last." She turned and looked at Leira. "Oriceran is home and an old threat has come back. I need your help."

"Whatever you need." Correk bowed before his queen.

"I'm sure you will play an important role but it's not your allegiance I need at the moment. It's yours, Leira. You possess magical talents not seen for a long time."

"Since Rhazdon, you mean." Leira was solemn.

"As a matter of fact, yes but fortunately on the side of the light and in service to others."

Turner raised his hand in the air, interrupting the queen. "If I may, there is a unique difference here. Rhazdon learned how to manipulate magic to her own will. Granted, she has the ability to sustain the poisonous effects of dark magic like no one we've ever seen before. But Leira is able to match that ability by following the flow of energy, not getting in front of it and wrestling it to do her bidding."

"May be able to…" The queen gave Leira a pointed look. "Not a criticism, only a necessary observation. Rhazdon is battle tested with her magic and clearly is capable of great deception and manipulation. She was able to sustain youth over hundreds of years, even change her physical structure."

"And fool the prophets into doing her bidding." The king grimaced, rubbing his chin.

"She was disguised as the Gnome prophet, wasn't she?" *The prophets plotted to kill your son. I should have told them. Not tried to spare them from more suffering.* Correk grimaced and momentarily looked away. *It will have to wait.* "It explains the connection to the Dark Market. It also means there's a Gnome buried somewhere between here and their mountain homes. Someone should send word to the real Gnome's people."

"That was something we didn't know. We still don't know how far Rhazdon's plans have crept into our world... or yours."

"Rhazdon is also after the necklace, I'm sure of it and I think I know why." Leira stood with her hands on her hips feeling a swirl of emotions, willing herself to focus, remember her old training as a cop.

Facts are what matter. Look at the data. "Rhazdon has been working to build a new following on both worlds, to connect the two. That necklace is very powerful. Maybe powerful enough to open a sustainable portal. Like a gate but maybe not as stable. Still, enough to connect our worlds early. On her timetable. We have one more bit of information to add to all of this. We stopped a very powerful Wizard from stealing another artifact and we have good information that the Wizard was looking for a booster."

"For the necklace. Of course." The queen raised a fist in the air. "She's building an army on Oriceran and a following on Earth. She's working to turn the two sides against each other and fight her battle for her. The Oricerans are taught her betrayal and will fight against her but the humans on Earth will get a dose of her ability to save the day, even if she's the cause of the wreckage. Revenge and victory in one neat package. Wickedly twisted."

"Magical marketing, fuck me," Leira said in amazement. "We need to find that necklace and stop her from gaining momentum on Earth. Expose what the bitch is really about. I can start that ball rolling from within the bureaucracy. Controlling the message will be more powerful than magic." *The general will help get the word out.*

"I need the necklace back in our family and to see Rhazdon pay." The king said it quietly, with bitterness in his voice. "I've failed to rule my kingdom well. Dark magic has its hand on our throat, and it's been there for centuries, spreading like a weed." He looked up, determined. "Too many people in my family have suffered at this bitch's hands. I will give my life before I let it be anyone else. Leira, you are part Light Elf, which makes you part of this family. Will you stand with us? Will you fight alongside us and rid this world of this vile creature?"

"My home is in Austin, Texas in the United States of America on planet Earth."

The queen shook her head angrily. "You turn your back on us…"

"You jump to a lot of conclusions." Leira raised her eyebrows and lowered her chin. "We will fight alongside each other a lot better if you learn to wait till, I finish a goddamned sentence. I will fight but I want this understood. I fight for my first home and I do it as an equal, a peer. I serve no other government, no monarchy *and* I will not stop till Rhazdon is put down. For good this time. The bitch has it coming and then some. You want honesty, that's mine. Don't question it again or we part ways and I find my own allies."

Correk put out his hand to stop Leira as her eyes started to glow from anger but she stepped away from him.

"You've apparently never gotten to know a Texan America before but let this stand as your one and only lesson about this. Our loyalty to where we stand runs deep and we don't let any goddamn interloper run up on our territory without a fight. You came here because you need my help. Ask for it, don't demand it."

Turner Underwood smiled and rested on his cane. "I love the

smell of a rousing speech in the morning! Well put, my young student. My Queen I believe the ball is in your court. Are you willing to be humble enough to ask for help? Close your mouth, Correk. I'm an old Elf. I say what I want and always with respect. By now, the king and queen know that." He tilted his chin and arched an eyebrow. "Well, my queen?"

The queen drew herself up and laced her hands in front of her, breathing deeply. "We may never be close friends, but we can be warriors side by side in this battle. Will you fight alongside all of Oriceran? For Earth?" She bowed her head as Correk's eyes widened.

"Chill, Cousin." Leira rolled her eyes and gave a crooked smile. "Shake on it." She put out her hand to the queen. "After all, you're not in Oriceran right now. We have a deal."

The queen smiled, determined to win the coming fight, and took Leira's hand, shaking it. "We have a deal."

"Come on, everyone, don't be left out. You know you want to. Pile on." Leira held the queen's hand tight, waiting for the others. Turner slapped his hand on top, followed by Correk and then the king. "To Earth and Oriceran and the end of Rhazdon," said Leira as symbols rolled across each of their hands, spelling out their intention.

CHAPTER TWENTY-THREE

None of the prophets had returned to their room behind the post office since the Gnome was revealed as Rhazdon. The room's location was exposed to the world and besides, they could feel their influence slipping. There were murmurings throughout the town about what the prophets knew and too many questioned their loyalty.

"How could they not know that wasn't really a Gnome?"

"Come to think of it, she never really acted like a Gnome, anyway."

"Did you hear about the Gnome's doings with the Dark Market? My cousin told me, and he said everyone knew. They figured the prophets were in on it, making cash on the side."

"You think the prophesies are true?"

"No one can find Rhazdon. I'll bet they know where she is."

No one thought they were blameless.

Kiyomi turned in his robe and asked forgiveness of the royal family. Still, he held back the one secret he hoped they would never know. *I will take that to my grave, but I will fight with everything I have to save Oriceran. A living amends. It's all I can offer.* He convinced himself it was for the best, for everyone. *No need to cause further pain.*

The others met one last time at a tavern by the Rodania sea to the north of the Light Elves kingdom, near the Land of Terran.

"May the Light Elf king and queen never know of our involvement," said the Wood Elf.

"We should tell them everything, clear the air." The Kilomea pounded the wooden table with his fist, shaking the tankards.

"It wouldn't clear the air. Quite the opposite." The Pixie stood on the table sipping from a small thimble.

"We need to decide what our strongest intention is in this present moment. That will rule. Our efforts were all aimed at saving the beings of Oriceran from destruction when the last prophecy by the seer is fulfilled. The gates start to open soon." The Crystal sipped his beer, frosting the glass.

"He's right," said the Wood Elf. "Coming clean will splinter the king and queen's focus. We must find ways to repair our reputation and lead everyone to safety on Earth. There's still time."

"We will need to go home to our own villages for a while. Live in exile for a short time." The Kilomea growled, angry at himself. "I will take it under advisement that we say nothing for now, but I will not promise to stay silent forever. I've caused enough harm with secrets for more than one lifetime. Too many have been hurt."

The Crystal sighed, as a spray of snowflakes floated to the table, melting as they landed. "I agree with my friend. My silence may be temporary, at best. And I will spend the rest of my days making up for what I've done, whether anyone else ever knows or not. May I restore my family's honor someday."

"May we all," said the Pixie, rustling her wings. "To Oriceran and her people." She raised her thimble as the others raised their tankards.

"To Oriceran and her people."

"I'm going back to Oriceran, just for a little while to help the royal family and to see if I can track Rhazdon." Correk saw the disappointment in Leira's face but he was determined. The king and queen were ready to travel back through a portal and go home. "They're ready to go. Thank you for agreeing to fight with us, in your own style, of course." Correk gave her a crooked smile and put his hands on her shoulders. "I will return as soon as I can."

"Make sure you do. I've gotten used to hearing you snore in the next room, and Yumfuck will be beside himself if you're gone too long. Gather all the energy you can. We can't pick the battle place or even the day this time. Rhazdon has a complicated plan in play and it's hard to say what she plans next. From the stories of her Lady Godiva moment in the post office she wasn't broken up about being literally exposed. She sounded relieved, inspired even. Like the next phase of her plot was underway."

"Open a large portal and somehow keep it open. I'd swear that was impossible until I heard that an eight-hundred-year-old ghost had returned as a young looking woman."

There was a crackle behind Correk and sparks as a portal opened.

"Your ride is here. You better go. Don't hug me that's not necessary." Correk ignored her and hugged her anyway, smiling.

Leira patted him on the back. "Okay, okay, we're not fighting off anyone today, hopefully."

"If only to annoy you before I go so you don't miss me too much."

"No need to miss you. You're coming back soon. You gave me your word."

"Indeed. Keep up with your studies with Turner and tell the troll everything. Mara may be right. He's smarter than he's letting

215

on and if he has all the information, he can make better decisions if Rhazdon decides to make the next appearance on Earth first."

"A smart troll who's been playing the long game with us."

"Here's one thing I do know about trolls. They bond with whoever saves them but out of choice. It's not a guarantee. I know, I know, I left that out, but you got on my nerves more back then."

"A million years ago and a few adventures. Does this mean I don't get on your nerves anymore?"

"Far less…Ow, don't punch. Use your words. Ow!" Correk laughed as he held his arm. "At least take off that ring before you hit me. You have a pretty good right hook."

"I'm bringing Hagan and the Feds into this. Not a discussion."

"Wasn't going to argue. Earth has just as much at risk and without the knowledge of Rhazdon's history with violence and war. They have a right to know everything and make their own decisions."

"You should tell your father. He's one of the few beings that can mix magic and technology. Maybe there's an edge there."

"Or an even worse disaster. No, that will have to wait."

"It will be interesting to see what the magical beings who've lived on Earth for generations decide to do. Earth or Oriceran."

"It was easy for you. It may be for them as well."

"In the end, I'm fighting for the ability to choose for myself and give that same right to everyone else. It's ironic that the part of Rhazdon she cherishes most, the half of her that's Atlantean is from Earth originally, not Oriceran. You'd think this would feel more like home to her. I know, the same could be said of me. I suppose there's something to be said for where you're raised and what you know."

"In the end, it doesn't matter. Rhazdon has betrayed everything she's ever known and for her own ego. Beware an Atlantean of every stripe. They are rarely magnanimous."

"I've met one myself and there's room for improvement, but they can be persuaded. You better go."

Leira gave Correk a small push toward the portal. "Those things don't stay open for long and the last thing we need is for you to fall through some crack into the world in between. The dark mist isn't strong enough to tear open a hole just yet." *All those teenagers and a dark Wizard. That's not justice.* Leira gave a small shudder but shook it off.

Correk gave her a nod and turned to go, helping the queen back through the portal and shaking hands with Turner Underwood before he stepped through and closed the portal.

"Back to work, young lady. Let's see if this artifact works after all. Just because we know who we're seeking doesn't mean we won't find valuable information. I have a feeling being able to disguise your magic so Rhazdon doesn't see you coming may yet still prove to be very useful. Now focus…"

CHAPTER TWENTY-FOUR

The queen and king walked into the library's outer room ahead of Correk. The king patted Correk on the back. "They'll probably throw a few books at your head, but Gnomes are not known for holding resentments. They tend to deal with things and move on."

"They're too busy devising a new vault, anyway. Rhazdon broke in far too easily. We all got lazy, thinking she was dead. Even if she was, we acted like no one just as strong could ever come along. Leira is living proof that was wrong." The queen held up her hand to silence Correk. "Thank the two moons she fights alongside us. But if there's Rhazdon, and now Leira there may someday be more. We need to prepare better than we've bothered. I'm tired of losing and reacting."

Correk stepped fully into the room, his muscles tense, fully prepared to duck. The Gnomes were busy filing books and sending out late notices or working on the vault in the very back. A poppy on a bowler near the front noticed him first and blew a raspberry, baring its teeth.

"I deserve that one, given the Willen and the late book..."

Several more poppies noticed and joined in a chorus of

growling. The Gnomes noticed the chatter from their hats and turned, peeking around corners and coming out from behind the stacks to see what was the bother.

"Let's get this over with…" Correk pulled in just enough magic to reflect any flying objects headed his way.

The queen came and stood at his side, crossing her arms and glaring at the Gnomes. "I've had enough for a lifetime of any pettiness. Get it out of your system, Gnomes and surrender it."

The Gnomes glanced at each other, waving to the Gnomes in the back and came forward standing in a crowd at the edge of the library.

"This is new," said the king. "Correk, how late was that book?"

"Just a week or so, I'm sure of it. This can't be because of a Willen," he said, incredulous.

"Someone has to go first." The queen scowled at the Gnomes as the poppies drew back and closed their petals.

"No need to encourage them." Correk wondered how many he could fight off at once. *Steady, steady…*

The Gnomes, in unison, all doffed their bowlers, holding them in one hand as they went down on one knee bowing their heads.

Correk hesitated, looking through the crowd of Gnomes all huddled around the front, some in the aisles between the stacks. "What's this?"

An older Gnome lifted his head and put his bowler back on top. "We have a common enemy now. Rhazdon has killed at least two of our kind. That much we know. And he sullied our reputation breaking into the vault."

"She broke in…" said the king.

"Really?" said the queen. "Take a beat."

"Right, right."

The Gnomes looked up, confused.

"Rhazdon is really a woman," said the queen, lifting her chin.

She took a deep breath. "It's a lot on top of a lot of secrets and lies. You were saying?"

"We are one of the oldest magical beings on Oriceran dating back before anyone can remember. Light Elves were not around when we were great warriors and fought to protect our kind. We are ready to do so again. We will leave a skeleton crew to guard what's left of the library. The rest of us are going with you to find Rhazdon and justice."

"Not necessary…"

The Gnome shook his head. "Queen Saria, we are of service to the Light Elves, but we are not indentured or subjects of yours. We choose to be here. We choose to fight. We're not asking for your blessing. We're going."

The Gnomes stood up, forming straight lines, pushing into the outer room.

Correk and the king bowed, and the queen gave a curtsy. "We are honored to have you by our sides. It seems I'm to learn a thing or two about working as a team today." The queen straightened out the folds in the front of her long dress.

Correk stepped forward and put out his fist for the Gnome to place on top in the Oriceran custom. Several of the Gnomes rushed forward and placed their hands on top, letting out a battle cry. "We fight with honor and to the end!"

As the noise subsided the elder Gnome leaned closer to Correk beckoning him with a finger. Correk leaned closer.

The Gnome harrumphed and gave a hard nod. "A month's ban on checking out a book."

"Seems fair." Correk straightened back up, doing his best not to roll his eyes.

The king was moved by the Gnomes' gesture. "Our forces are growing. Go back to Earth and help them organize, Correk."

"There are groups that we still need to make sure are with us."

"I'll talk to Perrom, myself. You have my word," said the king. "Help Leira spread the word on Earth among the magical community at least that Rhazdon lives and help them prepare. Not all may live but we must finally find peace for both worlds."

"Especially since the gates will start to open soon and the humans are growing increasingly aware of us. Go, the king is right. The prophets have meddled in Earth business already and many may have seen through their antics. That was bad enough. At least the celebrity lived and was healed quickly. If Rhazdon creates mayhem on Earth, it won't matter if we point out she comes from their planet. They'll see it as a lie and fight all of us. Go. We know how to inspire others here to join us. Rhazdon has made that fairly easy."

"Of course," said Correk, reluctantly. "As you wish."

"Gather as many as you can. There may not be much time. I can feel the energy from Prince Rolim's necklace right here." The queen held her fist to her chest. "Every time someone tries to use it, I know, and the energy is stirring. Whatever Rhazdon has planned, it won't be long now."

CHAPTER TWENTY-FIVE

"Clever of you to hide the necklace where there's no kemana and the altitude saps energy. Harder to tell where it is. Harder... but not impossible." Rhazdon stood menacingly over the cowering Wizard. She had managed to trace the necklace to his house but not the exact room. "I'm kind of short on time, your lucky day."

They were in the Wizard's large living room by the roaring fire on the outskirts of Denver, Colorado. The tentacles on her head were rolling in waves over her shoulders, warming themselves. The Wizard sat in his leather wing chair contemplating his options. Measuring his own dark magic. *First people in our clan start disappearing, now this.* He wasn't sure what to do.

"You can see how much sense I'm making, right?" Rhazdon smiled, her eyes an icy black. She was dressed in thigh-high suede boots and dark brown leather pants with a sage green tunic belted at the waist. Her old clothes from her days on Oriceran centuries ago, altered to fit her curves. *Finally able to take them out of storage.*

The only concession to being on Earth was the long mauve winter coat, held open by her hands on her hips. "You hand over the necklace your family took from me and fight by my side. Or you die here and now, and I tear this house apart looking for it. Your choice, of course. I like to be fair."

A Witch appeared at the doorway, holding out the necklace.

"Wise woman. Part of the decision has been made. Now the rest." Rhazdon tilted her head. "Fighting with me or dying to stay home?"

The Wizard swallowed hard. "We fight with you, of course. I'll see to it that the other families understand."

"There you go." Rhazdon took the necklace, feeling the current of magic pass through her. "Beautiful," she whispered, admiring the diamond shape with an O cut in the center.

The Wizard stood up, gripping the chair. "Rhazdon…"

His wife shook her head, but he had to know.

"What is it? Let him speak."

"There are plenty of stories about you. Legends, passed down through my family."

"Flattery, not a bad start."

"All of them talk about how you wanted to form alliances. You were interested in building a new kind of world for magical people. You wanted us to have respect. Your followers mattered to you. Has all of that changed?"

Rhazdon clenched a fist at her side, gripping the necklace tighter as the energy flowing through her head mixed with the pulse of dark magic that filled her veins after so many years of waiting to come out of hiding. It made her feel lightheaded, almost giddy. *Almost.* "It's all I ever wanted," she said between clenched teeth. "We deserve at least that much. Recognition for who we are, what we can do! I always had the best of intentions…"

She looked into the fire, lost in memories over eight hundred years old. "There was a time when Atlanteans were everywhere on this world. They were respected by everyone on Earth. We advanced technology beyond where the humans have managed to take it to this day! But no one cared." She shook her head, looking back at the Wizard. "They wiped out my kind. The only safe place to live was on Oriceran… in hiding." A smile came back to her face, curling her lip into a sneer. "But today's a new day. There are new followers in the magical communities around Earth and some on Oriceran. We can let the past go and rebuild. Find some closure."

"Then why the battle?"

Rhazdon felt the surge of anger and sent a fireball into the center of the hearth making the flames explode out into the living room. "Do you think this is my idea? Is that what you're saying? I'm defending myself! Just like before…" she hissed. "They are coming for me. No room at the table, again. No one can let me live in peace, gather a few followers. So be it. It is what it is. We defend our rights."

The Witch stamped out embers on the Persian rug as the Wizard stood between his wife and Rhazdon. "Where do I tell everyone to meet?"

"A favorite kemana of mine called Enchanted Rock. There's a certain half-Light Elf I need to meet and greet. I've heard great things about her, and I have a feeling if we don't size each other up and get it over with this will only drag out forever. Tell them to be there tomorrow night. I'll make sure to send Leira Berens an invite, so she doesn't miss our meeting. This shit is going down."

CHAPTER TWENTY-SIX

Leira felt the tug of energy pulling at her and the swirl of dark energy. "Rhazdon is doing her best to get my attention. She's been sending out waves of darkness since yesterday. I keep having visions of Enchanted Rock. Subtle wench." She stood in her living room surrounded by her mother and Nana and Correk. The troll stood on the back of the couch wearing his cowboy hat and red boots, watching Leira pace.

There was a knock at the door, and everyone looked up, startled out of their thoughts. "Feels like *deja vu* all over again." Mara answered the door as Toni piled in, followed closely by Jack and Larry.

"Hey, I brought Eric and Jim," said Molly, following them in, talking in her typical loud volume. "Eric explained the minutiae of battle to us on the way over. We're ready!"

"Because we've lost the will to live and are willing to fight our way out of taking him home."

"The battle's not here, is it? You have a lot of humans out there. I'd swear that dame with the red hair is one of us, but I checked. Human!"

"Jack, you came too." Leira recognized the owner of the Jackalope.

"Wouldn't miss it! Rhazdon's alive and a woman! Crazy ass trip! I shut down the bar, and we all piled into cars. There's more coming. It looks like you're having a party."

"This one is going to be hard to get past the regulars at the bar. They'll think I left them out."

"We'll call it a family reunion. Celebration of Mara and Eireka coming home. As a matter of fact, let's go have a beer with them. Introduce ourselves." Toni was already headed back out the door.

Leira whispered to Correk. "Is this a good idea? When worlds collide. Kaboom…" She held out her hands, pulling them apart.

"Probably not, but they're already headed out there. If you haven't noticed, we keep doing things that, if we thought about it, we'd realize are impossible and shouldn't work. Should never work even with magic. We're about to try again. Let's go have a beer with everyone who thinks of themselves as your family. Holidays are going to be very busy for you. That eating holiday, Thanksgiving, how did you celebrate it last year?"

"With Estelle at the bar eating creamed turkey over rice and a beer with a little cigarette ash mixed in. It was a slow year." She followed Correk out the door but turned back to the troll. "You good here?"

The troll smiled and shrugged.

"You ready for what's coming?"

The troll let out a soft trill and flexed the muscles in his arms.

"In case there's no time later I want to tell you something. I'm glad you're here. I know you had to choose to follow me through that portal. I'll bet you didn't expect so much danger. Regrets?"

The troll let out a cackle. "No regrets at all," he said. "I know a winner when I see one."

Leira's eyes filled with tears. "You little shit, you can talk." She smiled through the tears, determined to tell him. "Don't take too many risks tonight, okay? I know you can grow to be big and scary, but you don't have to prove anything."

"Life is risk, Leira," he chirped. "If you don't take the risks when they appear, you never really live." He waved at her, smiling and grabbed the remote. "Yumfuck!"

Leira gave him a crooked smile and wiped her face on her sleeve as she softly shut the door. "Love that little shit," she whispered.

"Leira!" The regulars all lifted their glasses calling out her name.

"You brought the party!" Kimberly smiled and got up from her seat to hug Leira. Estelle was on her riser opening bottles and stacking them in front of people before they could order, a cigarette dangling from her mouth. All of them were wearing royal blue shirts with the name, *The Ice Cold Pitchers* on the back.

"We won the pre-seasoner!" Mike's face was flushed with excitement.

"Nice place!" Toni grabbed a Shiner Bock and passed it over to Larry.

"I hit a double." Paul picked up four beers at once, passing them around to the others.

Estelle took out her cigarette and blew out a perfect smoke ring and smiled. "We do alright."

"Should we order nachos?" Craig waved at Estelle.

Mara took a long swig from her beer. "We can only stay for one beer. We have a…"

Leira cut off Mara before she could finish. "Work party. Can't say more than that."

"Good call," whispered Correk. "You're catching on. They're all family."

"We get it," said Scott, winking. "Paranormal secret stuff."

"Where's that cute Alan Cohen?" asked Mitzi. "Will he be at the party?"

"Wouldn't have it any other way." Alan Cohen came up behind

Leira followed by the agents, Mark and Gail from her team. "Now this is a party." Mitzi and Janice both tried to hand him a beer.

She looked up just in time to see Hagan barreling through the door from the restaurant.

Estelle poured two fingers of bourbon and slid it toward Hagan as he got close to the bar and he picked it up, drinking them back in a long gulp.

"One second." Leira held up her hand to Alan and went around him to the end of the bar.

"Hagan, I was going to tell you."

"After the show, apparently. Nice way to treat a partner."

"This didn't seem work related."

"Is it magical shit on Earth?" He shook his head, his eyes wide. "Seems like the job description I was given. You ever pull something like this again and I'll..." he shook his head. "I don't know what I'll do but it'll be something. Look kid, you don't protect me from jack shit. I signed up for this. My choice. Thank goodness the general has a little more common sense and knew to send in everything you got."

"Everything?"

"Yeah, those two wacky Witches are on their way. They said they'll meet us at the rock. They're sounding the alarm at some place called Hilldale. Said you'd understand. More recruits I take it. Rhazdon sure knows how to pull people together. You know, Lois and Patsy are good assets, I'll tell you. Can wield a wand." Hagan grew serious. "Nobody is standing down for this one. Too much is at risk. I like my way of life. A yard I hate to mow, a wife I love, the occasional fried food I have to fight a troll to keep. It's a good life. No one gets to take that from me without a fight. Here you go..." He pushed his glass toward Estelle as she went by refilling it, barely slowing down, smoke circling her red bouffant.

"I like her, she's got style."

"She has that effect on the good guys and scares the shit out of everybody else."

Hagan chuckled. "Maybe she should stare down this Rhazdon. Is the tiny guy coming? Of course he is. How about I go get him and we get this show on the road."

Leira felt another swirl of darkness surround her, tugging at her even harder. "No time like the present. Seems they're ready for us."

"We gotta go people!" Hagan put two fingers in his mouth and gave a sharp whistle. A groan went up from the regulars and there were promises to come back and spend more time. Everyone took their turn hugging Leira while Hagan slipped away to the guest house and collected the troll.

"Come back real soon!" Mitzi waved and blew a kiss as Leira went through the gate. She smiled and waved back.

"Can my mother and grandmother ride with you?" She looked at the large SUV parked behind her Mustang.

Alan nodded, "Of course."

"Leira, you go with them. Go with your team," said her mother, pushing her in the small of her back. "We'll squeeze in the Mustang. Hagan will drive us."

"At last! Throw me the keys, kid! Good omen for me already." Hagan held out his hands.

Leira whispered to her mother. "Really? Right now? You're thinking about finding me a man."

"You have to grab opportunities when they appear, and you don't seem to have many quiet moments anyway. Go or I'll start telling stories about you from when you were a baby."

Correk smiled. "See you there, Cousin."

"You too, okay. I see how it is. Fine."

"You have your PDA jacket with you? I brought mine." Hagan went and got it out of his car, jogging back.

"Not official, not really. Not going to wear it this time. Fine, let's go."

"You can sit up front with me." Alan hit the button to unlock the door. "We'll lead the caravan."

"My mother has plans for you."

"Most mothers do when they meet me. I'm very charming."

"And calm under the circumstances."

"Doesn't pay to worry. I'm trained, I'm briefed and I'm ready. Now, in this very moment, my goal is to enjoy every second. That way…"

Leira got in the car and shut the door, watching him walk around. The other agents piled into the back. She looked over her shoulder at all the people piling into cars and minivans and trucks and felt a tightness in her chest. *One magical creature threatens all of this. Please let me be ready… if it's the last good thing I do.*

CHAPTER TWENTY-SEVEN

The parking lot was already full when they got there with cars that had license plates from all over the country. Alan found a space under some trees by the road near the exit. "I like to have my getaway car pointing out at times like this." He smiled and got out of the car. *Enjoy every minute for as long as you can.*

They gathered in the parking lot as a hush came over the crowd. They could hear the murmur of voices from just over the ridge on the high plateau. All the magical beings in the group could feel the hum of the collective dark energy that was amassed not far from where they were standing.

The troll climbed down from Hagan's shoulder and ran to Leira as she bent down and scooped him up, putting him on her shoulder. "Look out for Hagan, tonight, okay?"

Correk came and stood by her side. "Are you ready?" He gave her hand a squeeze.

"I thought Turner Underwood would be here." She looked over the heads of the crowd.

"He must have his reasons. You're ready. Trust the energy and let it lead, even when your instincts tell you to take back your will... trust."

"The fight starts here and now. We take it to them." Leira centered herself and put out an intention to let the energy stop Rhazdon by any means necessary. *Hollow bone.* Her arms lit up with fiery symbols reading out information, changing shape as rapidly as they appeared.

Her eyes glowed as she let the magic flow through her, gathering in intensity. She let it lead, breathing evenly remembering what Turner taught her, following behind the energy. *Make space for it.* She walked forward, surrounded by her friends and family as they made their way up the side of Enchanted Rock.

The magic spread out, filling the air, rolling over the giant crystal. The magic helped Leira see Rhazdon standing on top of the rock before she got there. The tentacles on Rhazdon's head turning in one motion as Rhazdon looked in the direction of the approaching magic, smiling. "At last," she whispered into the stream. "A worthy opponent… or ally. It's not too late to join me."

Rhazdon was surrounded by Witches and Wizards with wands at the ready, determined to stay standing.

Leira resisted the urge to respond. *It's just bait. Rhazdon wants me to tell the magic what to do. Limit the power.* She focused on her breathing, looking in every direction inside the magic, even as she came to the top of the crystal kemana.

The magic was giving her a view in every direction, all at once. She felt a rush of wind through her chest and stopped at the edge of the crystal, finally facing Rhazdon as Correk joined her.

"I knew your grandfather." Rhazdon pointed at Correk, teasing him. "He fought well. Not well enough but better than I expected. Too bad about dear old dad too. Two Elves cut down in their prime."

Leira felt his anger and hesitated, wanting to grab him by the arm, but she heard Turner Underwood's voice in her head. *Stay the course, focus.*

The magic poured over the rocks, gaining speed, intertwining with the darkness surrounding Rhazdon, weaving itself into the black and shimmering mist.

Suddenly, Rhazdon's face took on a confused look, and she lifted her arms only to be yanked off her feet.

"Strike!" Mara yelled the order, sending out fireballs aimed at the Witches in the back of the crowd behind Rhazdon. They wouldn't be able to easily return fire without hitting their own comrades. Larry, Jack and Molly touched each other's shoulder, combining their energy sending out a golden line of barbed wire, wrapping it around the ankles of approaching Witches and hurling them off the side of the rock.

Alan gave the signal to Gail and Mark to move down off the rock and flank the witches and wizards. "Use lethal force. Don't take chances. If they so much as look at you, shoot."

The troll dropped off Leira's shoulder and ran between every-one's feet to Hagan, growing in size till he towered over everyone and let out a deafening roar. He advanced on the rock, his arms outstretched batting people off the rock with a swipe as more came clambering up to replace them.

"There must be hundreds!" Hagan followed just to the troll's right, shooting anyone who came close, but the bullets veered off into the horizon. "Not good," he muttered, still trying to get off a good shot. He reloaded as quickly as he could.

Rhazdon picked herself up off the ground, the smile gone from her face, standing with her legs far apart, leaning forward with her arms outstretched. "Enough!"

Leira felt the dark magic take on a sharp edge cutting through her energy. The pain cut into the middle of her body. The old scar ached as it glowed red. She gritted her teeth, the pain pushing into every part of her body. *No matter what, don't give into the urge to tell the magic what to do. Keep the intention.*

The darkness pushed at her, tearing at her from the inside. *I can't hold on much longer.*

A fireball shot by her, close to her shoulder making her see small dots of light in front of her eyes. She glanced over, her eyes almost shut from the searing pain and saw Correk fall back. *No!*

Leira tried to reach for him, interrupting the flow of magic through her and felt the dark magic slam into her chest. It threw her against the rock, knocking the wind out of her. She looked over the edge of Enchanted Rock in time to see Yumfuck steadily marching backward, defending the magical beings behind him, his fur singed in places.

None of us will make it. I failed. Turner I failed. She rolled to her side, determined to rise. *If I die, I'll do it standing on my feet.* It felt as if her bones were breaking under the weight of the dark magic.

She saw Rhazdon advancing on her mother, already assured of victory over Leira. Eireka stood in front of Mara as she passed energy through her daughter. Eireka stumbled backward, teetering on the edge of Enchanted Rock, and looked at the thirty-foot drop to the rocks below.

Leira got to her knees, nearly blinded with the pain. *I will rise. I can do this.* She screamed out in pain just as her mother started to fall.

A scream came out of Leira she didn't know she could do, rising from her depths. *I am tired of losing. Not again!*

Just as Eireka fell backward, a blue wave of magic encircled her, lifting her back to her feet.

Rhazdon whipped around, surprised. Queen Saria stood at the far end of Enchanted Rock, the king by her side.

Climbing just over the top of the rock came Patty and Lois, helping each other to the top. Behind them an army of Kilomea and Light Elves and Gnomes were fighting their way to the top. All of Hilldale was climbing onto the plateau. They were battling their way from the entrance to Hilldale, cutting off the dark Witches and Wizards, flanking them.

Leira felt the tears on her face watching the Jersey Willens come scurrying into view followed by dozens of their cousins.

"You can do this." She felt a heavy hand on her shoulder and heard the tapping of a cane. "Get up and let the energy help you. This was your lesson to learn. Magic isn't about what you can do. It's what we can all do together. Come on, let's get the fucking bitch. She's getting on my last nerve." Turner Underwood put out his hand and helped Leira to her feet.

"I thought you weren't coming."

"I'm the Fixer, kid. I always arrive at the moment I'm needed. It's a hard and fast rule."

Leira looked back at Correk's still body and wanted to go to him but Turner pulled her away. "Not yet. Finish this. Focus." She took a step and almost fell again. Her left leg was broken and there were cuts all over her body. "Focus."

She limped to the queen's side, pain shooting up her leg with every step. She was doing her best to keep most of her weight on her right leg.

Mara quickly pulled Eireka back onto the rock, holding her tight as Rhazdon turned to face the queen.

"You're no match," Rhazdon sneered.

Queen Saria took a long look at Rhazdon, taking in everything about her. "You killed my son. You banished my father-in-law to an unforgiving place." She said every word coolly and evenly. All the anger was drained out of her. "If there was ever anything good about you, any sanity in your cause your twisted magic has drained it out of you." The queen swallowed as her voice caught, tears in her eyes. "It's a hard thing to find out, isn't it Rhazdon. You are alone in this world. For eight hundred years no one has wanted to touch you, know you, comfort you."

Rhazdon raised her arm in anger at the words, ready to send a fatal blow to the queen.

"Do you know what happens when you spend that much time listening to your own bullshit?" The queen raised her hands for the last battle. "You forget a very basic rule about all of life.

Oriceran or Earth. Love trumps everything." She looked at Leira, tears on her face. "Ready?"

"Yeah, I am. Together." It started in the back, down on the grounds behind the plateau. Every creature touched the being closest to them, sharing the energy, passing it through until it reached the queen. Hundreds of them all connected by one source.

The queen smiled at Leira, her eyes glowing brightly, and she reached out and touched Leira as her entire body began to glow.

Turner Underwood stood just behind the king. "Let us all go out there with you."

Leira faced Rhazdon, tasting blood in her mouth and raised her shaking arms, burn marks etched across them. "For Correk," she whispered, "my family. With honor and to the end." She gasped, startled as the energy lifted her off her feet, passing through her as it swam out toward Rhazdon, enveloping the Atlantean, suffocating the darkness, sapping her energy.

Rhazdon's eyes widened as she slowly began to age. She looked at her hands as the skin grew looser and dark spots appeared and screamed in rage. "No! No! No!"

Leira limped slowly toward her, inching her way pulling away from the queen, even as the connection remained.

She stopped right in front of Rhazdon and looked her in the eyes as she reached up and ripped the necklace from her and held it aloft. "Mine hag."

Rhazdon recoiled covering her face with her hands.

The few remaining dark witches and wizards abandoned their posts and fled, falling as they ran away. Rhazdon grabbed on to a wizard as he ran past her, her tentacles shriveling on her head as he helped her off the plateau. Leira let her go. *I hope she lives for a hundred more lonely years.*

Slowly, the magic eased and Leira dragged herself slowly to Correk's side and fell to her knees, quickly running her hands over his body searching for a sign of life. "I don't even know what a fucking sign of life would be in a Light Elf. Wait! There! There!"

"Out of my way kid. It's my turn. If there's a flicker, I'll give the spark." Turner Underwood placed his large hands over Correk's chest, symbols lighting up on his skin.

Leira read them as fast as she could but some of them, she had never seen before. She looked up at Turner's face. "There's something different about you."

"So I've been told, kid."

Correk stirred, taking in a sudden rush of breath. "Don't move, Correk. You took more than one direct hit. A rather sturdy fellow, though."

Leira threw herself on top of Correk, hugging him, still clutching the necklace.

"Not recommended but, okay. We'll play it your way this time." Turner pulled himself to his feet, leaning on his cane. "Looks like we lost some good people."

Leira looked up, scanning the rock and saw Toni kneeling, running her hands over a body, sobbing. "Larry! Larry!"

"Too late for that one." Turner shook his head.

The rock was littered with bodies from both sides. The magical beings from Hilldale were already collecting the dead, carrying them back toward the entrance.

"They'll give everyone a proper burial out of sight from the humans. It'll give everyone the chance to celebrate their lives and grieve their dead without having to lie about any of it."

A Kilomea picked up Larry and cradled his lifeless body while Toni hung onto his hand and sobbed.

The Jersey Willen keened as other Willens helped carry his grandmother off Enchanted Rock. "I've never seen a Willen fight like that for anyone but another Willen. You matter to these people," said the queen.

Leira looked around at the destruction started by the theft of a necklace. She held out her arm and opened her hand.

"This rightfully belongs to you and at long last I'm grateful to be able to finally give it back to you. Prince Rolim's necklace."

The queen smiled softly and carefully picked up the necklace slowly bringing it to her chest, feeling the energy from her son, once again. "Thank you, for everything."

"I took on your case and said I would solve it." Leira gave a crooked smile. "Now, it's done." She hobbled toward her mother and grandmother, wincing with each step, determined to look over the side, afraid of what she would see. *Please be alright.*

Scrambling up the side was the five-inch troll, rushing back to her side. Leira bent down, crying out in pain and scooped up the troll, putting him back on her shoulder. "Yumfuck!"

"Show me where Hagan is. Did he…"

The troll pointed at Hagan reading a Wizard his rights, his face beet red and a burn mark that parted his hair right down the middle. Alan Cohen was sitting on a rock as Gail made him a makeshift sling. He looked up and waved to Leira as the darkness finally came over her and she fell backward against the rock, hitting her head.

Leira sat up in her hospital bed, her leg in a cast as Hagan told the story again to anyone in the room who would listen. "Most amazing thing I ever saw!"

Eireka smiled and brushed the hair off Leira's forehead. "Correk will be back soon enough. It was the right thing to do, sending him home to Oriceran. He needed help that doctors here can't give him. Magical help. He came close to not making it."

"It's already been a week. I miss the sound of him eating Cheetos."

Eireka smiled and kissed the top of her daughter's head. "Focus on getting better. You all have a lot of adventures left. The general has already checked on you a few times. I think he's trying to be polite but is itching to send you somewhere. He wouldn't tell me."

"Who are those flowers from?"

Eireka pulled out the card. "Alan Cohen and the team. Hmmmm."

"Still not a good time, Mom." Leira threw a plastic spoon in Hagan's direction to get his attention. "Aren't you supposed to be at an anniversary dinner with Rose?"

"Yeah, sure, I gotta go. Why do you think I'm in this monkey suit? I have the best bride ever. She insisted I come see you first, and she's meeting me at the restaurant. Love that woman. How she puts up with all of me, I don't know. Alright, I'm outta here. I'll stop by tomorrow. Maybe this time I'll bring you doughnuts. Tell you the rest of what you missed. The memorial they had at the Jackalope for Larry was very moving. They said they'd do it again when you're up to it so you can say your goodbyes too. Oh, and I can tell you about Lois. Geez, that lady! There were some good skirmishes down below. Wands slicing through the air!" Hagan was still talking as he wandered out of the room.

Leira smiled a crooked smile as she watched him go. *I think I can.* She shut her eyes and rested her head back against the pillow, taking a deep breath, centering herself as the magic crept inside of her, flowing out as she set an intention.

Hagan was surprised when every light he got to was green and a parking space opened up just in front of the restaurant. A man with a pushcart rolled past Hagan on his way inside with the last few roses for sale.

Rose was already waiting at the table, smiling at Hagan as he came in holding the flowers.

"Wow, the best table. Must have taken one look at my beautiful bride and put you right here, front and center. Good thing I wasn't here yet!"

Rose laughed and took the flowers. "They gave us champagne! Can you believe it?"

"Your favorite, too. How did we ever get so lucky?"

"Must be magic," said Rose. "Happy twenty-five years of playing with you. I wouldn't have it any other way."

Wolfstan Humphrey sat with his back to the bar, leaning with one elbow. He wanted a clear view of the door that was up a few steps from where he sat.

"Did you bring it?" he asked, looking the scruffy man up and down. *Shops at Target, playing at being a bad guy.*

The undercover FBI agent held his hand open to reveal the artifact. "I told you I was good for it. You bring the money?"

Wolfstan reached into his pocket and pulled out an envelope, dropping it into the agent's hand as he exchanged it for his prize. *Another piece of the puzzle.*

Nearby, agents rose from their tables, guns drawn and aimed at Wolfstan. The Light Elf smiled and gave a wink, pulling the shadows around him, snatching the envelope. His arm was the last thing to disappear.

The undercover agent lunged forward with his arms out, swinging, but came up holding nothing. "What the fuck just happened? We had him dead to rights." He ran up the few stairs, scanning the small bar, and pushed through the door out onto the street. Nothing.

"Sonofabitch. Somebody call General Anderson. Let him know, mission failure."

The story is far from over. Leira's adventure continues in
DEALING IN MAGIC.

Please turn the page to read a Bonus Short Story, *Christmas at Estelle's.*

CHRISTMAS AT ESTELLE'S

CHAPTER ONE

L eira Berens sat on her couch with her left leg propped up on pillows, sidelined from work at the Paranormal Defense Force. There was a stiff white plaster cast on her leg, stretching past her knee and she was under doctor's orders to take it easy for at least another week. Leira's partner at the PDF, Felix Hagan suggested she get a nice red cast or something in green to match the Mustang. "You could do both and you'd be your own Christmas ornament." Leira had given him a determined dead fish look and he dropped it. To start with, Leira didn't do *taking it easy* very well.

She was already missing Correk, wondering if he was alright and Hagan knew not to push things. Not this time. The battle with Rhazdon was too close and there were losses this time. Leira winced at the memory of her mother almost falling over the cliff.

The troll was sitting on her stomach and was busy pouring Pop Rocks into his mouth until his cheeks were stretched out as far as they would go. He opened his mouth and looked at Leira as the candy ricocheted around just behind his sharp little teeth, making a racket. He was doing his best to entertain her.

Her mother, Eireka came out of the kitchen and let out a laugh watching Yumfuck's head jiggle from the momentum of the candy.

Eireka had moved back into the guest house for the time being and was doing her best to take care of Leira and let her stream of swearing roll past when she was helping her get up off the couch. A flash of pain would go across Leira's face as she clenched her teeth, but she didn't complain. Not if you didn't count the string of motherfuckers or sons of bitches.

Eireka looked at her daughter as Leira leaned back and stared at the fading orange, circular stains on the ceiling. Eireka followed her line of sight and gave a *tsk* at the stains. *All those years alone has made you stoic,* thought Eireka, a pang in her heart. She looked around at the living room, at the couch and the red velvet chair. "It's already the holidays and there's not a single Christmas decoration to be found. Where's that old box of ornaments? I haven't seen some of those in years."

"Mom... leave it alone."

Eireka paused, watching Leira. "I know you miss him."

Leira looked up at her mother. "Correk, his name is Correk." She said his name softly. "Has there been any word?"

"Not yet. He was alive after the battle with Rhazdon and when they took him back through the portal. That's all we know for now but with all the magic on Oriceran..." Her voice faded as she let the thought go. "What about a wreath for the door?"

Leira took a long look at her mother and her face softened. "I know this is your first Christmas since you were released." Leira did her best to smile. "Sure, why not? Let's do a wreath. What about one with pine branches and a large red bow? We'll go classic." She shifted on the couch and felt a rolling ache mixed with an itch that had been bothering her for days, deep inside the cast.

She shut her eyes to focus and pulled in enough magic to run a thin stream through her body, soothing the broken bone in her leg. Eireka saw the symbols rolling slowly across Leira's arm and let out a deep breath, sending out her own energy to join her daughter's, soothing the ache deep inside Leira's bones. Leira let out a satisfied sigh as the magic swirled around the itch just behind her knee. Her mother's energy gave her an unfamiliar comfort.

The energy sensed something was wrong and surged, lunging forward as it sought out the break in her bones to heal it. Eireka sensed the presence of the stronger light and pulled back. "Turner Underwood was pretty clear about that, young lady."

"Well, now I don't have to wonder what you would have sounded like during my teenage years." Leira let the magic subside and glanced up at her mother. "Making up for lost time?" She gave her a crooked smile. "I won't try to fix the leg with magic. Turner said he wasn't sure it would heal correctly if I did that and I'm not going to take the chance. Not on that at least. I can be a little patient." She held up two fingers just inches apart.

"A little," chirped the troll. "Able to tolerate waiting... a little." He poured more Pop Rocks into his mouth.

"Where did you get those?" asked Leira, as the troll offered her some. Leira held out her hand and poured some into her mouth, feeling the fizz and pop. Her mouth puckered from the sour candy.

"Nana got those for him, of course. I left your grandmother on her own at our place. The furniture is rearranged by now, for sure and there's an off chance she's using that deck of cards to read the neighbors' fortunes. Probably cheating with a little magic, too." Eireka saw the look on her daughter's face.

"Sometimes I forget you were a detective. I missed most of that. Don't worry, I don't think she'd charge anyone for their so-called reading. I think she just likes watching their faces when she tells them a few things that she shouldn't know."

"Nana told me that she met some of their dead relatives when she was in the world in between and is passing along messages," said Leira. "She can't knock on a door and say, hey I met your

Uncle Bob. He said the earring you lost rolled behind the dresser and he forgot about some money that's in an account at a bank in Wichita. The readings are her cover. Nana is clever."

"You get that from her. Very resourceful. Doesn't hurt that she's using a deck of cards that was made on Oriceran and has a little magic stored in them."

Yumfuck looked up surprised from where he was sitting on Leira's stomach.

"That's right, I know about the cards." Eireka arched an eyebrow as she smiled. "Mom thinks she's sly. Best to let her keep on thinking it even if she's going to Oriceran again. I don't know everything she's up to or if you're involved...." She pointed at the troll who clamped his mouth shut and reopened it just as fast with another loud rattling of exploding candy. "But secrets always have a way of coming out, my furry friend."

"Nana's traveling through portals again. Even after the world in between. Now, that's ballsy."

There was a loud, sharp knock at the door and Eireka went to answer it, ignoring the insistent "No," from Leira.

Eireka stopped at the door and waited, looking back at the troll who reluctantly slid off Leira's belly and walked slowly into the bedroom, shutting the door as the knocking resumed. "He's got the guilt thing down cold," whispered Eireka. She opened the door wide to find most of the regulars standing in a line at the door. "Hi guys, must be lunchtime. Come on in." She stepped aside to let Craig and Scott pass by her.

The regulars had been streaming in and out of the guest house located behind Estelle's bar, since Leira was released from the hospital a few days ago. They came tramping in as an orderly group, leaving casseroles or beer and staying just long enough to sign her cast or chat for a moment.

Estelle was always keeping a watchful eye from the patio, a cigarette held firmly between her lips as the smoke swirled around her red bouffant. People entered in groups of four and after a few minutes were expected to move it along while everyone else waited just outside the door. Eireka smiled and glanced over at Estelle, giving her a wave. Estelle answered with a nod and blew out a long trail of smoke, staying right where she was, a hand on a bony hip.

Estelle had only visited once, late at night after the bar was empty, giving a soft tap to the door. Leira had still been awake, staring at the ceiling again and was grateful for the distraction. "Come in." She could smell the cigarette smoke even through the closed door. It was Estelle's calling card.

Estelle came walking in and quietly got a chair from the kitchen without saying a word. Leira was used to the intrusions from Estelle over the years when Leira was on her own. She seemed to always know when to barge in and when to keep her distance.

Estelle pulled the chair up close to the couch and sat down on the edge, leaning close in the darkness to get a better look at Leira. "How you doin' kid?" She made a point of not taking a drag on the lit cigarette. A small concession to being inside the guest house.

Leira looked just over Estelle's shoulder and saw the troll standing on the kitchen counter, peering around the door frame. His pale fur was silvery in the moonlight coming in from the windows. He pulled back, into the shadows as Leira focused back on Estelle.

"My brain thinks I can get up and go do something, but the body is a little more reluctant," Leira finally said. She pushed herself up onto her elbows, giving a low grunt, careful not to wake her mother. The troll peeked round again, this time holding a large piece of a Pop Tart between his paws, quietly nibbling at the edges. Leira made herself look over at Estelle.

"Sounds about right." Estelle's voice was low and gravelly. Her normal tone. "That itchy brain of yours will make you restless but it'll also get you off that couch a dang bit faster." Estelle sat back, her head tilted to the side as she scrutinized Leira. "You'll be okay. You've got some good Texas dirt in you."

Leira looked over at Estelle. "Don't you mean on me?"

"No, baby girl. Everybody's got to eat a peck of dirt before they die. Good for you. And if you're lucky enough to be from Texas, then you get that good Texas dirt in your blood. Something about the soil around here... if you get knocked down, you get twice as determined to get back up again and show everybody a thing or two."

Estelle leaned in closer to Leira till Leira could smell the mixture of Shalamar and cigarettes. It was oddly comforting to her after four years in the guest house. Made her feel rooted to the world. *I need that.*

The image of Correk being carried off the battlefield flitted through her mind and she felt a strong wince in her leg, flinching as she pulled back from Estelle. They had explained the broken leg as an accident running down a bad guy off his meds. Correk's absence was told as an assignment for the Feds that they weren't allowed to talk about in any detail. He wouldn't be back for a while.

Estelle watched the jerk of pain pass through Leira's body and sat back, her thin red lips firmly pressed together. "Listen here to these instructions. You don't do it alone," she said, finally. "I know you won't ask for a lot of help. I get that and I admire it. You got a lot of giddyup in you. But it's also true that a lot of people see you as family around here and they'll be stomping through here in no time to check on you and show a little kindness. Let 'em. People find their own ways to tell you they love you, but you have to be willing to hear it. It's a gift right back to them, too." She spit out the last words with emphasis, nodding her head hard and almost biting the cigarette in two.

"Now, let me sign that dang cast." Estelle had pulled out a black marker and made an oversized E followed by the rest of her name in a swirl. She penned her name right on top of Leira's knee with a nice smudge where a few cigarette ashes had dropped. "There you go, much better." She had slapped her thighs with satisfaction, more ashes dropping to the floor.

Leira had let herself relax back into the pillows without answering her, drifting off before she could say anything else. When she opened her eyes again it was morning and Estelle was gone. *Still not sure she's entirely human.*

Since then, Estelle had been both encouraging the regulars to stop by and monitoring their visits.

The regulars knew not to linger in Leira's small living room, or they'd be on Estelle's list. If they did, they'd earn a month's worth of side eye through the smoky haze that could chill someone to the bone. That and slow service on beers. Craig and Scott hustled in and signed their names, gave a few well wishes as Craig set down a six pack of Shiner Bock. "I owed you a few beers," he said, smiling as they made a quick retreat back to the bar. The cast was becoming covered in signatures. Cassidy pulled out a few markers in different colors and drew holly leaves and berries right next to her name.

Mike made a last-minute suggestion that they could help Leira to the bar and prop her up there as Mitzi and Kimberly shook their heads. But he plowed ahead until a low growl emerged from Estelle outside.

"That was a first," he muttered quietly as he patted Leira on the shoulder, his eyes wide. He quickly signed his name and walked past Estelle who blew a large, smoky O over his head as he passed.

"Damn, it's like she was marking him as he went by," said Craig, a chill going down his spine. Once the last of the regulars were firmly ensconced at the bar again and Eireka shut the door, the troll emerged from the bedroom, scrambling up the side of the couch and perching himself on the cast. He dangled his legs over the edge and let out a soft trill as he picked up a pen Cassidy had forgotten and covered his paw in ink, pressing down, leaving a tiny imprint.

"A Yumfuck Christmas," trilled the troll.

"That would involve a lot of eating." Leira plucked the troll off her cast and held him in the palm of her hand. "Your first Christmas too. I guess I can do a better job of at least not getting in the way of everyone else's ho ho ho."

"Fa ra ra ra ra." The troll smiled.

Leira looked at the troll and smiled. "My favorite movie of all time, no matter what time of year. A Christmas Story. Good one Yumfuck." She held him closer to her face. "No parties, though. Deal?"

"Deal." He crossed his paws behind his back and smiled at Leira.

CHAPTER TWO

The regulars stepped away from Leira's door and made their way over to their favorite spots at the long outdoor bar on the other side of the patio. They sat at the bar chattering about work and the mid-winter bowling season as Estelle walked around to the back of the bar. Everyone was making a point of not looking back toward the guest house. Estelle got up on her stool and wiped down the bar top as a couple tried to get her attention. "No, honey, not yet. Finish your conversation." She cocked her head as if she heard something interesting inside and hopped down, walking into the bar and taking a sharp turn toward the kitchen past the large pink Christmas tree decorated in white and blue ornaments. The couple looked at each other and looked around as Mitzi smiled back at them.

"I swear she's got the hearing of a bat," said Paul.

"Wait a minute till we're sure she's really gone." Craig leaned to the left on his stool, trying to get a better look inside. "No sign of her."

"That Pepto Bismol tree. You think that's ironic?"

"It's retro."

"She's out of sight in the kitchen. She can't hear us or see us."

"I mean, I get the white lights everywhere. Half of them she keeps up year round. Kind of makes sense."

"Should we bring presents. Maybe do a Chinese gift exchange? Or a Secret Santa."

"There's an elf on the shelf inside that moves around every night."

"No kidding..."

"No Secret Santa. We're doing this for Leira. Brighten up her place. Brighten up Leira. Stay on mission."

"Have you seen the large balls of light on the fence out front? Estelle has a vision. That pink tree is cool."

"Let's hurry up and finish before Estelle gets back. Someone has to figure out when Leira's place will be empty."

"Or we just storm the place and set up right in front of her, ignoring her swearing."

"I don't even hear it anymore. She says, motherfucker, and I say, fine, how are you."

"You think Correk might make it back in time for a party?"

"Not likely. They made it sound like he was undercover somewhere."

"I'll bring a baked brie and ginger snaps. Everybody always loves it."

"How does a tall drink of water like that go unnoticed?"

"Not unnoticed. Undercover. Put your tongue back in your head, Mitzi. You look like Lemon."

"Estelle's got better things to do. She's all the way inside, not paying any attention to us. She can't hear us."

"Doesn't mean a thing." Kimberly's eyebrows shot up as someone came out the door to the patio, but it was just a couple of University of Texas students headed for the corn hole game. "You'd think we were a bunch of kids."

"That's just because we want to break the rules for once and do something for Leira. You saw that living room." Cassidy's eyes grew wider at the memory. "Not a lot of decoration on a regular day."

Mike leaned across the bar, keeping an eye on the windows and filled his glass from the tap. He sat back and drank down half, hiding the evidence. "Getting away with shit is half the fun."

"You always leave such a huge tip. What exactly are you getting away with?" Craig shook his head.

"This is Estelle's place and we are here by invitation. I'm risking banishment." He gulped down the last few swallows, not willing to risk it.

"To God knows where. You'd have to try one of the bars down the street and fight through the millennials. No beer is worth that."

"He likes to live on the edge."

"It's more like the edge of a butter knife."

"Fuck you, Craig and your little spreadsheets too."

"Don't insult a man's spreadsheet."

"Can we focus for just a second here on Leira? Men."

"I know what I'm going to get her for Christmas. A framed picture of us. Give her something to look at." Mitzi nodded her head, determined.

"Normally, doesn't matter. She's hardly ever there except to sleep but now Leira's stuck there for the duration. We should do something. Liven it up for her. Hang on, I'll make a spreadsheet." Craig pulled out his laptop.

Paul looked over his shoulder. "That's like your diary, isn't it? Your entire life in a spreadsheet. Is your sex life mapped out in there? No?"

"I'll get the tree," said Mike, eyeing the tap again.

"Don't do it, dude. Estelle can sense a disturbance in the force as small as a flea peeing. It's not worth it. You should take up freestyle rock climbing or parachuting instead. Less dangerous," said Scott.

"Get the tree from the lot over in front of the Whole Foods.

They have the nice, full ones." Mitzi broke off a piece of a cracker and opened her large purse. Her small dog, Lemon poked his head up as she fed him the cracker. "I can get the lights and some decorations. I wonder if Leira has any."

"Does anyone have an idea of when we'll do this? We have a snowball's chance in hell of talking Leira into it," said Kimberly. "It's gonna' have to be when she's out and that hasn't happened much lately."

"Her mom is there, and she likes us." Craig looked up from his laptop. He was busy typing in everyone's name and making different columns. "Who's bringing food?"

"I can make my famous chili," said Cassidy, raising her hand.

"I'll make cornbread." Mitzi broke off another piece of the cracker, feeding it to Lemon.

"You feed that dog regular dog food too, right?" Kimberly looked inside the large purse as Lemon looked up and let out a sharp bark.

"Craig make those empanadas you brought to the last potluck!" Mike started to lean over the bar as Estelle passed by the window and looked him dead in the eye. He froze and held her gaze, not sure what else to do. She squinted, pausing by the window before moving on to somewhere further inside the restaurant. "Felt like something passed over my grave." Mike's face was ashen.

Craig let out a laugh and clapped him on the shoulder. "We should tell the regulars from that other bar. What was it?"

"The Jackalope."

"That's right, that place. Make it a real party."

"I'll call them. I got Toni's number. Really liked her. There was something about her."

"First we have to figure out how to get in there to even decorate the place and then we have to grow large enough balls to throw the party and damn the consequences from Estelle." Scott held out his hand. "Come on, pile on. We're either all in or all out. Who's with me?"

"Fuck it, I'm in." Mitzi slapped her small, pudgy hand on top of Scott's as Craig put down his laptop and covered her hand completely with his large, leathery hand. The others, one by one quickly put their hands on top and quietly Mike said, "All for one..."

"And one for all..." they echoed back.

"What in the sam hill tarnation are you people doing out here? You didn't go start a team without me, did you?" Estelle was back on her stool behind the bar, pouring Mike a drink and shoving it in front of him in one fluid motion. He started and slid awkwardly off his stool, catching himself before he fell all the way to the floor.

"She always knows..." Cassidy whispered in his ear.

"Bat hearing," whispered Paul.

Estelle regarded all of them and put her fingers around her cigarette, taking in a long drag and letting the smoke out slowly. "You making plans for the holidays?"

Mitzi hummed the first few bars from the Exorcist under her breath.

"Dinner with the family."

"What he said." Craig slowly shut his computer and put it away as everyone went back to talking about the warm winter or watching the nearby corn hole game.

"Uh huh." Estelle let out a grunt and stepped down from her stool without taking her eyes off them. She waited a second and turned to go inside. A sly smile spread across her face, deepening the wrinkles around her mouth. "Bout time," she muttered just out of earshot, the cigarette bobbing in her mouth. "Party would be nice."

CHAPTER THREE

"Come on, I don't think the doctor meant for you to never leave that couch. It's been nearly a week. You've worn a pattern into the floor from here to the bathroom and back." Eireka stood over her daughter, her hands on her hips. Her boyfriend, Donald stood just behind her, waiting for directions from someone.

The troll stood on the back of the couch watching the movie, Ratatouille. He kept moving every time Eireka or Donald moved so he could get a better view of the screen. The movie was almost at his favorite part where the rat finally got to cook up a storm. The troll let out a contented sigh as Leira looked up at him. He looked back at her and raised his little paws. "Go on, go. Shoo, get outta here," he squeaked.

"Is that your Bronx accent?" Leira wet a finger and held it up in the air. "It's a cold day." Yumfuck let out a cackle.

"How can you tell from the couch." Eireka pressed her lips together.

"The blast of air that came in when you opened the door."

The door opened suddenly as Eireka looked at her daughter.

"Don't look at me. I didn't cause that one." Leira held up her hands in protest. "I'm in plaid, flannel pajama pants. I can't fit anything else over this giant thing. Bring the food to me."

Mara came bustling into the guest house, kicking the door shut behind her with her foot. "Sorry about that. The door got away from me. Why aren't you up yet? Get your ass off that couch. It's starting to become one with you. It's not an attractive look. Enough already." Mara sent out a stream of magic to Leira that rolled over her skin, tickling her arms and running across her belly, surrounding her in a warm embrace. "Let's try that new Greek place. You can prop your leg up just as easily there. Get up before I levitate you."

"Is that a thing?"

"Drag your ass and find out!" Mara smiled broadly and put out her hands like she was about to cast a spell.

Leira sat herself up higher and hesitated. "I want to see if you can do it." A crooked smile appeared on her face. Her hair stuck straight up in the back where she had been lying down. Mara waved an arm as her eyes lit up and the magic wove itself in a circular pattern underneath Leira's ass, slowly lifting her into a standing position. Leira grimaced from the pain of shifting but didn't resist. She knew it was time and guided her leg over the side.

Donald came alongside her as she threw her arm over his shoulder. He watched the golden and purple swirl of magic, mesmerized. "Can't say that isn't cool. You doing okay?"

"So far, so good. Nana, if you could do this all along..."

"I was waiting to pick my moment. Where's your crutches?"

The troll bounded off the couch and scrambled underneath, pulling out a crutch. He was covered in dust as he ran for the bathroom while everyone waited. There was the sound of something metallic hitting the floor followed by the troll yelling, "I'm fine, no worries." He finally appeared holding the crutch over his head, covered in baby powder, shaking off a fine silt with every step. Leira looked at him and let out a snort. "It never bothers him to be covered in all kinds of crap."

"You forget how strong the little booger is." Mara took the crutch from him and brushed off the top. "You done good. I'll bring you back some stuffed grape leaves." The troll let out a trill and climbed back onto the couch leaving a track of small white footprints.

"World's smallest yeti," said Donald, glancing over his shoulder. "I can help you out to the car. Hell, I can even carry you but that doesn't seem like it's really you. Ready to give the crutches a try?"

The troll let out a cackle and looked at Leira, winking. She gave him a dead fish look but he was already entranced by the movie again. She took the crutches and steadied herself. "Open the door for me. Once I get started, I want to just keep going." She put the crutches out in front and easily swung forward, ignoring the ache in her leg as she easily crossed the living room and out the door.

"Why that little fucker! She's been boondoggin us this entire time. You've been getting out!" Mara smiled and winked at the troll. "You kept her secret. I can respect that. Wondered how the crutch got into the bathroom on its own."

The troll lifted the edge of the cushion and showed the wrappers from the food trucks down the street.

"So this isn't her first outing. She just wanted to be alone for a while." Eireka arched an eyebrow and took off after her daughter. Donald followed closely behind as Leira easily made her way toward the gate.

"Hard to keep a Berens woman down, especially when we get hungry. We'll be back when we're back." She waved to Yumfuck as she pulled the door shut behind her, not bothering to lock it.

The troll settled back on the couch and let out another contented sigh followed by a cackle. "A cooking rat! Too funny!"

CHAPTER FOUR

Mitzi saw Leira swinging easily across the patio on her crutches, maneuvering her way out of the gate, closely followed by everyone else. She couldn't believe her luck. Just when she thought she was going to have to enlist Estelle and confess everything the guest house was empty. Guests were all coming in a few hours whether Mitzi had pulled off her part of the plan, or not.

Her hands were shaking as she texted Craig and Mike, 'Coast is clear, bring the tree through the gate... Just this once. Tell the others to get a move on. We have two hours. Tops.'

"Estelle will pitch a royal fit but it has to be done. Can't very well drag a spruce through the middle of the bar." Mitzi wrung her hands, watching the inside of the bar through the windows for signs of Estelle. The red bouffant made it easy to spot her through any crowd but it was nowhere to be seen. "I am just having one helluva lucky day today."

The door to the gate swung open and Mike came through carrying one end of the tree, closely followed by Scott with the other end. Cassidy and Kimberly were behind them carrying bags of decorations and food as Craig brought up the rear with a large crock pot.

"We are cooking with gas." Mitzi ran ahead to open the door to the guest house, keeping her eye on the bar. "Hurry, hurry." She waved frantically as she opened the door.

The troll looked up from the couch and saw the backside of Mitzi waving her arms. He dove behind the cushions just as she turned around to look inside the living room for a good place to put the tree. He pulled himself along under the cushions, his mouth open taking in old crumbs and lost popcorn kernels. "Yum!"

Mitzi startled and turned around again, looking in every direction. "Huh..."

She didn't have time to think about it as the tip of the tree poked her in the back. "Right over here!"

She got out of the way as Mike and Scott came barreling through with the tree, momentarily getting stuck. "Turn slightly to the left. No, the other left."

The troll came across a penny and bit down on it, tossing it aside as he kept going till he reached the arm of the sofa. He peeked out from the back of the cushion and waited till everyone was focused on steadying the tree. Mike and Paul were fussing with the tree stand as Scott held it steady and the women stood back a foot to see if it was straight. Yumfuck saw his chance and made a break for the bedroom.

Craig came back from the kitchen with a scowl. "I think Leira might have mice in here."

"For another day, Craig. We don't have much time. Help us get the lights on this thing."

"I'm gonna go see if Leira has any ornaments in this place. Remind her of her childhood. Well, the good parts anyway."

"Mitzi, stay out of her stuff. That wasn't part of the plan!"

Mitzi wasn't listening and even grabbed Cassidy by the arm, pulling her along with her to check closets. They ventured into the bedroom as the troll slid under a pillow and watched them dig around in the back of Leira's closet. "Jackpot! Help me pull this out." Mitzi and Cassidy dragged out a plastic bin as Kimberly came in to help them. "Look, there's a whole box of ornaments. I remember these glass ones from my childhood. They must be Mara's."

"Look at this one..." Kimberly pulled out an opaque blue glass ball with a thread of gold looped at the top. She slid the loop over her finger and held it up for the others to see as the light caught it, sending rays of light dancing over the walls. "That's beautiful," she said, breathless. Mitzi and Cassidy stopped what they were doing and stared at the dancing streams of light.

"Has to be one of the prettiest ornaments I've ever seen." Kimberly's mouth hung open and her eyes were wide. They were all hypnotized by the light.

"Shake a leg, ladies!" Craig knocked hard on the door, knocking the women out of their reverie.

"What? Oh, right. Two hours! Get a move on!"

"Pretty sure that was you frozen like a statue. What's that you have there?"

"An ornament I found in Leira's closet buried in a box. It's a stunner."

"Let's put it near the colored lights on the tree. Right in the center!"

"I think it's some kind of prism. Imagine what that'll look like with all the different colors."

Yumfuck slid out from under the pillow and went to the closet, looking in at the box that was filled with some of Mara's old clothes from before her time in the world in between, along with a few things from Oriceran.

"Interesting." The troll went to the bureau and carefully slid open the bottom drawer, hanging off the knob, his toes barely touching the ground. He reached in and pulled out a disposable phone that Mara had given him, just in case. He thought about texting Mara to let her know but hesitated. He went to the edge of the door and peeked around, watching everyone laughing and jostling each other as they decorated the tree. "Nah," he whispered, a smile on his face.

Instead he punched in a different number and sent a text. *'Party over here. Bring donuts. Yumfuck.'*

He went back to his corner by the door and watched the room transform as garlands were hung along the walls and mistletoe hung near the front door. The troll smiled and smacked his lips together. He watched Mitzi hang the blue glass ornament on the tree right in the front and made a round 'O' with his mouth. "Very interesting. Everybody will get their party on."

CHAPTER FIVE

K imberly took a look around the room and smiled at what they had done. "Looks like Christmas threw up in here. Perfect!"

"Who's the kid sitting in Santa's lap?" Cassidy picked up one of the small gold frames lined up on the side table.

"That's my sister's kids. Thought it added a nice touch. I'll need to get those back later."

"Oh, I like the holly around the candles. That's a nice touch."

Mike lifted a slat on the blinds and peered through just in time to see the gate open. Leira elbowed it and pushed through, the others still chasing behind her. "She's here! Do we hide?"

"This isn't a surprise party!"

"Besides, all of us in her home will be enough of a surprise..."

"May we all live through it."

"She's got crutches so be ready to duck."

All of the regulars from Estelle's stood still, waiting for the door to open. Leira came barreling through, almost pitching herself into Scott and Craig.

"Surprise!" yelled Mitzi, holding out her arms.

Leira turned around like she was going to head back out the

door but Eireka and Mara were already behind her, blocking her exit. Don came in and looked around, his eyes widening. "You guys have been busy."

Leira turned around and around, balancing on the crutches as she looked at the decorations and the hopeful faces on all of these people she came to see as friends. As she turned, she saw the smiles on her mother and grandmother's faces and she thought about the last Christmas in this house.

It was empty. She looked over at her grandmother and mother. *I had no idea where you were, and I thought you were crazy.* The regulars were looking at her, smiling but no one was coming any closer. *And I kept my distance from all of you. Estelle brought over that plate of warm turkey and sat with me while I ate it. That was it. I think I even got called in to work a homicide. Everyone looks like they're waiting for me to say something. Correk.*

His smiling face flashed in Leira's head. She heard his voice in her head, cracking a joke and reminding her that she was among friends and to take her hands off her gun. She smiled at the thought as her eyes glistened. *He would love this.*

"I love it," she shouted. She made her way over to the tree and hugged each one of them, doing her best to balance on the crutches and leaning into the hug.

"You love it? A hug! Okay, I can do that." Craig looked surprised as Mike gave a shrug and shook his head.

"I told you this was a good idea," said Kimberly as she nudged Mitzi in the ribs. Mitzi pulled a tissue out of her sleeve and wiped her eyes. "We should have done this sooner."

The knocks at the door started and didn't stop as the guests kept piling into the little guest house till they had to leave the door open. Everyone from the Jackalope came with Toni leading the charge carrying a platter of salami and mozzarella.

"I got the invite and left the bartender in charge tonight." Jack was smiling broadly as he carried in two cases of beer from Adelbert's Brewery. "How about I set these in the kitchen? There's more on the way."

"You know, I have beer." Estelle stood in the doorway as everyone froze. The smoke swirling up from her cigarette partially hid her face.

"I think I just peed a little." Mike did his best to steady himself putting a hand out against the wall.

"I could make diamonds right now," said Craig, clutching a handful of tinsel.

"Well, come on. Let's get this party started. Did somebody forget the music? Lucky for you people, ya'll have me." Estelle smiled as she squeezed one eye shut from the smoke and pushed a button on a remote control. The sound of Michael Bublé singing, *Santa Claus is Coming to Town* filled the patio. "Now, it's a party. Give me one of those beers, Jack."

"Estelle, you bring those wings?"

Jim and Molly did a slow waltz around the room. Don leaned in toward Eireka and whispered, "That looks like a pretty good idea." Eireka smiled and put out her hands as Don waltzed her outside to the patio. Mara followed them out and no one noticed as she made her way out the gate and down the block.

Leira made her way to the couch and slowly sat down as she watched everyone laughing and talking, the noise level picking up till it was hard to hear. Someone handed her a beer and she took a swig, smiling at the party she finally managed to throw in her house, even if she had nothing to do with any of it.

She glanced over at the tree and spotted the troll sitting among the branches tucked back against the trunk. She was about to go rescue him when she saw Hagan pushing his way into the party. He was carrying a stack of pink boxes from Voodoo Donuts.

Hagan made his way over to the couch and sat down as Craig relieved him of the boxes but not before Hagan reached in and pulled out a kruller.

"How'd you hear about this party?" Leira pulled off a piece of his kruller and popped it in her mouth.

"Yumfuck sent me a text. It was too strange to miss. Wasn't sure it wasn't a ploy to get me to bring donuts but as long as I get a few, win win. Besides, with you down there hasn't been a lot to do and Rose is pretty tired of seeing my mug around the house all day. Seemed like a good time for a visit. Where is the little guy? Keeping a low profile?"

"Sort of. Look closer at all the ornaments on the tree." Leira hooked a thumb in the direction of the tree.

Hagan peered more closely, squinting till he spotted the furry five-inch troll. "Think I can make his party a little better. Hang on." Hagan hoisted himself off the couch and went to stand near the tree, acting as if he was admiring the ornaments as he pushed a piece of the kruller onto the branch near the troll. He gave the troll a wink as Yumfuck blew him a kiss with his tiny paw and licked the piece of donut.

Hagan went and sat back down next to Leira.

"I think you've found a new best friend. Should I be worried?" Leira gave Hagan a crooked smile.

Hagan feigned surprise and pressed his hand against his chest. "Am I your best friend? Your life may not be what you hoped. Come on, we all know that tall, blonde and pointy is your best friend. I'm your favorite partner. No, no protests. That's the title I want. We catch the bad guys together." He leaned in closer and whispered, "Even the magical badasses." Hagan took a look around the party as his eyebrows went up. "You know, I've been to my share of parties in my day. Even Christmas ones that lend a certain amount of good cheer to them, but I don't think I've ever seen a friendlier bunch having such a good time and so early into the booze. You got a good vibe, Berens. I'm not surprised. It was buried underneath all that hard ass all these years. Nice to see it coming through." Toni passed through the living room, handing Hagan a beer as she did, waving at Leira.

"It's been quite a year." Hagan held up his bottle as Leira clinked hers against it.

"It's been quite a year, alright. What's amazing is we're almost all here to still talk about it."

"Amen to that." Hagan took a long drink from his beer as he remembered all the close calls that year. "Some epic battles and one very special family put back together. Helluva year."

Mara hurried back down the sidewalk hoping the party was still in full swing. She had only been gone for a few hours on the Earth side of things and not too much longer over on Oriceran. There was something she needed to do that was going to be her Christmas gift to her granddaughter. A smile spread across her face as she almost broke into a run, her long dark hair swaying down her back, held together by a large silver clip with an O carved in the center.

She could hear the party before she even got to the gate. Mariah Carey was blaring over the loudspeakers as she got to the patio that was packed so tightly with people that Mara had to work her way through the crowd. "I guess you wait years to throw your first party, no one wants to miss it. Good for you, Leira."

Mara finally made her way to the door of the guest house and back to Leira who was still perched on the couch, a plate of food in her lap.

"Nana! I was wondering where you were. Thought you might have met someone."

"Honey, that's not out of the realm of possibilities but I wouldn't miss my granddaughter's first real party."

Leira paused with the beer almost at her lips and thought about it. "Fuck, I think you're right. This is my first party. I guess I'm officially a grownup now. Hey, where have you been?" Leira gave her a broad, loopy smile. Mara knit her brows together, about to say something but brushed it off. "How many beers is that? Never mind, I have something for you."

"A Christmas present? It's not quite Christmas Day."

"You can have this one early." She reached into her pocket and pulled out a Polaroid picture. It was Correk, sleeping in his bed.

The smile faded off Leira's face as she stared at the picture.

"He's fine, just sleeping. Getting better every day. Stronger. I had to get his friend, Ossonia to take the picture. I couldn't make it all the way to the room but..."

Leira cut her off, throwing her arms around her grandmother, clutching the picture. "Thank you," she whispered into her grandmother's neck. "Thank you." She squeezed her tighter as she looked at the picture over Mara's shoulder. She sat back, still looking at the picture. "He's alive."

"He's alive. Merry Christmas, Leira and thank you."

"For what?" Leira looked up at her grandmother.

"For all of this." She pointed at all the people in the room and out on the patio. "They're all here because of their love for you. You made a family even when your own was hard to find. You have a big heart, granddaughter. I thought it was only fair that someone help it not break. Correk is fine. Your friend will be back before you know it." Mara smiled at glanced up at the tree as two people dancing jostled the tree, sending the blue glass ornament spinning and the light dancing along the walls.

"Hey, what is that doing on there?" Mara got up and went and looked more closely. "Well, no wonder this party is such a positive rager. Someone hung an artifact on the tree." Mara stopped it from spinning and felt the hum through her fingers. "This little sucker is working overtime."

Toni stopped at Mara's elbow and laughed when she saw what Mara was touching. "That thing will be responsible for a few August babies. You know what that is, don't you? Puts out a steady stream of good wishes and a loving feeling." Toni let out another loud laugh. "Shhhh... Let's let this be our little secret. Nothing like a love hangover. May it last till the New Year and help everyone start it off with a general feeling of peace on earth and good loving toward all men."

The troll settled down on the branch, nestled back behind a large Santa and licked the chocolate donut Hagan had brought over from the boxes in the kitchen. There was a thick smear of chocolate across his lip and a swath of chocolate across his belly as he wrestled the donut into his lap. He smiled and watched the artifact spin as Mara gave it a twirl, spreading the light all across the room and sweeping out onto the patio. "Merry Christmas to all, and to all a very good night," he said, as he opened his mouth wide and bit down into the donut. "Yum.... Fuck..."

Get sneak peeks, exclusive giveaways, behind the scenes content, and more. PLUS you'll be notified of special **one day only fan pricing** on new releases.

Sign up today to get free stories.

Visit: https://marthacarr.com/read-free-stories/

AUTHOR NOTES - MARTHA CARR
UPDATED JUNE 6, 2020

These are kind of strange author notes to be updating almost three years later in the middle of a pandemic, mixed with a recession and run through with protests. There were also the Australian fires at the beginning of the year. Yeah, that was this year too.

But reading again about that moment when I was down to just the hotel keys in my hand and how peaceful it felt is a good reminder. I was still okay and slowly but surely things changed. By the way, a few months after I was in that hotel was when I was diagnosed with terminal cancer (clearly they were wrong – over ten years later...). Things kept piling on, but it was a very personal journey and this time I'm walking it with everyone in the world.

I suppose I can do right now what I chose to do then. See how I can still be of service on a local level. Try not to make everything about me. Not give up and instead wonder what good thing may happen next. Sharpen my sense of humor and look for things to be grateful for on a daily basis. Call level-headed people when I need to be redirected back to gratitude and out of frustration or resentment. Gather friends around me and find fun things to do that are still affordable. All those sentences add up to a belief in a connection between me and each one of you that is worth preserving and even nurturing. Frankly, the friendships I developed during those few years of personal weirdness are still the strongest ones I have and they are all family to me. Another good reminder. Maybe, if I'm open to it again, I will gather even more new members of my family that have gone through this shared experience and I will cherish the new ties for all the years to come. More adventures to follow.

Original Author Notes, September 26, 2017:

Here we are at the fourth book, the fifth title and life is already changing for me. That lifelong dream keeps unfolding and I get to interact with fans on a daily basis. We share stories about children and grandchildren with each other, triumphs over adversity, dreams we're still working on – and a lot of selfies with troll mugs.

I keep finding myself thinking about 2009 when the Great Recession was in full swing and being a newspaper journalist was going the way of the dinosaur. (And that was my backup profession). I was on an assignment ghost writing a memoir for a man who had been in South Africa's version of the Navy Seals and at one time, owned diamond mines in Africa.

I was staying in a local Hampton Inn in upstate New York, spending my days following him around, asking copious questions, learning his speech pattern and weaving together his story. At one point, I found myself sky diving with him, and then there was the moment I was waving at James Gandolfini. It was a very high end neighborhood.

But in that same point in time I had reduced what I owned down to almost nothing in order to start over. The recession had taken its toll by then and I was making ends meet one day at a time.

There was this moment after a long day of work and I was in

the elevator in the motel that I looked down at the room key and rental car key and realized these were the only keys I had in the world. At that particular moment, for the first time in my life, I had no fixed address. There was even a weird moment when my iPhone stopped working and the thought occurred to me that without it no one could find me.

Strangely, I was okay and even felt a little liberated from taking care of things for a little while. The offspring was grown and in another state, fortunately doing fine and I didn't have a dog. There was no one to answer to and nothing to go check on. It was as if the world slowed down just a little and the choices were all wide open.

Fast-forward eight years and here I am in my own home filled with furniture again and the good dog, Lois writing books about magic in Austin, Texas and a swearing troll. That same feeling keeps coming back to me lately. A kind of freedom and a world full of options.

The last time was from stripping away everything and getting down to the essentials that could fit in a suitcase, living in the present moment. This time, it's from watching my dreams take off and seeing it's not a fluke, not temporary. This is here to stay. Kind of like having a handful of keys and I'm just finding out what they're going to unlock. Big THANK YOU to everyone who's on this ride with me – that's all of you fans! Just like Leira is learning – I've come to see over the past eight years the sweetest part of this whole ride are the people who are on it with me and you guys are really showing up.

By the way – Magic Mike reminded me to say – there was a two-star review from someone perturbed about the 'f-bombs' in the series who said they were returning the book in protest... That has inspired me to double-down on them in this one in their honor.

Aloha everyone!

AUTHOR NOTES - MICHAEL ANDERLE

UPDATED JUNE 23, 2020

Pandemics, recessions, Australian fires, and the list keeps going on and on.

Things to be thankful for is the enjoyment of watching Martha grow into the successful author she was on the inside, and have it occur on the outside. With your support and encouragement, she has been living the truth of a thirty-year effort to publish well and have fans support her ride through it all.

It hasn't been easy, goodness knows that. However, she has walked through it in a unique and impressive way and has garnered much wisdom helping people in her life through the years.

Where I've been more introverted and insular Martha had written syndicated newspaper columns distributed through hundreds of cities.

Pretty damned impressive.

If you get a chance to meet Martha in person, take advantage of the opportunity to ask her questions. She is insightful and cares. Your question doesn't have to be about writing and publishing (although it certainly can be). She is a fountain of information and enjoys sharing!

But, throw in a question about her family tree for good measure.

Original Author Notes, September 26, 2017:

First, let me say 'THANK YOU' so much for not only reading the story, but reading these author notes in the back as well!

Martha called me the other night when she was "words complete" for this book. For us, words complete is when your story is done, and you just have editing passes to do.

She told me how writing this book had been more difficult due to both wrapping up the threads to complete this part of Leira's arc, and lay the groundwork for our next four books.

Next four books.

As many of you know, I come from a whale reading background. That term – whale reader – is something I coined a couple of years ago when I focused on other readers like myself. Readers who read at least fifty books a year.

You know, at least one book a week, and you get two weeks off? Occasionally, I would go through four or five books from Friday night to Sunday night... Or Monday morning, early.

Here at LMBPN Publishing, we focus on one major 12 book arc. We break these twelve books down into three arcs of four books each.

If we fail to hit the mark with a series, we know we can wrap it up in four books. If one of our collaborators has something else they need to do, then they (and we) need to be able to conclude the series.

Now, having spoken about the twelve book arcs as my preference, it can be a *negative* to do longer series from a financial standpoint.

Many readers will try a new book 01, but the longer the series, the more hesitance new readers have to start with the series.

Books, 01,02 or 03 come out? No problem. Book 09, 12 or 15

comes out? That's a problem. Readers are already feeling fatigue to complete a series before they even get started.

Plus, it's a lot easier to plan out a trilogy and write it (without screwing up) than pretty much anything past somewhere between five and eight books. I have received a LOT of comments about how surprised readers have been that The Kurtherian Gambit, for example, is still awesome and they are just on book nine of the series.

Here, Martha has been working to complete the first arc of the Leira Chronicles. We designed three major arcs, each of four books, to set the Oriceran Universe and create the machinations of the political and business spheres within the universe for our collaborators to understand what is going on, and how they can play inside it.

Going back to Martha's call to me, she was discussing wanting to lay out the core ideas of this quadrilogy (4 books, right?) and how the larger world was reacting to what Leira happens to be in the center of at the moment.

So, I suppose what I'm trying to express as we go from book 04 to book 05 is that we have come to the end of our first arc for Leira, Hagan, Yumfuck, Correk and the rest of our characters. We have a minimum of eight more books planned out.

If you keep doing what you have been doing (loving the books, sharing with your friends, and buying Yumfuck mugs and basically telling others to stuff it, he's a Troll what are you expecting him to say then we will continue writing these stories about a family.

It might not be the kind of family that we recognize with a mom, dad, two point three kids and a dog.

But, this family has a troll.

I think that about trumps everything else we can say, right?

Because, in the end, they care about each other and will die for each other... You keep loving, we will keep writing.

The crazy shit that we have been able to do is because of YOU.

And yes, I'm happy the lady returned our book for the language. I'm *also* happy she lives in a country that allows my favorite troll to work his damned hardest to open the fridge, and finally...*finally* get it open to suffer having a big-ass boot close it and then looks up at the elf who towers over him and yells...

"MOTHERFUCKER!"

Ad Aeternitatem,

Michael Anderle

Creating crazy-ass characters since 2015

For Hire: Teachers for special school in Virginia countryside.

Must be able to handle teenagers with special abilities.

Cannot be afraid to discipline werewolves, wizards, elves and other assorted hormonal teens.

Apply at the School of Necessary Magic.

<u>**AVAILABLE ON AMAZON RETAILERS**</u>

If smart phones and GPS rule the world - why am I hunting a magic compass to save the planet?

Austin Detective Maggie Parker has seen some weird things in her day, but finding a surly gnome rooting through her garage beats all.

Her world is about to be turned upside down in a frantic search for 4 Elementals.

Each one has an artifact that can keep the Earth humming along, but they need her to unite them first.

Unless the forces against her get there first.

<u>AVAILABLE ON AMAZON AND IN KINDLE UNLIMITED!</u>

OTHER SERIES IN THE ORICERAN UNIVERSE

SOUL STONE MAGE

THE KACY CHRONICLES

MIDWEST MAGIC CHRONICLES

THE FAIRHAVEN CHRONICLES

I FEAR NO EVIL

THE DANIEL CODEX SERIES

SCHOOL OF NECESSARY MAGIC

SCHOOL OF NECESSARY MAGIC: RAINE CAMPBELL

ALISON BROWNSTONE

FEDERAL AGENTS OF MAGIC

SCIONS OF MAGIC

THE UNBELIEVABLE MR. BROWNSTONE

OTHER BOOKS BY JUDITH BERENS

OTHER BOOKS BY MARTHA CARR

JOIN THE ORICERAN UNIVERSE FAN GROUP ON FACEBOOK!

BOOKS BY MICHAEL ANDERLE

For a complete list of books by Michael Anderle, please visit:

www.lmbpn.com/ma-books/

All LMBPN Audiobooks are Available at Audible.com and iTunes. For a complete list of audiobooks visit:

www.lmbpn.com/audible

CONNECT WITH THE AUTHORS

Martha Carr Social
Website:
http://www.marthacarr.com
Facebook:
https://www.facebook.com/groups/MarthaCarrFans/

Michael Anderle Social
Website:
http://www.lmbpn.com
Email List:
http://lmbpn.com/email/
Facebook
https://www.facebook.com/LMBPNPublishing

www.ingramcontent.com/pod-product-compliance
Lightning Source LLC
Chambersburg PA
CBHW031647100726
47898CB00006B/2014